CURRYING DEATH

CURRYING DEATH

A KENZIE KIRSCH MEDICAL THRILLER
BOOK ELEVEN

P.D. WORKMAN

 **PD WORKMAN**

ISBN: 9781774687789 (KDP Paperback)
ISBN: 9781774687796 (KDP Hardcover)
ISBN: 9781774687819 (Lulu Paperback)
ISBN: 9781774687802 (Large Print)
ISBN: 9781774687826 (Digital)
ISBN: 9781774687833 (Auto-narrated audiobook)

ALSO BY P.D. WORKMAN

She Was At Risk

He Drowned in Memory

Their Walls Were Empty

They Came for Him

They Sought Vengeance

She Was Their Target

His Fear Was Real

She Was Out of Reach

He Was Deceived

She Once Vanished

Parks Pat Mysteries

Police Procedural Set in Canada

Out with the Sunset

Long Climb to the Top

Dark Water Under the Bridge

Immersed in the View

Skimming Over the Lake

Hazard of the Hills

Knows the Hills

Spanning the Creek

Sanctuary in the Stream

Echoes of the Engine

Bench with a View

Beneath the Icy Depths

Grounded in the Wind (Coming Soon)

Reservoir of Secrets (Coming Soon)

Peril in the Blooms (Coming Soon)

AND MORE AT PDWORKMAN.COM

To the survivors
and all those left behind

1

Kenzie was bent over her computer finishing up her notes and reports on the death of an elderly man, Casey Earl, when Dr. Cook approached her desk. He walked with a sense of purpose but did not have a stack of paperwork in his hands, so Kenzie straightened up expectantly. She brushed a few dark curls away from her face.

"What's up?"

"Feel like attending a death scene?"

"Sure," Kenzie agreed. She saved and closed her documents and started to tidy her desk. "What have we got?"

"Man found dead in his apartment. Paramedics were called to the scene. Nothing they could do; he'd been lying there dead for some time."

Kenzie nodded. Probably not anything too unusual about it. Someone who had died in his sleep, maybe a heart attack or stroke.

"How long is 'for some time'?" she asked cautiously. It could be anywhere from a few hours to a few weeks, and she wanted to be prepared for what she would find.

"Sometime today," Dr. Cook told her with an understanding grin. It always threw her for a loop when he smiled like that. He had the face of a movie star, not an experienced pathologist. Most of the time, she didn't really see his good looks anymore. They had worked together for a few months while Dr. Wiltshire was on medical leave and, once she'd worked over a few dead bodies with him, her consciousness of his appearance had faded. She didn't notice it unless he did something like smile at her in that relaxed, understanding way.

Whew. Zachary was lucky she didn't believe in office romances.

"Nice and fresh," Kenzie approved. "That's good. Looks like natural causes?"

Cook pursed his lips. "I will leave that up to you to determine; I would not want to bias you in any way."

Of course not. Kenzie nodded her agreement. "I'll let Carlos know we've got a transport. He and George can stand by for when I am done."

"I already paged him. He should be there by the time you're ready for him."

"Great." Kenzie opened her mouth to ask for the address when a text arrived on her phone. When she swiped the screen to reveal it, she saw it was the information she needed. He must have sent it as he had approached her desk, but it had taken a minute to arrive. She read the address and nodded. "Okay, thanks. I'll get on this."

If it was pretty clear that it was a natural death, Kenzie should have the death scene cleared and the body back at the medical examiner's office within a couple of hours.

Kenzie parked her "baby," a cherry red convertible, in front of the apartment building, ignoring the tow-away zone. The parking permit hanging from her rearview mirror identifying her as being from the medical examiner's office would prevent her car from being impounded. At least, it should. She popped the trunk to retrieve her small scene-of-death kit. She would be quickly in and out. The body would not need to be autopsied immediately. It might not require an autopsy at all if the man happened to be elderly and his doctor informed her that he had a history of heart disease or was being treated for some other potentially fatal condition.

There was an elevator to the third floor. A good size for transport. Everything looked like it would fall into place, and they would not have any difficulties. She walked down the hall to apartment 302 and found the door standing open. Peering in, she could see the paramedics standing in the living room chatting while waiting for her arrival. She nodded and stepped in. She was not familiar with the paramedics, so she introduced herself. They would not expect a stranger to walk in off the street but, sometimes, people got overly curious and stepped into death scenes without authorization.

"Dr. Kenzie Kirsch," she advised them, holding out her hand. "Assistant Medical Examiner."

"Oh, doctor." The female paramedic shook her hand. "Thank you for getting here so quickly. Sometimes we have to hang out for hours."

Roxboro was a small town, so they really shouldn't have to wait a significant amount of time at any death scene. Except that being a small town meant that there were a limited number of people who could do the job and, if there were several deaths to attend to in a day, there might be a delay in getting to one of them. But that rarely happened. But Kenzie didn't know the paramedic, who might have moved there from the city, where it was more likely that she would have to wait for a death scene investigator to arrive.

"Great, well, if you would like me to—" Kenzie stopped herself and studied the two other people in the room. A young man and woman in their late twenties or early thirties. The man's children? Grandchildren? Maybe one of them was a nursing care provider or aide? "Hi. I'm sorry. I'm Dr. Kenzie Kirsch. Medical examiner's office. Are you the ones who discovered the body?"

They both nodded.

"I'm Rachel Evans," the young woman introduced herself. She hugged herself tightly. "This is kind of weird. I'm a nurse practitioner."

"Mr. Robertson's care worker?" Kenzie asked expectantly.

"No." She shook her head vigorously, her eyes widening. "No, I was his girlfriend."

"Oh, I'm sorry." Kenzie's cheeks heated. How much younger than Robertson was his girlfriend? She didn't like putting her foot in her mouth like that. She should know better than to make assumptions. "I just assumed when you said you were a nurse..."

"No." The pretty blonde was flushing as well. "I should have told you. I don't know why I said I was a nurse before I told you about our relationship. I just mean, that's what is so weird. I deal with sick people, deal with death all the time, but I feel like... I don't know. It was just so surprising to find him like that."

Kenzie nodded understandingly. "It's not the same when it is someone you know. If he wasn't in your care, you didn't think of him that way. Had he been ill for a long time? Actually—" Kenzie held up her hand to prevent Rachel from answering the question. "Let me examine the body and the scene before you say anything. I don't want to be influenced by anything else." She turned to face the other person in the room, the young man. "And are you...?"

She didn't want to put her foot in it again by asking him if he were Mr. Robertson's son, so she left the sentence hanging, waiting for him to complete it.

"I'm his roommate."

"Oh, okay." Kenzie felt uneasy as she looked toward the bedroom. If the girlfriend and the roommate were both in their early thirties, then she might have been wrong in her assumption that the man who had died had been elderly like Casey Earl, whose file she had just closed, or even middle-aged. He was probably around their age. "What did you say your name was?"

"Alex Collins."

"Okay. If you would just stay out here..." Neither of them appeared to be inclined to follow her into the bedroom. "Which room is it?"

"Last one at the end of the hall."

K enzie nodded and stepped away to examine the body. She didn't want to be influenced by anything else they might have to say. One of the paramedics, the woman, trailed along behind her. Always best if there were two witnesses to corroborate each other's testimony if there were ever any questions as to what had taken place at the death scene.

Kenzie went through the door standing open at the end of the hall. The room was warm, the blinds drawn, like he had still been sleeping, maybe feeling sick. Or maybe he was a shift worker. He could be a medical professional like his girlfriend, someone she had met on the job.

Robertson was still in the bed. The paramedics had not moved the body to the floor to examine him or to do CPR. They knew a dead man when they saw one. Robertson lay as if asleep, partially on his side. He was a young man, like his girlfriend and roommate.

It was a queen-size bed that took up most of the small room. There was already a faint odor of death. He had been there most of the day, if she had to guess just by the stuffiness of the room. She moved closer to him, pulling on gloves. In the artificial lighting, his skin seemed to have a yellowish cast. He was overweight, puffy and bloated, his belly hanging out from under the t-shirt he had worn to bed. Someone who had not, at first glance, taken good care of himself.

Kenzie touched his neck to confirm death. His flesh was waxy. Rigor had set in. Nothing about the body suggested that it had been moved after death. Kenzie looked slowly around the room. There were several pill bottles on the side table, which she examined one at a time. A statin for high cholesterol. An SSRI antidepressant. Xanax for anxiety. All prescribed by the same doctor.

Kenzie pulled evidence bags out of her scene-of-death kit and sealed each one individually. She looked through the drawer of the side table to see if there was anything more. She found over-the-counter remedies. Antacids, allergy pills, painkillers, cold and sinus. The same as she would find in practically any bedroom or bathroom cabinet. She bagged each one.

Pulling out her phone, Kenzie looked up the prescribing physician online and called his office.

"Dr. Brandon is with a patient at the moment," the receptionist advised. "Did you want to set up an appointment?"

"This is Dr. Kirsch from the medical examiner's office. I need to talk to him about the death of one of his patients."

"Oh, dear!" the receptionist sounded concerned. "I'm sorry to hear that. I will have him call you back. Can I get your number? And the name of the patient so he can review the file before calling you?"

"Patient's name is Scott Robertson." Kenzie gave her phone number. "If I could get him to call me back as soon as possible. I am at the death scene right now, and I don't want to release it until after I have talked to Dr. Brandon."

"I'll try to have him call you before his next patient. We do have a busy practice…"

"I understand that. And hopefully, he does not have the ME's office calling him about too many of them. It is quite important that he take the time to call me back."

"I will let him know."

Kenzie sighed. "Thank you."

There wasn't much else for her to do. She would do a full examination of Robertson in the morgue, but it appeared that he had not been in good health and there were no preliminary indications that it was anything other than a natural death.

The room was not exactly neat, but there was no sign of any violence there, either. No sign of a struggle. Robertson was in bed, where he had likely been since the night before. There were no visible injuries. His laptop sat on his desk, along with his phone and a few other items that any self-respecting burglar would have taken.

As she looked around the room, there was a noise in the closet. Kenzie froze, her heart racing.

Was there someone in there? Even though she had been thinking of a burglar, there was no sign of any burglary. If it had been burgled, why would the thief have stayed in the room for hours to risk discovery by the girlfriend or roommate? Obviously, he couldn't show himself once they had shown up, and then the paramedics had come, and then Kenzie, so there hadn't been any time in which someone could sneak out since the time the body was discovered.

Kenzie had heard of cases where a burglar had fallen asleep in the middle of his burglary and been discovered at the scene. She looked at the bed, but there was no sign that anyone had been sleeping there other than Robertson. She didn't think that a burglar would have lain down next to a corpse. But then, she wouldn't have thought they would lie down at all, much less fall asleep in the midst of a burglary.

"Is somebody there?" she asked in a loud voice.

The paramedic, who had followed her to the bedroom but was stationed outside the door due to the lack of space inside the room, stuck her head in the door.

"Did you call me?"

"No, there's... I think there's someone in the closet."

The paramedic looked at the door, closed most of the way but still slightly ajar. She turned and shouted back to the others in the living room. "Is there anyone else in the apartment?"

Kenzie could hear Rachel and Alex coming down the hall

toward them, arguing about something. It sounded like an old argument, something they had hashed over many times before and barely had the energy to get mad about now.

"You know she isn't allowed in there! You're supposed to keep track of her," Rachel insisted.

"I do. Who left the door open? It wasn't me."

"You're not supposed to let her roam everywhere."

Alex marched into the bedroom, forcing Kenzie to step back so that she was squeezed against the bed. He paid no attention to her and walked over to the closet door, pulling it open with a whoosh.

"Cuddles!" He snapped. "Get out of there! You know you're not supposed to be in there!"

Kenzie couldn't help grinning as he bent over to push things around the bottom of the closet, coming out with an armful of fluff.

"This is Cuddles," Alex said unnecessarily. The fluffy tricolor cat glared at Kenzie, ears folded back. "Sorry. She's not supposed to be in here; she must have snuck in while we were calling the paramedics. We were both kind of in a panic. We weren't expecting... something like this."

Now that he had retrieved the cat, he stopped and stared at Robertson's body on the bed. His cheeks turned pink and he swore.

"I didn't mean to just barge in here like that. I kind of forgot myself... I'm sorry." He shook his head.

"If you could just step out with Cuddles, that would be great. We don't want her contaminating the scene or getting in the way."

"I told you!" Rachel was saying in the hall. "If you're going to have a cat, you need to keep it shut in your room. It can't just be wandering all over the apartment. I told you before that she aggravates Scott's allergies!"

She suddenly went quiet.

"Well, she isn't going to aggravate them anymore, is she?" Alex sighed. "I *am* sorry. I said that. Neither of us was watching her when we went to call the ambulance and answered the door. She just snuck in. It was unintentional. Normally, she couldn't get into Scott's room; that was why she was so curious about it."

"She shouldn't have the run of the apartment. You shouldn't have even gotten the cat while he was living here. It's common courtesy. You talk to the people in the household before you bring an animal in. Scott would never have agreed to a cat. His allergies were so bad."

So Cuddles was the reason for the antihistamines in the side table. Kenzie felt sorry for Robertson, who had not been in good health, to have had this additional trial to deal with. Not just the allergy, but the ongoing fight with his roommate about it and the contention between his girlfriend and his roommate. It wouldn't have been easy for him to deal with on top of his illness.

"Why don't we go back out to the living room," she suggested. "It is going to be a while before I can transport the body. I may as well ask a few questions while I am waiting."

3

Everyone seemed a little reluctant to shut the door of the bedroom and leave Robertson on the other side alone, but Kenzie didn't see what benefit there would be to staying with the body while she asked her questions. It would just creep them out, and they would be too awkward to answer her openly, constantly distracted by the body in front of them.

Even in the living room, she might still run into this problem. But it would not be as much of a distraction. Kenzie got everyone to sit down. "Do you want coffee or tea?" she suggested. "A soft drink? Anything to help you to just relax for a few minutes. I know this is a very strange, tense situation for you."

Rachel agreed to a coffee and got it for herself. The paramedics turned down any refreshment, as Kenzie expected, and Alex seemed irritated by the whole business. Eventually, they were all sitting down, the smell of freshly brewed coffee in the air, with some semblance of relaxation, even though Kenzie could tell Rachel and Alex were both tense, sitting rigidly instead of relaxing into the sofa and chairs.

"I'm very sorry that this happened to you," she sympathized. "It must have been very upsetting to discover Scott like this. Can you tell me about his health in the last few days? Did you know that he was ill?"

"Of course I knew he was ill," Rachel snapped. "We have been trying for months to get him the medical help that he needed. But *this* ill? No, I had no idea that he was in any immediate danger. I thought... you know, he's young and vital and he would get through it. We would get him stabilized on medications, and the symptoms would go away, and he would have a good quality of life."

"When was the last time you saw him?"

"Last night. I was here for a while in the evening, before my shift. He didn't really want company; he was feeling pretty low. I did the best I could, and then... I went on shift at the hospital. I called him a couple of times today, left messages for him, but he didn't answer. I came over when I knew Alex would be getting home."

"You don't have your own key?" Kenzie asked.

"Well, I don't live here."

"And you don't have a key?" Kenzie persisted, noticing that Rachel hadn't actually answered the question.

"I do. But I wanted to talk to Alex and see how Scott had been doing. I didn't want to just come here like I owned the place. Especially if Scott hadn't invited me over..."

Kenzie nodded. She wasn't sure that Rachel's explanation tracked, but she was probably telling the truth about wanting to ask Alex how Scott had been. If the man had been in bed all day refusing to take calls, then there was reason for her to be concerned about his condition.

And all the more reason to come straight over after her shift rather than wait for Alex to get home.

"So the two of you got here together? Or was Alex home first...?" Kenzie looked at Alex for his answer.

"I got home first," Alex agreed. He shrugged his shoulders. "So what was I supposed to do? I knew Scott wasn't feeling well. I called out to him, but he was lying in bed with the door closed and the shade drawn, so I didn't want to wake him. I figured he needed some rest. If he could sleep, that was the best thing for him."

Rachel did not look as though she agreed with Alex on this matter. She clearly thought that he should have kept track of Scott and made sure he was okay. He should have known earlier that Scott had passed away.

"What time was that?"

"That I got home? I don't know. One o'clock, maybe. I had a morning shift. Rachel texted and said she was coming over and could we please talk. Then she got here…" Alex met Rachel's eyes. "About an hour after that? Two o'clock?"

Rachel nodded. "Yes. About that."

"I just said… that I didn't know how he was doing, he was sleeping, and she could see for herself how he was."

Kenzie nodded. She waited for Rachel to take over the narrative.

"I said we should talk to him together," Rachel said, her eyes flitting around the room. "See if he needed to go to Emergency or something like that."

"So you thought it was more than just the flu."

"I didn't think it was a stomach bug," Rachel corrected. "The flu is a respiratory illness, and it can kill people who are weaker and not in as good health. Scott has not been well lately and, if he did get the flu or another virus that affected his lungs or his heart, it could be bad."

Kenzie leaned forward. "How bad *was* Scott's health?"

"If you talk to his doctor… he just needed to lose some weight and get more active." Rachel looked at Kenzie to see what she thought about this.

Kenzie thought back to the medications. "Obviously, there might be some dietary issues. But if he was severely depressed and having other health challenges… I suspect it was more than just obesity."

"He didn't die from obesity," Rachel asserted.

While Kenzie was not yet able to say exactly what had killed Scott, she thought that Rachel was probably right. It took a lot of factors presenting in just the right way for obesity itself to kill someone. It was almost always something associated with obesity. Diabetes, heart disease, cancer, hypertension. It was rare for someone simply to die from the excess fat and the way that it weighed the body down and constricted the organs.

"I don't know yet what he died from. Can you tell me about what other health challenges he was experiencing?"

Rachel rolled her eyes. "What challenges *wasn't* he having would probably be a shorter list. The things that his doctor was the most concerned about were Scott's cholesterol and depression. He said that if Scott could get up the motivation to get out and start walking, that everything else would go away."

"What else?"

"He said that Scott was just stressed out. Being tired and moody, his skin breaking out, the weight gain; he said they were all just symptoms of stress and his body telling him that he needed to handle it better."

Kenzie nodded. "Had you noticed a lot of changes?"

"Not all at once. It was all... it kind of crept up a little at a time. You know how it is. Little changes that happen over a period of weeks or months, and then you look at a picture from a year ago and realize how much things have changed."

"Do you have a picture I could see for comparison?"

"Uh, sure..." Rachel pulled out her phone and started thumbing through her photos. "Just give me a few minutes to find a good one."

"Did *you* think he was stressed?"

"Well, yes, I know he was stressed. He was stressed because the doctor said it was all in his head and all he had to do was get out and walk every day, and all of the weight would fall off, and his stress would melt away, and he would feel better again. He was stressed because he felt so rotten all the time. It didn't help that his allergies were in high gear because of that cat."

She shot a look at Alex, who shook his head. "You can't blame it all on me. She's just a cat, not the plague."

"A cat that Scott was allergic to. If it wasn't already bad enough that he was losing his hair and his skin was breaking out and he was gaining weight. He could hardly drag himself out of bed every morning."

"Cats are supposed to be good for your mental health," Alex pointed out. "They are supposed to make people less stressed and depressed. They increase your endorphins or something."

"*Not* if you are allergic to them."

Kenzie made calming motions with her hands. She glanced at her watch, hoping Carlos would be there soon and Doctor Brandon would call her back. She was as impatient as Zachary when it came to waiting for something to happen.

"Okay. I understand that the cat was an additional stressor. Scott was allergic, and that could cause a lot of issues, especially when he was already feeling sick. I'll make a note of that and take it into consideration during my investigation."

Rachel leaned back in her chair, arms folded in front of her, and nodded her approval smugly. Alex rolled his eyes and shook his head. The cat in his arms decided she'd had enough of having to sit and listen to the humans argue, and twisted and wriggled around until he finally let her go. She headed back down the hallway toward the bedrooms. A good thing that Kenzie had shut the door to Scott's room.

"When was the last time you talked to Scott or saw him alive?" she asked Alex.

"I don't really know. I know I saw him yesterday, but I don't know when the last time was. This morning..." Alex rubbed his chin, fingers rasping against his five o'clock shadow, "Well... I talked to him through the door. Said goodbye to him. But I never went in to see how he was doing. I don't know... if he was alive or dead when I left."

He cleared his throat and looked around, trying to find something to focus on. If he'd still been holding the cat, he could have lavished attention on her and pretended that he wasn't feeling so crappy about not keeping better track of his roommate that morning. He was feeling pretty bad that he hadn't even gone into the room to make sure that his friend was still alive.

"I'm sure if you had realized how ill he was, you would have gone in to check on him," Kenzie soothed. "You had no way to know this little bout of flu or whatever it was would lead where it did. How has everyone else been feeling?" Kenzie looked from one to the other. "Have you or your friends all had anything recently? Sometimes viruses just get passed from one person to another…"

Alex shrugged. "Yeah, we've had our share of colds and other bugs. Nothing that sent anyone to the hospital. Do you think we should have taken him to the hospital? Would it have made a difference? They would have just sent us back home, wouldn't they? They don't want you going to the emergency room with a bug. It has to be something really life-threatening."

Kenzie nodded. With the way that emergency rooms were overwhelmed lately, people were being told *not* to go to the hospital. Just stay home and get better there. "It's hard to know what to do. And I'm sure that you would have taken him to the hospital if you had known he was in real trouble."

"Could he have just died in his sleep?" Rachel asked. "Like, his heart just stopped?" She sighed. "I'm a nurse. I know it doesn't just stop without a reason. But some deaths by cardiac arrest are very peaceful, aren't they? They just don't wake up."

"I can't even guess at this point," Kenzie told her.

She was relieved when her phone rang.

4

It was Dr. Brandon's office. Kenzie made a motion to excuse herself from their company and walked back down the hallway to Scott's room. She closed the door, sealing herself in with him.

"Dr. Kirsch speaking."

"Dr. Kirsch. My receptionist said that you were with the medical examiner's office? My name is Emil Brandon. Dr. Emil Brandon."

"Yes. Did she tell you the patient I was calling you about?"

"Scott Robertson."

"Yes, that's right. Did you pull his file?"

"Yes, I have it in front of me."

"Would you make yourself a note to send me a copy of it, please?"

"Is that necessary?"

"Absolutely. I need to see his previous medical records. Of course you know all of that history comes into play when I am trying to make a determination of the cause of death."

"You don't know yet?"

"I'm still at the scene. There is nothing that clearly indicates cause of death on gross examination. I will need to examine him properly when I get him on the table. In the meantime, I need to find out everything I can about the history and what happened up until this point."

"Was it suicide? Did he take pills?"

"Not that I can tell. But Mr. Robertson did have several prescriptions close at hand. Was he suicidal?"

"I don't know. Maybe. He was depressed. Low energy, couldn't focus on things, couldn't get up the motivation to get out of the house and be active."

"How much of that was due to his physical symptoms and what was due to depression?"

"How can anyone tell? People who are depressed often have physical symptoms. People with physical ailments often get depressed."

"What was your diagnosis? How many times had he come to see you with these issues?"

"I don't know how many times. Maybe three or four. But he didn't seem willing to take responsibility for his own health, to make the changes I recommended. People want a magic pill—a quick fix that lets them continue their habits without making any lifestyle changes."

"Sure," Kenzie agreed, keeping her tone neutral. "But we can't always tell what they are doing or not doing. If someone does what you suggest and doesn't show any changes, you assume they haven't followed through."

Dr. Brandon said something unintelligible, like he was talking to someone else with the receiver covered up. Then he returned, his voice clear.

"Is that all then, Dr. Kirsch? I'll send these records to you; I don't know if they will make any difference to your investigation; I don't think he was that sick. I'm afraid I would tend toward a suggestion of suicide. He didn't seem to be getting any better since I prescribed him antidepressants. Some people do not respond to medication."

"Or not the first prescription," Kenzie pointed out. "How long had he been on it? Did you try something else?"

"Some medications take a number of weeks to reach full efficacy. I like to give it six or eight weeks to see if it is making a difference."

"So he had been on the SSRI for less than two months?"

She could hear him flipping pages in a file. A paper file, not a computer record. Some people liked to have hard copies of everything.

"Looks like closer to three months," Brandon said. "He should have been back here for a review so we could make an adjustment. Change the dose or try a different medication."

"He hadn't been back to see you in the last month?"

"Yes, but with different complaints. Frequent urination. Headaches, a feeling of pressure. Nothing that tied together in a way that I could make a diagnosis. I ordered a number of tests, but it doesn't look like everything had come back yet. Sometimes the labs are a lot slower than you would like."

"I'm sure that's true," Kenzie agreed. Her lab tests could often take weeks, but no live patients were waiting on the outcome. "You had some of them back?"

More turning pages. Brandon muttered. "Liver enzymes. Kidney function lower than it should have been. Multiple systems, like maybe he was reacting to one of the medications. Unfortunately, some of the psychiatric drugs can be very hard on the liver and kidneys. Once I had everything back, I would have called him to go through the results. See if we needed to switch things around. But these things take time, and I guess…"

"Robertson's time ran out," Kenzie said flatly. She couldn't fault Brandon for not trying to hurry things along faster. The system could be notoriously slow. Kenzie always laughed at TV medical shows where all the test results came back in minutes or, at least, the same day, so that the proper diagnosis of an incredibly rare disease could be made by the end of the episode. In real life… those people would probably have to wait years for a correct diagnosis. If they were lucky and actually got one.

"I'm very sorry to hear it," Dr. Brandon said with what sounded like real feeling. "As medical professionals, we should be used to the fact that we can't properly diagnose or treat every patient. That we will lose some of them. But it is still very difficult to face."

"Well, if you send that file to the medical examiner's office, I would be extremely grateful. The sooner I get it, the sooner I can make a ruling. Just like you waiting on your lab results. And if you think of anything else or want to bring anything to my attention, please feel free to call. Sometimes a patient says something, or you get a feeling from them that points you in a certain direction, even if you were unable to prove anything."

"Of course, of course," Brandon agreed. "Good luck."

As Kenzie opened the door, she could hear voices at the front door. Not just in the living room this time. And she knew the voices. Carlos and George. Her transportation team. She walked out to meet them as they brought a gurney in the front door and had to move a few things to the side so they had a clear path through to the hallway and bedroom.

"Doctor," George greeted with a nod. "End of the hall?"

Kenzie moved out of the way. "Yes. Bit of a tight squeeze. You might need to leave the gurney out here and carry him to it."

They nodded and didn't tell her they were the experts in sorting out a situation like that. But of course they were. She sometimes helped with the transportation, but she was far less skilled than Carlos and George. They would suss out the situation quickly enough and figure out how to approach the move.

"He's a big guy," Kenzie warned. Also unnecessary.

"You're finished with everything in here?" George asked as he moved into the bedroom and looked around. "Nothing else that needs to be collected or documented?"

"If you could take a couple of overhead shots of the body. Other than that... unless there is something unexpected underneath him, I think we have everything we need."

George and Carlos moved together in a sort of choreographed dance. No words were spoken, and they seemed to anticipate each other's movements without any instruction.

5

Kenzie looked at her watch. It had taken some time to get everything done, and there wasn't much point in her returning to the medical examiner's office. She would only have a few minutes there, unless she decided to work late and start on the autopsy. But Zachary was supposed to be home, so she needed to spend time with him. And the body was still in rigor. It would be much easier to do the autopsy the next day when rigor was released.

She called Dr. Cook to let him know that she was going to return home from the scene. She had already cleared everything off her desk and locked it up, so she didn't need to go back to take care of anything. It could all wait until the next day.

"I'll see you tomorrow then, Kenzie," Dr. Cook told her. "You have a good night."

After seeing the transport crew off, Kenzie headed for home. She tried calling Zachary, but he was not answering his phone. Maybe with a client, or maybe just so focused on whatever he was doing, he hadn't noticed the phone ringing. Cell phones were a great convenience, but Zachary sometimes didn't pay any attention to his, even with the volume turned up. When he was hyperfocused on something, an earthquake probably couldn't shake him. Not that they got earthquakes in Vermont.

The snow was off the ground and they had entered what locals tended to refer to as "mud season." The state was on the verge of spring, but it would be a couple of weeks before everything greened up and it looked like the Vermont on postcards.

"I'm home," Kenzie called out as she emerged from the garage into the kitchen and hung up her outerwear. There was no response. She pried off her shoes and looked through the doorway into the kitchen. Zachary was not sitting in his usual place on the couch with his laptop computer.

She raised her voice. "Are you home?"

There was no reply, only stillness. No sound from the shower or anything else to indicate that he was home and just hadn't heard her. Kenzie took a short walk through the house to confirm it was empty.

She opened the calendar app on her phone and switched to Zachary's calendar. He didn't always remember to put his appointments into it. Sometimes, Heather picked up commitments that Zachary had forgotten and added them to it. Kenzie tried to add any dates or other joint appointments to make sure that he was aware of them. As long as he remembered to look at his calendar, of course.

She was in luck, and his calendar showed him out at a meeting with someone named Kymchuk. Kenzie wasn't familiar with the name. Not Zachary's mechanic or dentist or other professional service she was aware of. Maybe a new client. That would explain his not answering his phone when she had called.

The meeting might go later than planned but, if it ran on schedule, Zachary should still be back in good time for supper. He might already be on his way home. She didn't bother checking their location-sharing app and started dinner preparations.

Her instincts were right and, within ten minutes, she heard Zachary letting himself in the front door. After a brief door-locking ritual, he made his way to the kitchen.

"You beat me home!"

Heedless of the hot pots on the stove, Zachary reached around Kenzie and gave her a quick hug and kiss. She moved back from the stove and snuggled into him for a minute. An aromatic blend of garlic and tomatoes filled the room as she simmered the sauce.

While he often looked like a homeless bum—quite intentionally so—today Zachary wore a fresh, collared shirt and khakis and still smelled faintly of shaving cream. Definitely a client meeting. She kissed him and withdrew to check her pots and make sure that the pasta was not about to boil over.

"Who is Kymchuk? New client?"

Zachary nodded. He undid the second button on his shirt to loosen it further, getting comfortable. He turned to the cupboard to get out the plates and set the table.

"Yeah. Initial meeting today. Everything looks good. Paid a retainer. I'll set up the file and get my notes down..." He was clearly planning the administrative steps out loud that he would need to follow to open the file. Administrative work was not his strong suit, but his sister Heather, now working as his administrative assistant and junior investigator, would make sure that he followed the new file checklist and wrote down all of the information she needed to open the file, set up the timekeeping and billings, and all of the behind-the-scenes stuff that was not Zachary's forte. Having raised two kids with ADHD, Heather had a lot of good, practical solutions up her sleeve to help keep Zachary on track, and seemed to enjoy doing it.

Kenzie put a colander in the sink to strain the pasta as soon as it was cooked.

"What kind of file?"

"Interesting one..." Zachary added cutlery to the table setting and stood there looking at it for a minute, lost in thought.

Kenzie let it go. He would undoubtedly fill her in once he was ready. When they were sitting down at the table and he didn't have to focus on his chores and everything else he needed to remember. They worked together in silence while Kenzie finished the hot dishes and Zachary pulled together a salad he probably wouldn't touch.

When they were sitting down at the table and Zachary had a mound of chicken penne arrabbiata in the middle of his plate, he picked up the conversation as if there had been no lull.

"Mostly surveillance work. Client suspects that his daughter may be having domestic problems and wants some physical evidence."

"Domestic problems?" Kenzie repeated. It was obviously the client's turn of phrase, not Zachary's.

"Thinks the husband is abusive," Zachary clarified. "Wants to know for sure."

"So you're surveilling them at home? Seeing if you can catch him in the act?"

Zachary nodded and shoveled food into his mouth. He caught a look from Kenzie and dabbed at the sauce on his face with his napkin. He chewed for a minute and went on with the conversation.

"I'll get some bugs and micro cameras set up and be able to monitor the situation in the house from a distance," he told her. "I won't be in harm's way."

Kenzie was glad for this reassurance. She had pictured him watching through windows, rushing in to try to interfere when the daughter's spouse decided to lay hands on her. If he was just watching or recording remotely, she didn't have to worry about his tackling an abusive spouse himself. He could call the police or provide the footage to his client without ever having to get involved in the situation physically.

"How will you get bugs and cameras into the house?" she asked suspiciously. That seemed like a dangerous prospect in itself. Especially with someone suspected of being violent.

"He works during the day. I should be able just to use cameras that stick on the outside of the window and never go into the house but, even if I need to go inside, no one should be around during the day."

"That's good." Kenzie helped herself to more salad. She was trying very hard to eat healthier and lose a few of the pounds she had put on the last couple of years. "I don't want you getting in this guy's way."

"Yeah. And, of course, I'll be doing background on him. See if there are any previous arrests for violent behavior, track down a few former girlfriends and see if they will talk about him."

"What does the dad expect to get out of this? Does he think that he'll be able to talk her into leaving the relationship?"

"That's the idea." Zachary shrugged. "He hopes he'll be able to talk her into moving back home if he explains that he knows what is going on. Sometimes, people are afraid to leave because they don't want people to know about the abuse. If he already knows what is going on... maybe she will be okay with talking to him about it and he'll be able to talk her into coming home."

Kenzie nodded. "I hope so. It's nice that he is trying to help her, but there might be better ways. Hiring a private detective to look into her partner is probably not the best approach."

Zachary shrugged with one shoulder. "I'm sure he's also trying to get through to her in other ways. Or will, once he knows whether he's right or if he's just seeing things because he doesn't like the guy. If I go back and tell him that no, there's no indication that the guy is actually abusive... maybe he can just move on and focus on his relationship with his daughter in other ways."

Kenzie's mind drifted to Scott Robertson. So far, she had only talked to the girlfriend and the roommate. Next on her list would be Scott's family, if he had any. Talking to immediate family was never easy. Robertson had been so young to die of a heart attack or whatever other illness he was suffering from; it was sure to be a shock for the family. Hard to get past that.

"How was your day?" Zachary asked.

Kenzie glanced at him and saw he was studying her carefully. He had probably noticed her attention drifting away from their conversation and knew she had something else on her mind.

"Got a callout this afternoon. I thought it was going to be an elderly man who had died in his sleep. That was what the call sounded like when it came in. But it was just a young guy. Twenty-seven."

"Wow. Yeah, that is young. What was it? Did he just die in his sleep or was it something else?"

"I'll do the autopsy tomorrow. I'm not sure at this point. He had health concerns, but I don't know for sure what it was that actually caused his death. Maybe a virus. Maybe something undiagnosed. He'd seen the doctor a number of times but didn't get far. The doctor ordered some lab tests recently, but they weren't all back yet, so he wasn't sure what the patient was dealing with."

"You don't think it was anything other than natural causes?"

"No red flags or alarm bells. No sign of violence. Not the kind of person who appeared to be involved in drugs or a gang. More the intellectual type. I would say introverted, but that's just my sense. I would have to talk to more friends or family members to get a better sense."

"Yeah. Maybe he was just... frail."

Kenzie grimaced. That did not seem like the right word to apply to Scott Robertson. Words like frail or vulnerable made him sound delicate, and he had been a hefty man. But it might still be correct. Given the number of things the girlfriend had said were bothering him recently, it seemed like he had been vulnerable to something.

6

The cat inhabited Kenzie's dreams.

She didn't know why she couldn't get the animal out of her head. She was not an "animal person." She had never had a pet growing up. During her sister Amanda's illness, no one had the time to take care of an animal too. Even if they had the time and money for it, there was just no more emotional space for something like that.

Kenzie had been shocked when her mother had adopted Lola, a dog that had been adjacent to one of Kenzie's cases. She had never known that Lisa had any interest in animals. Apparently, she had been wrong.

The cat kept worrying her. There was no reason why Kenzie should be concerned about Cuddles at all. She wasn't Robertson's cat. His death would not impact her life negatively. In fact, now that Robertson was gone, the cat would have the run of the apartment rather than being confined to a certain room or locked out of one of the rooms. Her life would be better with Robertson out of the apartment.

But every time she dropped off to sleep, the cat was there. Sometimes it was yowling outside the window and Kenzie was trying to call it inside to keep it safe from whatever hazards were out there for a cat. Somebody could hurt it. There were animals out there even though they were within the town. Even more dangerous, there were cars.

Sometimes in her dream, she was trying to catch the cat inside the house. But it always kept ahead of her fingers, and she was never able to grab it. The house grew bigger and more twisted and complex in her dreams, giving the cat more dark hiding places and making it impossible for Kenzie to ever find her. She saw the cat in the closet again, back in Robertson's room. Digging around. Trying to pull together a little sleeping nest? Looking for something else? Agitated by an unusual smell? Something dangerous? Someone who wasn't supposed to be there or who she thought was a danger to her people?

Had the cat even liked Robertson? Who knew if she considered him one of her family members or not.

"Get over here!"

Kenzie startled herself out of sleep shouting at Cuddles as she tried to catch her again. She woke up Zachary, who was not a good sleeper and rarely got more than a few hours of sleep.

He jolted awake beside her and turned over. "Kenzie? Are you okay?"

"I'm fine," Kenzie tried to smooth things over quickly. "It was just a dream; go back to sleep."

But he didn't close his eyes and go back to sleep without saying anything else. He moved closer to Kenzie and put his arm around her in a comforting hug. "Are you okay? You had a nightmare?"

"No... not even a nightmare. It was just... a dream. A silly dream about a cat."

"A cat?" Zachary chuckled. "What about a cat?"

"There was this cat at the call I went to this afternoon. It was nothing; you should just go back to sleep." She tried again to persuade him to try to go back to sleep instead of staying up talking with her about something so inconsequential.

He put his head down on the pillow, still holding her enfolded in his embrace. A car drove past the house, tires swishing on the wet road.

"What did the cat do?"

"Nothing. Well, first it scared me because it was in the closet and I thought a person might be hiding in there somehow, even though it had been hours since the patient had died. But it was just the cat. And then there was an argument between the roommate and the girlfriend, I guess the patient was allergic to cats and the girlfriend was really angry about the roommate bringing an animal into the apartment. But the cat itself was fine. I'm not worried about it."

"It was just strange enough to make it into your dream."

"Yes," Kenzie agreed. She didn't tell him that it was in more than one dream; that would just convince him that it was more significant than it was.

The only significance was that Kenzie would be performing the autopsy the next day and Cuddles had been at the scene when Robertson had died.

"Why would the roommate buy a cat if he was allergic? Didn't he know about it? Or did he not start being allergic until later?"

"I didn't get any details, to be honest. I assume he knew he was allergic already, or the girlfriend would not have made such a big deal of it."

"Yeah." Zachary snuggled against her. "And what were you dreaming about it?"

"It was outside and in danger, and I needed to catch it to keep it safe."

"But you're not worried about the cat?"

"I really am not! It wasn't even the patient's cat. The cat is fine."

They stayed like that for some time, and Kenzie started to drift off to sleep again. She was aware of Zachary loosening his grip and withdrawing from her. She was just on the edge of sleep, too far gone to call him back and tell him to stay with her.

Besides, he wouldn't. He might stay a few minutes extra, but he would still get up and go to the living room to work. Now that his sleep had been interrupted, he was unlikely to go back to sleep again.

7

Kenzie felt far from well-rested when her alarm went off in the morning. She hadn't ever found that restful state of sleep, but had been in and out of consciousness, restless, with her mind working away, all night. Maybe she was coming down with something.

She got up anyway. There was plenty of work to be done, and she didn't want to end up feeling rushed because she had slept in. Even though Dr. Cook was perfectly okay with her setting her own hours, he was a morning person and was nearly always in the office before her. Unlike Dr. Wiltshire, who typically arrived later and gave Kenzie time to get everything sorted out before he came in. She preferred to be the first at the office; it made her feel more in control of her day. With Dr. Cook already there when she arrived, she always felt like she was playing catch-up, even if he didn't mind her taking a bit of time to organize herself in the morning.

She felt a little better after her shower, though she knew she would probably hit a low-energy slump before noon, and it would be a struggle to focus on her work after lunch. There was fresh coffee in the kitchen, and Zachary looked up from his computer work, not so immersed in it that he didn't notice her arrival.

"How are you doing?" he asked immediately.

"I'm fine. A bit tired, that's all."

"Any more cat dreams?"

Kenzie rolled her eyes and took her first sip of coffee. "Too many," she admitted.

"Strange. I've never known you to dream about cats before."

"No, I don't think I have. I don't know if it is just because this one scared me or what."

She had a few more swallows of the piping hot coffee. "How about you? Did you get any more sleep?"

Looking at the puffy bags under his eyes, she was pretty sure the answer was no.

Zachary shrugged. "I slept for a couple of hours before that. Once I wake up, there isn't much point in trying to go back to sleep."

"So, no."

"No." Zachary picked up a large travel mug he'd set on the side table, well away from the computer, and took several large swallows of what was probably lukewarm coffee. "I'll get caught up tomorrow."

"You're not doing surveillance tonight?"

He shook his head and put the coffee mug back away. "No. The subject works day shift, sleeps at night. Once he knocks off for the night, I'll be done. Probably by midnight."

"So you won't be here between supper and midnight?"

"No, that will be prime time for friction between him and his wife. Sorry about that…"

Kenzie shrugged it off. She couldn't expect Zachary to be with her every evening. Not as a private investigator. "You have a job to do. It isn't like you're out every night. Just… be careful. Really careful. You know this guy might be violent. You don't want to get in his way."

"Don't worry; I'll stay out of sight," Zachary assured her. "I'll be monitoring the feeds from around the corner."

Kenzie was well-caffeinated by the time she got to the office, even though she knew it was likely to contribute to a crash later in the day. She took a quick look for any emails, messages, or voicemails that had come in since she had left the office for the Robertson call the afternoon before, then went to Dr. Cook's office.

"Are you going to join me on the Robertson autopsy? I'm going to get right to it."

Dr. Cook looked surprised, knowing that she usually spent more time on the computer first thing, but he nodded. "Sure. You're ready to start now?"

"Yeah. Let's get to it right away."

"No problem." He took a quick look over everything on his desk, then stood up. "I'll be right behind you."

Kenzie went ahead of him to the morgue, where she checked to ensure Scott Robertson was all ready to go. George had prepared the body for her, collecting any trace evidence or swabs before washing it down so that she could start immediately.

Kenzie put on her protective gear and reviewed her scene notes while waiting for Dr. Cook. When he was dressed and waiting, she clicked the floor button with her foot to begin recording. She announced the date, time, their names, and the patient's name and file number.

Observing the scale markings on the autopsy table and the weight on her screen, Kenzie dictated Robertson's height and weight. As she had expected when she first saw him, he fell within the definition of obese. And the amount of body fat he carried confirmed this, unlike in a bodybuilder who might be within the weight category for obese but not be fat.

Robertson had a large belly and significant adipose tissue deposits on the chest. His skin had a yellow cast. Kenzie opened his eyes to observe that they, too, were yellow. Despite prematurely thinning hair, his round face and acne made him look younger than his twenty-seven years. He would not be mistaken for a teenager, but he had a boyish look that tugged at Kenzie's heartstrings despite her efforts to remain detached.

Rachel had found a picture of Robertson from a year before,

which Kenzie had logged into the computer records for the file and brought up on one of the big screens now.

Rachel was right about Robertson changing a lot in the past year. The man in the picture from a year ago was considerably slimmer, clear-complexioned, and had thicker hair, though he did have a slightly receding hairline.

Dr. Cook studied the picture from a year ago. "Some significant changes."

"Yes," Kenzie agreed. "He'd been to the doctor a number of times in the past year, trying to figure out what was going on."

"I would suggest a hormone panel and liver enzymes."

Kenzie agreed and made the appropriate entries on the computer file to put them on the list of tests to be performed.

"Anything else?" Dr. Cook prompted.

Kenzie pressed her finger into the puffy flesh over Robertson's ankle. When she released the pressure, an indentation remained in the flesh.

"Significant edema," Kenzie observed. "Kidney panel?"

"Definitely." Dr. Cook's eyes traveled over the body. "There are signs of damage to multiple organs here. Significant damage."

"Yeah." The internal exam was likely to be pretty grim.

"What medications was he on?"

Kenzie listed the three prescription medications that had been on his bedside table and the over-the-counter meds in his drawer. Dr. Cook nodded. "The more medications, the higher the chances are that he ends up with something toxic to his liver. Acetaminophen is one of the worst offenders, especially when combined with alcohol. People have been conditioned by the media to think they can pop them all day, every day without negative consequences. People think that it's the most benign drug of all."

"I looked up the prescriptions, and they are all known to be toxic to the liver."

"Most medications are if taken in large enough doses. And if you're stacking up multiple medications..." Dr. Cook shrugged. "How close were they to the bed? How many pills did he take before he went to sleep?"

"They were right beside the bed. Within reach. But nothing looked out of place. He didn't finish off any of the bottles. He hadn't vomited. I don't *think* it was suicide, but we haven't even started the internal exam."

"He's taking an SSRI antidepressant; that is the first thing to look at. Young people, in particular, can have increased suicidal ideation with SSRIs. He's not a teenager, but he's still young enough. Had he ever attempted suicide? Did he have therapy? Did his doctor just prescribe the pills without any other resources or follow-up?"

"We can test to see how much of each medication is in his blood and his stomach."

Dr. Cook agreed, and Kenzie added them to the list of lab tests to be done. They would figure out what had killed him, one way or another.

"Are you ready to proceed?" Dr. Cook prompted.

Kenzie knew that she was delaying the inevitable, looking for ways to postpone the postmortem, and that it wouldn't help her to do so. It had to be done. If she didn't want to do it, Dr. Cook could complete it, but Kenzie didn't want to give it to someone else to take care of. She just wanted Scott Robertson *not* to have died and be lying on her table. She wanted him to have survived, figured out what was wrong with him, and found a way to regain his health and settle down with his girlfriend and have little Robertsons running around the house.

Instead, he lay dead and cold on her table.

"Yes. Let's just roll him and check his back first."

With his heft, it took both of them working together to roll him onto his front so they could visualize his back. There was nothing remarkable. Livor mortis had settled into the expected areas, and there were no marks, bruises, grazes, or needle marks. Nothing to indicate that he hadn't just died in his sleep while he lay in his bed.

Kenzie had kind of been hoping to find something else, but she hadn't expected to. They turned him onto his back again, and she made the Y incision. It took considerable effort to slice through the layers of skin and fat. The adipose tissue was bright yellow and marbled with blood vessels.

She retracted skin and muscle tissue with care until she exposed Robertson's rib cage and abdominal cavity. Dr. Cook handed her surgical shears, and Kenzie went to work on removing ribs to expose the viscera below.

Liquid oozed out of the various tissues. He was waterlogged, everything oversaturated. The edema might be caused by kidney failure, congestive heart failure, or both. Kenzie dictated her findings while she examined the thoracic cavity.

She looked at the heart, taking multiple pictures before removing it.

"Heart is enlarged. Almost twice the usual size." Kenzie weighed and measured the heart and put it to the side for dissection. The heart had clearly been damaged by something, whether it was just lifestyle or the medications Robertson had been taking. Or maybe even by a virus. She would return to it later and detail the various abnormalities she found. There were likely to be several of them. "Coronary arteries show significant occlusions," she observed as she set it aside, able to see distention of the arteries and the yellowing atherosclerotic plaques with her naked eye.

8

"Shall we take a break?" Dr. Cook asked, noting the time.

Kenzie stretched her muscles and rolled her shoulders. The work of a postmortem wasn't as easy as they made it look on TV. It was physically taxing. "Yeah. That would probably be a good idea. I need a breath of fresh air."

"Let's take forty-five? Take a walk, rehydrate, grab a snack..."

"Okay." Kenzie was already peeling off her gloves and other protective gear as she headed for the door. "See you back here after."

She was out the door before Dr. Cook even left the table. She had been absorbed in the work of the postmortem, but she definitely needed the break that he had suggested.

The work was physically more challenging to perform with an obese patient. She'd had her share of them in the past, so it wasn't a new experience, but it was always more difficult to move, cut, and lift a larger, adipose-ridden body. She was sore, and she wasn't even halfway through it yet.

Robertson's case might not be as disturbing as an abused child dying of massive injuries or an elderly person starved to death, but the young man dying in his prime despite having reached out for help repeatedly bothered her in its own way.

She took the elevator up to the main floor of the police station and went outside without putting on a jacket. The brisk, fresh air felt good. And, mud season or not, she was going to take a walk around the block and just revel in being alive and able to enjoy the nature around her. She slipped in her earbuds and called Zachary.

She didn't know whether to expect him to answer or not. It was pretty hit-and-miss as to whether he would be easily distracted from his work by the ringing phone or not even notice it because he was focused on something else.

"Kenzie!" Zachary sounded cheerful and pleased to hear from her. "How is your day going?"

"It's good. Just need to take a breath and relax for a few minutes."

"Sure. How is Dr. Cook?"

"He's good."

"You haven't decided you're tired of him yet?"

He said it jokingly, but Kenzie thought Zachary was slightly jealous of Dr. Cook and worried Kenzie would fall for his good looks. She couldn't help that she spent a lot of time with the guy or that he was good-looking. She thought that Zachary was pretty secure in their relationship—as secure as someone so riddled with anxiety could be—and that his jokes just showed his need for a bit of reassurance now and then.

That was what she hoped, anyway. She didn't have any way to change how he felt about Dr. Cook.

"You know how it is with bosses," she told him lightly. "Unless you work for yourself, you don't get to choose them. You just do your best to get along and work together efficiently."

"You don't get to pick your boss when you work for yourself, either," Zachary pointed out. "You're stuck with the guy. And sometimes my boss is crap."

Kenzie laughed. "Your boss can be quite the taskmaster sometimes," she admitted. "And occasionally gets distracted or changes priorities on a whim."

"Occasionally?"

They both laughed. It felt good to let go and just enjoy each other's company for a few minutes, even if it was over the phone. Thank goodness for technology. She didn't have to be alone, even when she was alone.

Kenzie was feeling better when she returned to the basement to resume the autopsy. Her desk phone was ringing and, rather than letting it go through to voicemail, she picked it up, since she was right there.

"Medical examiner's office."

"I'm supposed to talk to someone there about my brother."

Kenzie didn't recognize the voice. She sat down to take his information for Dr. Cook. "Of course. Who is calling?"

"This is Kirk Robertson," he paused awkwardly. "It's about my brother, Scott."

"Yes," Kenzie swallowed. She wasn't about to tell him that she had Scott on the table right now and was just about to go back and continue the postmortem. "I am the Assistant Medical Examiner and attended at the scene. I'm going to have some questions for you, and I wonder whether you would be able to come in and have a short meeting?"

"Questions?" Kirk repeated suspiciously, "What kind of questions?"

"I am looking for family history, Scott's medical history, how he was when you last saw him, that sort of thing. We like to make sure that we have the full story before making any ruling."

"Why? You think someone killed him? That's ridiculous."

"No, I didn't say that," Kenzie said quickly. "We just need to know anything you are aware of to do with his health. Sometimes, there are things that you can't see just by looking at the... physical evidence. Sometimes, you don't know what to look for unless you are aware of the person's history. Even little things like allergies or heart disease in the family can be clues as to what to look for."

"It seems to me that's your job, not mine."

"Of course. That is what I am working on. And I have spoken to his doctor and asked for his medical records. But sometimes a patient doesn't tell his doctors all of his symptoms, or the doctor doesn't write them all down, or there is something that seemed insignificant at the time but might have had an unexpected outcome…"

Kirk huffed out an impatient breath. "Well. I suppose we'll have to meet, then. I'm not available today."

"Do you have some time tomorrow? I will try to accommodate your schedule."

"I really don't see the need."

"Were you close?" Kenzie asked. Sometimes, the people who seemed insensitive were actually the ones who were the closest, trying to push the pain away. Kenzie hoped to remind him of their relationship and maybe break down the barriers. "I'm sorry to have to intrude on you at such a difficult time…"

"We hadn't seen each other in years," Kirk said. "Two, three, I don't know. We aren't a lot alike. Didn't really enjoy doing the same things together. We just… drifted."

His words rang false to Kenzie. She nodded slowly, trying to come up with an appropriate comment. "Things can be difficult between brothers."

"Yes," Kirk agreed. "Since our dad died… well, things have been tied up in probate court and Scott just would not back down and let things go through quietly. Everything had to be done his way, you know? That's how it is with the younger brother. He was spoiled."

"That must make it very difficult. How long has your dad's estate been in probate?"

"A couple of years. If Scott would just stop fighting over every little thing, it would be able to go through."

"Uh…" Kenzie cleared her throat. If he had been wishing that his brother would just roll over and stop fighting, he had gotten his wish.

"I didn't mean for it to sound like that," Kirk said immediately. "It's just that it has been such a fight. I just wanted it to be over."

"Yes. Of course."

"Tomorrow would be fine," the man blustered, trying to cover up his embarrassment. "Afternoon? Maybe around three? I'll have to move stuff around at work, but I should be able to make it there in the afternoon."

"Sure," Kenzie agreed. "I will be happy to see you then. My name is Dr. Kenzie Kirsch."

"Right. I guess I'll see you then."

9

Kenzie returned to autopsy. Her timing was good, and Dr. Cook was just suiting up. She joined him in the ritual.

"How are you doing?" Dr. Cook asked.

"Good. I really needed that break. That was a good call. How about you?"

"Good to clear my head," Dr. Cook acknowledged with a nod. "This can be a stressful job, and postmortems, in particular, can bring up unexpected emotions at times."

"Yeah."

"Self-care is important. If you are in it for the long haul, you have to take care not to burn out."

"Are you?" Kenzie asked curiously.

"Burned out?"

"In it for the long haul."

Dr. Cook smiled in understanding. "Since I am only here temporarily, you mean? *Overall,* yes. I am a pathologist, and this is what I want to do. But there are not a lot of medical examiner openings, and I tend to get restless when I have been in one place for very long. So, temporary assignments to cover for other medical examiners or help with overflow is ideal. So… long haul, but in short assignments."

"So if Dr. Wiltshire isn't able to come back, you won't be staying here?"

He considered this. "Not something I have considered," he said eventually. "I think Dr. Wiltshire will be back as soon as he is able. I enjoy working with you and it is a nice town. But I think I'll be moving on again within a few months."

Kenzie was reassured that he wasn't coveting Dr. Wiltshire's job and looking for a way to stay there permanently. Dr. Wiltshire would return as soon as his hand had healed and he completed the necessary physical therapy to regain full function.

"Got a call from our patient's brother," she told Cook, changing the subject.

"That's good. He's prepared to claim the remains?"

"We didn't discuss that yet. I want to ask him about their family medical history and anything we should know about from Robertson's history. You never know what might have happened in his past to contribute to his death. Things he might not have talked to his doctor about. We all have to decide what bits to tell our doctors and what is irrelevant. He might have misjudged and not revealed something important from his personal or family history. An allergy or drug interaction, some disease or disorder that runs in his family but is rare in the general population."

"How did he sound? Do you think he will be helpful?"

They both knew that some people had a head for medicine, even if they were completely untrained, and others were completely blind in medical matters, even with a scientific background.

"Hard to say yet. He wasn't happy about being called in. Sounds like they were estranged. Fighting over an inheritance."

"Ouch." Dr. Cook finished suiting up and stepped toward the table where their patient lay, waiting for them. "That's a tough situation for him to find himself in. He's probably experiencing a significant amount of guilt if they didn't part on good terms."

Kenzie nodded her agreement. "Yeah. Might be a difficult discussion."

They returned to the table. Kenzie took a deep breath and looked over the body and what remained to be done.

"The liver is going to be a mess," she predicted.

"I think that goes without saying. Just take it one step at a time."

Kenzie continued with the dissection, slicing down the diaphragm to reveal the liver, bloated and discolored, riddled with fat.

"He must have been in a lot of pain from this, don't you think?"

"Probably. Some people have a pretty high pain tolerance, but I don't imagine he was asymptomatic. You can see how jaundiced he was. I'm surprised his physician didn't admit him to the hospital."

"I assume he wasn't that jaundiced for his last appointment." Kenzie worked with Dr. Cook to cut the liver free. "His girlfriend is a nurse."

Dr. Cook stopped and looked at Kenzie across the body. "I'm surprised *she* didn't have him in the hospital."

"She said she hadn't realized how much he had changed, but she must have seen the jaundice. She knew he was seeing his doctor. Maybe she thought that if it was that serious, the doctor would know what to do."

"If she was a nurse, she should know better," Dr. Cook said with a twinkle in his eyes.

Kenzie chuckled. The nurses she knew were all very competent and had saved a doctor's bacon more than once. As a medical student, she had learned that a good nurse was worth her weight in gold.

She placed the liver on the scale and shook her head as she dictated the weight into the record. "I don't know if a hospital could have done anything other than make him comfortable at this point. One of those medications, or the combination, just destroyed his liver."

"Or it could be a familial disease," Dr. Cook pointed out, "or a history of alcoholism or other drug abuse. Don't make assumptions.

Just because the medications he was on could cause liver toxicity, that doesn't mean they did."

Kenzie conceded the point. They would have to wait to see what the histopathology showed, what his liver enzymes and other blood tests showed,

"Hair analysis," she suggested, "I'd like to see a timeline of what drugs he was taking."

"Good idea," Dr. Cook agreed. "We can easily find out when he was prescribed the varying medications, but sorting out any alcohol, illegal drugs, and over-the-counter medications is going to be a lot more difficult. The girlfriend or roommate might be able to provide some observations, but hair strand analysis will be more accurate. Would you like me to prepare the hair samples?"

"Sure," Kenzie agreed.

Dr. Cook moved to Scott's head and bent close to him to cut strands of hair from as close to the scalp as possible. He packaged them for the lab while Kenzie went on to remove the kidneys, noting the weight and color and carefully documenting each.

"I will take blood and fluids while you do stomach contents," Cook told her. "Then we can move on to organ dissections and preparing tissue samples for the lab."

10

K enzie was relieved to set aside the Robertson postmortem and focus on other tasks. She needed to keep up with the rest of her work, and she really needed to be able to disengage from the Robertson case and think about something else. She would still have Robertson in the back of her mind, but she could let her subconscious brain work on that while she got caught up on the other reports that had come in and routine work that needed to be done. It was a slower time of year for the morgue, not like it was around Christmas and New Year's, but there was always more paperwork to be done.

She heard the elevator doors open and heels clicking down the hall toward her, so she put her finger on her computer screen to mark her place and looked up to see who it was. For an instant, she didn't recognize Rachel Evans in her nursing scrubs.

"Rachel. I'm surprised to see you here. You didn't need to come all the way down here…"

She was glad to see the woman, though. Kenzie had not been able to talk to her privately at the apartment, and both she and Alex had been in shock over their discovery.

"I really felt like I needed to talk to you," Rachel said, looking around. "I guess… is there somewhere we could sit down?"

"Of course," Kenzie agreed. "Just give me a minute to forward my phone."

"You're the assistant medical examiner *and* the receptionist?"

Kenzie shrugged. "Small town. I started off in an administration role, even though I have the medical training. I didn't have enough practical experience at that point and medical examiner positions don't open up very often. The position allowed me to learn more about how everything works, get my feet wet, and gradually get the experience I needed to be promoted into the assistant medical examiner role."

"You're pretty young to be a medical examiner, aren't you?"

Kenzie thought about Dr. Cook. He was younger than she was and her senior, with lots of pathology experience. "Well, most medical examiners are older," she admitted. "But you don't have to be. I think maybe... most young doctors like to start with live patients. But that was never my thing. I got the practical experience I needed to earn my medical degree, but my goal was always pathology."

Kenzie finished locking down her computer and forwarding the phones, and motioned Rachel toward the boardroom. "We can meet right here."

She let Rachel in, then shut the doors and they sat down to talk.

"I'm sorry to come by without an appointment," Rachel apologized. "It just seemed like too much to call ahead. I don't have a lot of mental energy for much right now."

"It's okay. I have the time. You didn't catch me in the middle of anything I couldn't put aside for a while. I'm glad that you came by. I was hoping to talk to you again, but I don't like to push people. Everyone needs time to mourn and to adjust to the loss. And there ends up being so much to do with funeral arrangements and finances and all."

Rachel put her hands flat on the table and looked down at them. "I don't have all that much to do, to be honest. We weren't married, so I don't have anything to do with the will and taking care of his estate. I talked to his brother this morning about funeral arrangements and if there is anything I can help out with, and it sounds like he isn't even going to have a funeral." Her eyes shone with unshed tears. "How could he not even have a funeral? What is he going to do? Just cremate Scott and not even have any kind of service for his friends? I know the two of them didn't get along, but…"

Kenzie laid a comforting hand on Rachel's arm. "You know… you don't have to have possession of Scott's remains to hold a memorial service. You don't have to be the next of kin. You can just call Scott's friends and invite them to a get-together to mark his passing. They can call other people who know him. You can put out a notice in the paper or on social media. You don't need his brother to agree to anything."

Rachel raised her eyes. "Really?" She thought about it. "I guess you're right. He can't do anything to stop me from getting together with a group of friends. It's none of his business, in fact."

Kenzie smiled. "That's right. And it can be whatever kind of get-together you want. It doesn't have to be a formal funeral—though you can have a religious talk and eulogy and all of that if you want to—it could be a dinner or a movie night or going to a baseball game together. Whatever you think Scott would have liked. Whatever you think his friends would appreciate."

"Yeah. I could. Maybe we'll get together and have curry." She laughed.

"Did Scott like curry?"

"He was obsessed with it the last few months, and the hotter the better. It was funny, because when I met him he didn't like spicy stuff. But his tastes had really changed."

"Really? How interesting. You don't see that a lot. Had you introduced him to a lot of new foods?"

"No, it wasn't anything to do with me. I don't know why his tastes changed. He just said… everything else tasted too bland. He wanted stronger, spicier flavors."

Kenzie nodded and made a mental note of this fact. Was it another symptom? Loss of taste? Sometimes medications did weird things with the taste buds. There was also some connection she vaguely remembered between depression and taste.

"Were there any other changes that you noticed in Scott? I'm sorry we didn't get longer to talk at the apartment, and I'm glad you came to see me. Looking at Scott's condition… I imagine he must have been feeling pretty bad toward the end."

Rachel wiped at the corners of her eyes, not letting the tears escape. "It was… to be honest, I wasn't there a lot of the time. We were sort of… things hadn't been going so well between us. I didn't know whether we were going to break up. Well, I figured we would break up; I just wasn't sure when or how. It seemed… kind of inevitable."

"Oh." Kenzie was sympathetic. "That must have been really hard. Did you just find that you were not compatible with each other? Was there someone else? Or maybe you were just going in different directions?"

"He had turned really moody. Not that I blame him; I understand that he wasn't feeling very well and, when you're that sick, you get crabby. But he was… he was *really* moody. Not just grumbling and groaning or snapping if I bothered him with something. But angry! He scared me a couple of times. I thought he was going to break something. Or that he would hit me."

"Oh, no."

"He never did, luckily. I had decided that if he ever hit me, that would be the end of it. I wouldn't put up with physical violence. But the other stuff… yelling, throwing things around, just raging like some wild animal… I couldn't understand where it was coming from and didn't know how to talk to him about it. He didn't even seem to realize what he was doing. He used to be such a quiet, gentle guy."

"And there weren't any new stressors in his life, something that might be setting him off?"

Rachel shrugged helplessly. "Well, sure, there were new stressors. All the time. He was really stressed out almost all the time. I wouldn't even know where to start."

Despite this claim, Rachel immediately launched into an explanation.

"He was trying to start a new business. I didn't understand all of the details; it was very technical, a start-up that had something to do with financial tracking and prediction... He thought it would make a lot of money. But he really wasn't cut out for that kind of work. The start-up, I mean. He was fantastic with numbers and really smart about high finance. But starting his own business, getting investors, having to be the face of the company and figure out all of the stuff about registering his business and doing the tax stuff, finding a place to set up in, and all of the other stuff that goes with running your own business, he just was drowning in all of that."

Starting his own financial firm sounded like a nightmare to Kenzie. If Scott was the introverted, geeky guy that Kenzie pictured, she could only imagine how difficult it would be for him to deal with banks, grants, financial aid, investors, and all that. He had been anxious, stressed, and depressed in a failing body, falling out of his relationship with Rachel. It was a huge amount to deal with.

"I want to ask you about something, and I want you to think about it, not just blow it off. I know this is a difficult question, because I have dealt with it myself. Was it possible that Scott was suicidal?"

11

Y ou think he committed suicide?" Rachel shook her head. But she didn't immediately argue the point, taking her time to think about it as Kenzie had suggested. "What do you mean you've dealt with it yourself? You've been that depressed?"

"No, my partner. I know what it is like to have a partner who is depressed and suicidal. He had to be hospitalized, and it was all very scary. That horrible feeling of not knowing if he was going to be okay. Of what I would find when I got home from work. Of where he was and what he might have done if I couldn't reach him on the phone."

Rachel was nodding along with Kenzie's narrative, relief on her face. "Yeah. It's really hard. I didn't know who to talk to. His dad died a couple of years ago, and his mom is... I think she's in Australia. She didn't seem to want anything to do with the boys. So his brother was here, but they were estranged. I talked to Alex, and he had his concerns about Scott too. But where do you go with something like that? You can't exactly call the police because you think that someone might be suicidal. What are they going to do about it?"

"There are hotlines, and you can ask for a welfare check done on someone if you are really worried. You can send the police to someone's house."

Rachel raised her hands in mute appeal. "And then what? What do you do after you've hung up the phone? What do you do after the police check and say there is nothing they can do? Or the doctor prescribes antidepressants and says that it is all in his head? What do you do when the answer to every medical question is, 'lose some weight and get more exercise'?"

Kenzie wasn't sure what to offer. "That sounds awful. You must have been very frustrated."

"Not as frustrated as Scott. I don't think he even told me the half of it. Though I stopped listening when he would start on a rant... I knew what it was about and I just tuned it out... told him I had to go, or turned on the TV... anything to distract him or drown him out."

"Did he talk about suicide?" Kenzie asked, bringing Rachel back to the original point.

"No, not really. I mean, he said he wished he was dead or that he would be better off dead. He would say that he'd do anything to get rid of the pain or just to be able to eat a bowl of cereal or *anything* without feeling sick. But he never said he was going to kill himself."

"He had a lot of pills. Would you know how much of each one he had a week or two ago? Would you know if a bottle was empty that should have been full?"

"No, I never tracked any of his pills. You might think that's weird because I am a nurse. I want to take care of people. But I didn't get together with Scott as a patient. I never wanted to be his mother or nurse. When he started having health problems, we both agreed that he was a grown man and could deal with the doctors and his medications and stuff on his own. Sometimes... I regretted that. Or told him he needed to ask his doctor about this issue or that... but I tried to stay out of it."

Kenzie, too, had needed to learn to step back and not get involved in Zachary's medical issues. The more she pressed him to take his medications every day, the more he pushed back. She would try to recommend something, thinking that it would greatly benefit him, and he would tell her that he had done it before and it hadn't worked. She would tell him that he needed to bring something up with Dr. Boyle, his therapist, and he would resist and tell her that it was not the real issue. Taking care of someone else, especially someone with a mood disorder, was exhausting. It had been hard to learn to take a step back and let Zachary take care of himself unless he asked for something.

"He didn't leave a note," Rachel pointed out. "If it was a suicide, wouldn't he have left a note?"

"No, not necessarily. The majority of suicides do not leave a note."

"Really?"

Kenzie nodded. "Less than half. And then there are the suicides that don't look like suicides because the patient didn't want his family to know it was suicide for one reason or another. Someone who steps in front of a bus, falls off a cliff, or confronts the police in a gunfight is rarely identified as a suicide."

"Right. I guess not." Rachel shook her head, frowning. "I really don't know, then. Can't you tell whether Scott committed suicide?"

"I still have a lot more work to do and tests to run. Our conversation is just one part of the investigation. I'll want to talk to Alex too, and Scott's brother, and anyone else he had close contact with. I'm trying to get a full picture of what Scott was like and what life was like for him. His doctor is sending me a copy of his medical file, and I'll be able to look up when he was prescribed the various medications and how much of each he should have left, and if that information matches what was on the bottles."

"But you won't be able to tell with things like Tylenol or his allergy meds."

"Maybe I'll get lucky and be able to find purchase receipts. But I'm not counting on it. You don't happen to know if he kept his receipts, do you? Or where he usually bought his Tylenol?"

"I don't know. The grocery down the street, probably. We didn't usually shop together. And I had been with him less and less. I just couldn't deal with his mood swings and outbursts."

"That's understandable. It must have been very difficult. If it hadn't been for the moodiness, do you think it would have lasted? You said you thought the relationship was on its way out…"

Rachel rummaged in her purse without answering, eventually coming up with a pack of tissues. She wiped her eyes and blew her nose.

"Things were not good. I think that if he had been healthy and it hadn't been for the moodiness and aggression…" She looked away from Kenzie. Her words suggested that she might be suggesting they would have stayed together, but her body language told a different story. There was no way they would still have been together. Probably the only reason they had still been together was because Rachel hadn't wanted to abandon Scott at the worst time of his life.

"He cheated on me," Rachel said finally, her voice flat. The emotion over losing Scott was gone, suppressed or overwhelmed by her outrage. "More than once. Me!" She gestured to herself. A pretty, petite blonde. Maybe the scrubs were not the most flattering clothes for her figure, but she was clean and well-groomed and obviously very smart. And Kenzie had seen Scott at his worst. Overweight, thinning hair, acne. He was smart, but he couldn't control his rage or, apparently, his libido. "How could Scott have cheated on me?" Rachel demanded. Her hands trembled slightly as she wiped her eyes.

Kenzie nodded. "It's hard to believe. And unfair. I'm sorry that you had to deal with that. You stayed with him, despite that?"

"I just… I don't know. I thought it wasn't fair for me to leave when he was sick. And with him being so sick, I knew he wasn't out with some other girl. He was done with that."

His health problems had seen to that.

12

K enzie was glad to be home. It had been a long day after a sleepless night, and she was ready to spend the evening relaxing and putting aside all thoughts of work.

She found, upon returning home, that she was alone again. As she should have known. Zachary had told her that his best surveillance period would be between the end of the workday and when his suspect went to bed. Zachary was probably sitting around the corner right now, watching the spy cameras he had installed on the windows and listening to the couple talk. Would they spend all night arguing and fighting with each other?

She quickly texted Zachary to let him know she was home and tell him to call or message her when he had some time. Nothing urgent. Hopefully, at some point, the young couple would just have the TV on, and Zachary could use the lull to give Kenzie a call so they could at least exchange pleasantries about their days.

Zachary had been a private investigator since Kenzie met him, and she had been very interested in his job and how it all worked. Their shared interest in law enforcement and justice had attracted them to each other. Zachary had needed Kenzie's knowledge of pathology, and she had been excited to work so closely with him to help him to solve a case that the police had failed to identify as a murder. It was exhilarating to be so closely involved with the investigation and yet working on their own.

So she knew from the start that there would be nights he had to do surveillance. Sometimes, he would be gone all night, and there was nothing she could say about it because she had understood the deal when they first got to know each other.

But she did wish that he was home to discuss the case with. Or to ignore the case and talk about other things. Maybe to sit down with popcorn and a movie like the couple he was watching were probably doing, cuddling on the couch and enjoying the warmth of each other's bodies.

It wouldn't be long before he was back. He would surveil the couple for a few days; then he would have enough information to report back to the woman's father, and he would take it from there. Zachary would be back to his regular schedule, and they could return to their usual routines.

It was funny that she was missing their little rituals and routines and felt at loose ends being by herself. She had always thought that the routines meant more to Zachary. He was the neurodivergent one who needed the structures and routines to keep his brain happy.

But she missed them too.

There were a lot of things that Kenzie had promised herself she would do when she had some free time. When she didn't have to be either at work or with Zachary and could pursue her own interests and activities. Chores, hobbies, friends to get in touch with, books to read… and she didn't feel like doing any of them.

But Kenzie's usual routine after a grueling autopsy was to have a long shower as soon as she got home, and then deal with supper and everything else afterward when she was clean and relaxed and all the sore muscles soothed by the hot water. And that was something that she would do with or without Zachary home.

Kenzie felt rejuvenated after her shower; her skin tingled from the hot water and her muscles were loose and relaxed. She scavenged the fridge after getting out of the shower. She had already put on her jammies, so she didn't want to go out shopping or to pick something up from one of the fast-food restaurants nearby. Likewise, she didn't want to order in and have to face the deliveryman in her PJs. There wasn't much in the fridge that interested her and she wasn't up to making anything complicated. She managed to find a small microwave dinner, one of those ones that was supposed to be low-calorie and good for her. She'd bought it around New Year's Day when she had been determined to lose some weight and get into better shape. That had been four months ago and it had been sitting in the freezer ever since.

But there was also ice cream, which helped round out her need for something sweet and chocolatey to make her feel better. Just a little spoonful. Or two.

As she swiped her finger around the inside of the bowl to catch the last few drops of sweet ice cream, she saw Zachary's car pull in front of the house. She looked at the clock in surprise. She hadn't expected him to be home before ten. He climbed out of the car quickly, checked the locks, and strode toward the house. What was wrong? Why was he home already and in such a hurry?

Kenzie headed for the door, the bowl still in her hand, and reached the entryway as Zachary pushed open the door, his face pale and eyes wide. He jumped back when he saw her standing right in front of him, instinctively raising his hands in defense.

"Kenzie!"

"Whoa. What's wrong, Zach?"

He lowered his hands slowly. He turned away from her, and she saw him swallow hard and then focus on the burglar alarm, punching in his passcode so that it would not go off. He turned back to her, eyes down at her feet.

"Uh, I was worried. I texted and called, but you didn't answer."

Kenzie patted her leg, realizing she didn't have a pocket—and therefore no phone. "I must have left it in the bedroom. I'll go get it."

"You're okay?"

"Yes. Everything is fine. You didn't come home just for that, did you? Just because I didn't answer right away?"

"Well…"

Kenzie didn't know what to think about that. She shook her head. "I would have gotten back to you. I was just eating dinner."

"I didn't know," his voice betrayed his frustration. "All I knew was that you were not answering. I thought maybe… something happened to you."

"Did you check your map app? You would have been able to see that I was at home."

"Knowing you are at home—or your phone is—is not the same as knowing you are safe."

They had been targeted several times at home. Kenzie couldn't exactly forget that. She should probably be glad that he had apparently not called the police or the security company to check on her, but had returned home himself.

"I'm sorry."

Kenzie left him in the front entryway while she returned to the bedroom to retrieve her phone from where she had set it down on the dresser before getting into the shower. There was a long trail of messages and missed call notifications on the screen.

"I'm sorry," she repeated as she returned to talk to Zachary in the living room. "I really am. I didn't mean to worry you. I texted you when I got home to let you know I was all right. I thought… you would appreciate that."

Zachary took a deep breath and let it back out. "I do. I just thought…" He looked down at the message on his phone, then read it aloud. "I'm home. Text or call when you can. It's urgent."

"What?" Kenzie looked down at her own phone. "That isn't what I said. I said *not* urgent." But there on her screen were the same words Zachary had read aloud. It wasn't just his dyslexia substituting the words he expected to see; it was right there in green and white. "I did, I said *not* urgent. It must have autocorrected."

Zachary let out a bark of laughter. "Dang autocorrect. You should have checked it! Or answered when I called you."

"I was in the shower. That's all. And then I was eating dinner. Didn't even realize that I hadn't picked it up when I got out."

"I think you've got it backward. *I'm* the one with ADHD, remember?"

Kenzie chuckled. She was glad he could joke about it, but his tone was still very stressed. He could probably see that it wasn't really her fault, just a technology fail, but he still wanted her to fix it somehow, to make up for the mistake.

"Well, since you are back from your surveillance early, maybe we could spend some time together," she suggested. "Some *quality* time."

Zachary rubbed his forehead. "I had not planned to be home so early tonight."

"I know. So, let's make the most of it. Tomorrow you can work later."

"I had it all planned out."

"I know. But I guess it wasn't meant to be. So you can get over it, right?" Now the stress was creeping into her own voice. Rather than trying to pull back on it, she doubled down. "It was just a mistake, Zachary. You have to be able to adapt to changes in your plans."

He looked at her, frustrated. "I do adapt to changes," he snapped. "I thought you were in trouble. I thought something was wrong. I can't just turn off that part of my brain."

"Okay. But you can see I am okay, so you can start coming down. If your anxiety is that high, then..."

She was about to suggest he should take his anxiety meds, but that would do no good. Nothing good had ever come from her telling him how to manage his own brain. She swallowed her anger and frustration, deciding that she was the one who was going to have to make adjustments.

"Then why don't you tell me what I can do to help," she suggested quietly.

Then she shut her mouth and waited. Since her instinct was always to keep giving advice until he blew up, this apparently surprised him, and he wasn't sure what to tell her.

"I think… I just need to take a few minutes," he told her awkwardly, and shimmied by her to go to the bathroom and shut the door.

He could have had the bedroom if he had wanted it. Or the office, which they shared. But apparently, he had sent himself to the bathroom. Kenzie took her bowl into the kitchen and put it in the dishwasher. There wasn't really anything else to clean up, since she had eaten the frozen dinner right out of the box and already put the fork in the dishwasher. Cleanup was so much easier when it was just one person, especially if she didn't actually cook anything.

13

Kenzie didn't know whether Zachary would want to stay home and do something with her or go back out and finish his surveillance. She told herself firmly that it didn't matter which he chose; she would be fine with it.

In case he wanted to stay home or was considering staying home, Kenzie turned on the TV and looked for something to watch together. They both liked movies, forensic shows or other true crime, and a variety of other shows. And Zachary was easy to please if he was working on his laptop while they watched, because he would more than likely hyperfocus on his work and not have a clue what was on the TV.

She turned the lighting down so it was a warm, golden glow, peaceful and cozy.

Eventually, Zachary returned. His face was damp from splashing water on it. His movements were no longer tight and angry, but were still awkward and uneasy.

"I didn't know what you would want to do," Kenzie told him. "Did you want to go back out or stay home?" She didn't emphasize either choice, trying to make it clear that he was free to choose whichever he wanted. If his brain would not let go of the idea of finishing his surveillance, he could go back and finish it. He wouldn't sleep if she imposed a decision on him and his brain refused to let his idea go.

Zachary looked around, his breathing slow and even. There wasn't anything to look at. He was just trying to regulate himself. A car drove by outside, and he watched it all the way down the street.

"I think… I may as well stay home," he told her in a calm voice. "If I go back, I'll probably only have another hour before he goes to bed. I may as well not waste my time going back and forth across town."

Kenzie nodded. "Okay. Did you want to watch something?"

He looked at the directory on the screen.

"Yeah, that sounds good."

After they had been cuddling for a while and it was obvious that Zachary was feeling better and settled down, back to his usual self, Kenzie broached the subject of his surveillance.

"So, how are things going with the new file?"

Zachary played with Kenzie's hair as she leaned against him.

"Not a lot of progress yet. Still checking into his background. Haven't caught anything on video, but they are definitely having some… tense discussions."

Kenzie felt a little guilty about their own tension. But that hadn't been her fault. It had just been a misunderstood text and Zachary's anxiety over whether Kenzie was okay. They did not have an abusive relationship. They were in couple's therapy to help them learn how to communicate better and to handle Zachary's trauma and mental illness. Their relationship was not in trouble and was not in danger of becoming violent. Every relationship had tension from time to time, and it was not unexpected that they would have more because of Zachary's emotional dysregulation and trauma responses.

"What have you found out about his background so far?"

"No criminal record. He hasn't changed his name or anything like that. As far as past relationships go, I am still working on that. It seems pretty obvious that he has a temper, but anger doesn't always lead to abuse. To physical abuse, anyway."

Kenzie was lucky not to have had to deal with any physically abusive relationships in her past. Many women did. And many men, for that matter. Zachary had dealt with a significant amount of abuse in the past, including an abusive relationship with his ex-wife Bridget. Kenzie wasn't sure if Bridget's abuse had ever escalated to physical violence, but the verbal and emotional abuse Zachary had suffered from her had been significant.

"What does your gut tell you?" she asked Zachary. "Do you think there is physical abuse?"

He was probably wound so tightly because of the tension he had already observed between the couple. Kenzie had no doubt that he would have a negative reaction to witnessing an argument or abuse. His brain was hardwired to protect him against any perceived threats. It would explain why he had immediately assumed that Kenzie was in trouble when she didn't answer his phone calls. If he had taken the time to think about it, he would have known that she would hop in the shower immediately after she got home. And obviously she wouldn't have her phone in there with her.

"Probably," Zachary admitted. "He seems aggressive. And if her father was seeing red flags, I think that's a pretty good indicator. Even if he hasn't seen any physical abuse himself, I don't doubt that what he sensed was real. If it hasn't turned abusive already, it probably will."

"It's good she has someone on her side. I'm glad she has a dad looking out for her."

Zachary nodded his agreement. "It's good to have people in your life who are looking out for you."

He had been alone for much of his life. For many years, his old foster father, Lorne Peterson, had been his only safe haven. But now he also had Kenzie, and his siblings were back in his life. And a small circle of cops and other friends who only wanted the best for him and would try to keep him safe from harm.

"It is," Kenzie agreed, tickling the back of his neck with a light touch. "You and I are both lucky to have people in our lives who… would do everything they could to make sure we don't get hurt."

He reached for her fingers, but she eluded him, grinning.

"Do you think it is affecting you? Watching them, waiting for him to start hurting her?"

She could feel him withdraw from her, sense the cooling between them.

"I guess *you* think so."

"I don't know. I'm just asking. You're pretty tense today. I just wonder if it is bothering you more than you realize."

"I won't let it affect me."

Kenzie didn't think he could control that. He could try to moderate his behavior and tell himself not to overreact, but he couldn't just turn his reaction off.

"Okay. I was just wondering if it was bothering you."

Zachary turned his attention back to the TV, staring intently at the screen, though Kenzie didn't know if he were actually seeing the movie playing out before him. She snuggled into him, not saying anything, and waited for his body to relax. It would probably be a good night for him to take an anti-anxiety pill and a sleep aid, but she didn't know whether he would or not. But she knew he wouldn't if she told him he should.

14

enzie sat down at the boardroom table and spread out the contents of the file before her. Dr. Brandon had sent her a photocopy of his paper file for Robertson, but it was not in any logical order. It was as if he had intentionally mixed the various lab reports and consultation notes together in the most confusing and misleading way possible. She had encountered this kind of passive-aggressive behavior from medical professionals before. Dr. Brandon had complied with her request to provide her with copies of his files, as he was required to by law, but that didn't mean he had to make it easy for her.

It wasn't that hard to spread everything out on the table and sort it into chronological order. Then Kenzie started to read through the items to construct a timeline.

Until a few months ago, all of Scott's visits to the doctor had been for incidental things. Antibiotics for an infection, flu shot, a rash that Brandon believed resulted from a contact allergy rather than dry skin as Robertson had thought. Pretty routine stuff.

The first one that hinted of a more serious problem had been about three months earlier, when Robertson had come in with multiple complaints. Fatigue, mood swings, and weight gain. From Brandon's somewhat cryptic notes, it looked like they had talked about stress and an allergy to the roommate's new cat. Brandon had advised him to take an over-the-counter antihistamine and to get more exercise.

Not an unexpected response. At that point, Robertson didn't show signs that it was anything serious. It *could* have just been overwork, a sedentary lifestyle, and an allergy to the cat. Being congested from a mild allergy would make it harder to get the sleep he needed and might reduce the amount of oxygen he was getting. That and stress would cause mood issues and fatigue. All easily addressed by some minor lifestyle changes.

But when Robertson had returned, his initial symptoms had not been resolved and he was having additional issues. He reported shortness of breath and chest discomfort. But he was young and had been in good health, and Brandon, reviewing the previous notes, recommended a stronger antihistamine and an inhaler to help keep his chest clear and the addition of an anti-anxiety medication to be taken as needed. The advice to get more exercise was repeated, as he had put on additional weight since his last appointment.

Dr. Brandon had been careful enough to order an EKG to check for heart problems and a follow-up appointment.

The next appointment had been a few weeks later. Robertson had been too busy to get the EKG done. This time, he presented with symptoms that were serious enough for the doctor to start to get concerned. The former symptoms had not subsided, and he now presented with edema in his legs and complained of having to get up several times in the night to use the bathroom.

Dr. Brandon repeated the order for an EKG, setting up an appointment for Robertson this time instead of leaving it for him to schedule. He also ordered blood tests to check Robertson's kidney function and lipid levels.

The EKG showed left ventricular hypertrophy and ischemic changes to the heart, suggesting reduced blood flow. His kidney function was low, but not critical. Referrals were made for both cardiac and renal consults. His LDL (bad cholesterol) levels were high. Brandon prescribed the statin at that point to manage the cholesterol and recommended strict dietary changes to reverse the cardiovascular issues. Kenzie assumed that Brandon's recommendations were probably pretty strongly worded at this point. Robertson was still a young man and, if he wanted to avoid a heart attack, he needed to make some significant changes to his lifestyle. Brandon had also added an SSRI at this point in response to Robertson's repeated complaints about depression and not wanting to get out of bed in the morning.

Kenzie was glad to see that Brandon had, in fact, ordered the appropriate tests and made referrals to specialists, and not just asserted that Scott Robertson was too young to be concerned about heart or kidney disease. But it had not been enough. Robertson's symptoms had developed very quickly, which suggested they were caused by something more than just eating too much fast food and not getting the exercise he needed. More was going on than just his work stress and allergy to Cuddles.

"How's it going?" Dr. Cook asked.

Kenzie jumped, not having heard his approach.

"Sorry, sorry," Dr. Cook apologized, chuckling. "I should know better than to sneak up on someone so absorbed in her work."

Kenzie took a few deep breaths, hand over her pounding heart. "No, it's okay. I just didn't hear you coming. I think we need to put a bell on you! You're too quiet."

"I am sorry. Just wondered how things were going. This is the Robertson case?"

"Yeah. There's a good paper trail showing Robertson's progressing symptoms and the doctor did order tests and prescribe appropriate treatment. But…"

Dr. Cook sat down and waited for Kenzie to pull her thoughts together.

"I'm still not seeing the initial cause of his symptoms. It happened pretty quickly, so we might be looking for a toxin. I don't think it was a virus or familial disease."

"Are you thinking of something environmental? A chemical he was exposed to? Maybe something at work?"

"It sounds like his work was all computer stuff, nothing industrial. Unless he had another job on the side. All of this was clearly not caused by his allergy to the roommate's cat."

Dr. Cook rubbed his chin. "Could it have been triggered by something he contracted from the cat? Toxoplasma gondii, cat scratch fever, or tapeworms? Or maybe some combination? Toxoplasmosis in an immune-compromised individual could cause multiple organ failure."

"Really? Do you think so?"

Dr. Cook shook his head slowly. "I *don't* think so, no. But it is a possibility. But if he started to suffer symptoms shortly after the introduction of the cat… it is something we should at least check."

"Aren't about ten percent of people in the United States positive for toxo?"

"Around that," Dr. Cook agreed. "And most of them will never even know it or have anything more than mild symptoms. But if there is a connection between the cat and his failing health, it could be toxoplasmosis or another zoonotic infection."

Kenzie added a few tests to her notes. "Okay. That would be weird, but you never know what you'll find in a case like this."

He agreed. "You certainly don't expect to die from someone adopting a stray cat, but there is a reason you are supposed to take them to the vet to be checked out right away. You never know what you might catch from a stray."

"I don't know how they got it or where it came from. Just that the girlfriend was really upset about it because Robertson was allergic and the roommate had decided to keep it anyway. Most places won't even let you have pets; I don't know what their landlord would have thought about it."

"Maybe the girlfriend should have called him. It would be the easiest way to get the animal out of the house."

Kenzie drew a line across her notepad to separate her timeline notes from his findings. "So tell me about what you found."

Dr. Cook had been working on organ dissections since early morning. Kenzie wasn't sure when he had arrived, but he had already been deep into his work when she got to the office.

"Well, as we could tell when we first removed them, the heart and liver were enlarged and riddled with fat. His heart also showed—"

"Left ventricular hypertrophy?" Kenzie suggested.

Dr. Cook raised his brows. "You move to the head of the class. Good guess?"

"He had an EKG that suggested it. Also suggested ischemic changes."

"His heart was not getting enough oxygen," Dr. Cook agreed. "All in all… with *just* the damage to his heart, he would not have lasted much longer without some kind of intervention."

"And how about the rest? The doctor did not test liver enzymes —at least not in the documents I have reviewed. Kidney function was reduced."

"We'll see what our liver enzymes test shows. But the gross changes to the liver are pretty extensive. Fatty liver, necrosis, and a few visible tumors. The histological analysis will show even more, I'm sure. Whatever attacked Robertson's liver was pretty toxic. I would not have been surprised to hear he worked with solvents. But no?"

Kenzie shook her head. "No, and nothing that I saw around the apartment, but I might want to go back and check again now that I have a better idea of what we are looking for."

"Yes. Might be a good idea. We don't want anyone else to be exposed to whatever it was."

Kenzie thought again of the cat and the dreams she'd had about it. That, combined with the issue of toxic chemicals, made her think of a cat with Spider-Man-like powers. She shook her head, laughing at herself. She obviously still needed to catch up on her sleep.

Dr. Cook cocked his head. "What was that?"

Kenzie covered her face with her hand, embarrassed. "Wild imagination. Mutant cats with special powers."

He snorted. "Did you stay up late watching movies last night?"

"Not that late. And no Spider-Man."

15

Kirk Robertson bore little resemblance to his brother, either before or after Scott's illness. He had red hair and a red face. Lots of broken capillaries around his nose suggested that he might be a drinker. He had rounded shoulders and a thick body that suggested strength despite the fat around his abdomen. The kind of guy Kenzie had seen pulling fire engines in contests of strength on TV. She showed him into the boardroom, once again neat and tidy after she had picked up all of Dr. Brandon's papers and filed them properly.

Kirk looked around suspiciously and lowered himself into one of the padded boardroom chairs. "I don't have to identify Scott's body or anything like that?"

"No. He was already identified by his roommate and girlfriend. They were the ones who found him. We have his government-issued identification, and everything lines up. We're not concerned with identifying him, just with figuring out the cause of death."

"I don't know how I can help you with that. I haven't had anything to do with him for a couple of years, I told you that. I'm not a medical professional. I thought you guys were the experts on that." His eyes flicked around the room. "I suppose this is such a small town that you aren't really trained to do this kind of thing.

Do you have another job? Like you're the mortician or something and just do autopsies on the side?"

"No. This is my full-time job. I am a trained pathologist, not the only one working out of this office. And there are plenty more around in Vermont who could help out if we ran into something that we hadn't seen before and needed some help. But TV shows like *CSI* and *Bones* have led people to believe that we can do a lot of things that we really can't. They make it look like the cause of death is always easy to determine, and you don't have to make a judgment call one way or other."

"And that's not accurate," Kirk guessed.

"Not at all. A lot of different mechanisms of death look the same, even though they have different root causes. Suffocation and anaphylaxis, for example. We might only know the difference if we are told that the patient had an allergy and we know that the allergen was present at the scene or in the stomach contents."

"But the guy with anaphylaxis would be all swollen up and have hives, and someone who was suffocated would have bruises inside their lips and petechial hemorrhaging," Kirk objected immediately.

Kenzie just looked at him.

"Okay, so I like my medical shows," Kirk admitted. "I guess that's exactly what you're saying."

"Yes. Your TV sleuths would always have enough evidence to tell the difference. Because it's a lame show if they can't actually figure it out. But in real life, not everyone with anaphylaxis shows any signs that can be discerned postmortem. Sometimes, the heart stops before anything else can develop. And not everyone who is suffocated has petechial hemorrhaging. And you can also get petechial hemorrhaging from coughing or throwing up. Or other extra-curricular activities."

Kirk nodded slowly. He leaned back in his chair, making it creak, as he thought it through. "Okay. So sometimes you need to know more from the people who knew the dead guy. Like whether he had allergies or not."

"Exactly."

"Well, Scott didn't."

Kenzie raised her brows. "Didn't…"

"Didn't have any allergies."

"Uh… I understand he was allergic to cats."

"Well, cats, yes. A little bit. Like hay fever symptoms. Stuffed-up nose, red eyes. I meant not like anaphylaxis. Nothing that would kill him."

"Allergies can change over time, getting more or less severe. But we don't think Scott died of anaphylaxis. I haven't seen any signs of that. He did have some pretty serious medical issues, though."

"Scotty? Really? He never seemed like the type. He was always pretty healthy growing up. Didn't miss a lot of school. Didn't fake sick like some of us," Kirk chuckled. "He was kind of… mama's boy, teacher's pet, golden child." He rolled his eyes. "I was not."

Kenzie smiled. "I've seen that dynamic before. You got in trouble?"

"Not very much. A little. Well, maybe more than a little. But since Scotty didn't get into any trouble, I had to get in enough for both of us."

"That makes sense." She smiled.

He was getting more relaxed talking with her. No longer so suspicious or defensive. He could see that she was a real person, not some bureaucrat or government official who was out to get him.

"Did either of you have any major illnesses growing up, Chickenpox? Strep throat?"

"No. Our parents believed in vaccines and handwashing, so we never really had any of those things to worry about."

"Anything inherited? Kidney disease that runs in the family or anything like that?"

"We're all pretty normal, I think. I still have most of my grandparents. One died in a farming accident. You know that our dad died. But that was not unexpected. He was a smoker practically from birth. Lots of coughing and wheezing for those last few years."

"Oh, I'm sorry to hear that. That can't have been very pleasant."

"Well, luckily, I wasn't home for the end stage. I'd hear him hacking away on the phone. Mostly just talked to Mom, and she would relay anything he wanted me to know. We all knew it was coming. I remember growing up…" Kirk stared off into the distance. "The way he smelled, that stale cigarette smoke that clung to him even if he had just stepped out of the shower. His yellow fingers. His breath. If I ever have kids, I'm definitely telling them how not-cool it is to end up like that. I'll probably traumatize them with gruesome descriptions, but they'll never touch a cigarette."

"I'm glad that it has fallen out of favor. Though the resurgence with e-cigarettes and vaping is concerning. I guess every generation has to try it for themselves."

"Not my kids."

Kenzie nodded.

"So… what was going on with Scott?" Kirk asked, finally sounding like he cared about him instead of being angry with him for whatever had happened with their father's estate. "It was such a shock to hear that he had died. I didn't even know he was sick."

"His decline was rapid. Over a period of a few months. Did you hear anything at all from him during that time? Or maybe your mother passed on information about how he was doing?"

Kirk's brow furrowed. "My mother has… disengaged from life since my father died. Or she's disconnected from us, at least. We occasionally hear something from her through the lawyers but, mostly, it's radio silence. She moved to the other side of the world. Australia. It's like she needs to find herself or something. Find out who she is now that Dad is gone."

"Is it because of the trouble over his estate?"

"Some of it probably is. I can tell you that she is not too impressed with us for our…" Kirk fished for a word. "For our childishness? Our selfishness?" He banged his hand down on the table with a soft thump. "But the terms of the will were unfair. I don't see how we could be expected to just walk away from the estate without anything."

"Did he leave everything to your mother?"

"No. He left a bunch of bequests to charities, some to Mom, and the rest he left to us in trust, like we were little kids. But he gave money to Scott for his business before he died. A *lot* of money. That should have come out of Scott's portion of the inheritance.

And some of the foundations he gave money to, they were funding Scott's research, so he double dipped that way too. He screwed me out of thousands of dollars."

"I see." Kenzie wasn't sure how to respond to the allegations. There wasn't anything she could do about it, of course. She tried to look and sound as sympathetic as possible. "I suppose that Scott passing away complicates things even more."

"I talked to Mom about it. Apparently, the way that Dad had the trust set up, if one of us died without kids, the money went to the survivor. So there's no point in taking the fight in probate court any further, since I would just be fighting against myself! The whole trust comes to me now. Which is how it should have been in the first place, since he had already spent so much on Scotty."

"Right. And you aren't interested in preserving Scott's legacy? Finishing what he started?"

"It's not my thing. I couldn't run it if I wanted to." Kirk shrugged philosophically. "Maybe his idea will be picked up by some other bright young student. But it won't be on my dime."

"Well, that's lucky for you, then."

Kirk frowned at her. "I didn't want my brother to die. I was fully prepared to duke it out in court. I would have won, eventually. The whole point of the trust and the provisions in his will were to give us equal amounts of his wealth. Not to give three-quarters of it to Scott. I would have won."

Kenzie nodded and didn't see any reason to argue or dig any deeper into it. Kirk could believe what he liked. There wasn't any way for anyone to know how it would have turned out if Scott had survived.

"Did your lawyer tell you that Scott was sick? Did you and your mother know anything about it?"

"I remember his lawyer using it as an excuse for him to get a couple of hearings delayed, but I put a stop to that. One delay I can understand, but if you are going to demand more than that, you'd better be at death's—" Kirk cut himself off and flushed scarlet. "I didn't mean it that way. I didn't mean I would have wanted Scott to die. Just... yes, I heard that he was sick, but I had no idea he was *that* sick. I didn't think it was anything. Maybe a bug. Maybe out drinking too late. I never would have thought that my little brother, in the prime of life, was going to die. It never even occurred to me."

"No, if you weren't in touch, there is no way you would have known how sick he really was. I don't know if *he* realized how sick he was."

"What was it, then? I never knew he was really that sick."

"The death investigation is still underway, but I can tell you that he suffered multiple organ failures. There was probably nothing anyone could have done, even if you had known about it a month ago."

"Multiple organ failure? What does that even mean? How do you get that?"

"That is what we are looking into. When I know... I will let you know."

"Okay, good." Kirk placed his hands flat against the tabletop, ready to push himself up. "That's it, then, right?"

"That's it for now. I may have other questions, though. I hope you will indulge me."

He shrugged and didn't agree or disagree.

16

K enzie's phone rang as she was getting ready to go home. She was tempted just to ignore it. Her workday was done, and she needed time to relax. But she looked at the name on the front of her phone and sighed.

Lisa Cole Kirsch

Kenzie swiped to answer the call. "Hi, Mom."

"Mackenzie. It's good to hear your voice. We haven't talked for a while."

Kenzie had to think about whether it was true or not, which probably meant that it had been too long. She needed to do better at keeping in contact with her parents. Look at Zachary. After being separated from his siblings for decades, rarely a week went by now that he wasn't talking to one of them. More than likely, he contacted several of them during any given week. They hadn't grown up together, had been estranged for years, and were now as close as any adult siblings could expect to be.

Kenzie had still exchanged several texts and emails with her mother but knew it wasn't the same.

"You're right, Mom. I haven't been keeping up like I should. I'll try to do better at that. How are you?"

"As well as can be expected. I was wondering if you have any plans for tonight. Maybe we could get together for dinner?"

"Oh…" Kenzie really wasn't up for a road trip. Especially when Zachary was more than likely unavailable. She had come to rely on him to help buffer her from her parents. He was good at running interference. "I don't think I could make it to Burlington today."

"Well, that's just fine, because I'm not in Burlington. I can come to you. Where do you want to eat? Do you have a favorite restaurant? Home? We could get takeout."

"You're here in Roxboro?"

"I will be by dinnertime. Can we make it a date?"

"Well… of course. I'm not sure that Zachary will be able to be there, though. He's got a job."

"I would be delighted to have some one-on-one time with my daughter. I can't remember the last time we did something like that."

"No, I can't either."

Kenzie always went to her mother, not the other way around, and Lisa often had an ulterior motive for wanting to meet. A fundraiser she wanted Kenzie to arrange. A speech she wanted her to make. Some favor or other. If she was coming to Roxboro without warning, she must really need something badly.

"Is everything okay, Mom? Dad won't be with you?"

"No, he is still at home. Just us two girls tonight."

"Sure. Of course. That would be fine."

"Where should we meet, then? Would you like me to make a reservation?"

"Do you like Thai?"

"Whatever you like, dear. Thai is always nice."

"Okay, then," Kenzie gave her the name of their favorite Thai restaurant. "I need to go home and change and make myself presentable." Lisa typically had a much later dinner than Kenzie was used to anyway, so she wouldn't expect Kenzie to be ready for a few hours. "Should we say… eight?"

"That would be lovely. I'll see you there."

Kenzie looked at her phone to make sure the call had disconnected, and thought about it. She had no idea what to think about Lisa coming to Roxboro to have dinner with her. Or coming to Roxboro for something else and wanting to have dinner with Kenzie while she was there. Last-minute dinner arrangements were not really Lisa's thing so, chances were, something else had fallen through. Or else the issue Lisa wanted to discuss with Kenzie was tantamount to an emergency.

Kenzie tapped Zachary's name on her favorites list and waited for it to connect. She would either talk to Zachary one-on-one or leave him a detailed voicemail. No miscommunications.

Zachary answered after a couple of rings. "Hi, Kenzie. You must be off work. Or else calling to say that you're working late."

"I am off work."

"I won't be home; I am doing that surveillance."

"That's what I figured. Believe it or not, I got a call from Lisa, and she wants to have dinner."

"Oh, okay. When? I'm not sure I'll be free this weekend."

"Right now. Tonight. Just her and me. She's on her way to Roxboro now."

Zachary was silent.

Kenzie waited and, when he still didn't say anything, she went on. "That's weird, right?"

"It's unusual for your mom. She didn't say what she wanted? If there was something wrong?"

"She just said she wanted some face time, but it seems pretty strange to me. And she wouldn't necessarily tell me straight out if something was wrong. She would wait until we were together to spring that on me. Do you think it's Dad? That he's okay?"

"He's not with her?"

"No. She said he was home. I can understand them not wanting to be everywhere with each other. They are divorced, after all."

But Walter had been staying in the family home since he had been forced to fake illness to escape entanglement with an organized crime syndicate. As far as the rest of the world was concerned, he'd had a couple of serious strokes and was not able to work anymore. Withdrawing from the rest of the world had not been easy on him. Or on Lisa.

"Yeah, that makes sense, actually. But you know, she probably had an event to come to somewhere close by and decided she would try to see you while she was here. It will just be a nice little visit and then she will go home. Or maybe stay in a hotel for the night and then go home tomorrow."

"Or in our guest room."

Zachary grunted and didn't make any comment. There wasn't really anything appropriate to say, so that was a wise choice. He couldn't say that he didn't want Lisa to stay over, but he knew Kenzie wouldn't want her to stay over. Still, he couldn't say that, because she might take it as being judgmental or dissing her mom. Kenzie sighed.

"Well, I'll let you know what the scoop is once I find out," she promised. "I just wanted to give you a heads-up so you know where I am if it goes late. And to see if you had any thoughts."

"Well, there's no point in assuming it is going to be bad…"

This from the man who catastrophized everything in his own life.

"Of course not," Kenzie said sardonically. "I'm sure everything will be just fine."

Kenzie tried not to worry too much about what Lisa wanted, repeatedly assuring herself that Lisa just wanted to have dinner with her daughter and she should not read anything into it. She had a shower and relaxed for a while before dressing for dinner. The Thai restaurant was casual dining, not formal, so she didn't need anything too fancy, but Lisa would expect her to at least be in a skirt, not blue jeans.

At seven-thirty, she left for the restaurant, which got her there in plenty of time in a small town like Roxboro. But of course Lisa was still there ahead of her.

Kenzie and Lisa kissed cheeks in greeting, they each complimented each other on their dresses, and they were seated by a waiter who clearly recognized that Lisa was of a higher class than normally patronized the restaurant and that she should not be kept waiting like their usual customers. They were handed their menus and, in a moment, were alone at the table, looking at each other.

The restaurant's interior was adorned with intricate artwork and softly glowing lanterns that cast warm shadows on the walls. The gentle hum of conversation mixed with soft music playing in the background.

"This is nice," Lisa said, looking down at her menu.

"They have a great range of dishes and are always busy," Kenzie said. "That's the mark of a great restaurant."

"Indeed. I meant it was nice to be together. You and I."

"It is," Kenzie agreed. She looked around. "How is Dad? I worry about him."

"He's just fine. He gets bored, but what do you expect? He's used to being out and about all day, meeting with people, having his dinners and special chats, making backroom deals and planning... oh, all that stuff. It's quite a shock to his system to have to be at home 'relaxing' all day. Some men are just not made out for retirement."

"Yeah. And he can't show his face too soon, or the Russians will know it was just an act, and they won't leave him alone."

"It all has to be kept very hush-hush. For as long as it takes for them to lose interest in him."

"And how will you know when they have?"

Lisa shrugged. "I imagine... when we stop hearing rumors. When people stop asking how he is and if he will be able to go back to work."

Kenzie nodded. That made sense. "So... this dinner isn't about him?"

"It isn't about anything. But if Zachary needs Walter for more research or other jobs, he would certainly not turn them down."

Kenzie laughed. "I'll be sure to tell him. There must be something he can research for him. And is Dad getting into any of those innocence projects?"

Lisa nodded. "Dipping his toes in. I'm not sure how much he can do for them anonymously. They want to know the qualifications of the person they're dealing with. But he does some searches and writing up cases for them. Clerk work."

"That's good. I'm glad he's doing something."

17

Kenzie and Zachary both arrived home at about the same time and were taking off their coats and shoes as they greeted one another. Zachary's brow was furrowed and he didn't ask Kenzie about her dinner with Lisa, so Kenzie thought she had better ask him about his evening.

"How did the surveillance go?" she asked, trying to keep her voice light. She didn't want him to think she was worried about him or that he couldn't manage his own business and cases. He was good at what he did, managing to lean in on his strengths and work around his challenges. She was always impressed at how much he had managed to do on his own. With Heather helping him out now, he had someone he could rely on for administrative support and keeping up with fee collection, but before, he had somehow been managing to do all of that himself, too.

Zachary scowled as he considered her question. Not angry at her for asking, but maybe worried or stressed about something that had happened that evening.

"Nothing that can be used against him yet," he grumbled. "The guy is a jerk, a real piece of work, but so far he hasn't done anything physically abusive while I've been watching. You can't exactly prosecute someone for being a jerk."

"Too bad. We could make the world a better place if you could get some of those people off the streets."

Zachary gave a smile that was more of a grimace. Maybe remembering how Bridget had treated him while they had been married. He was obsessive about her, and there was no way he would want her to be arrested for verbal abuse, no matter how bad things had been.

"You're okay?" Kenzie asked. "Seems like maybe you're a little stressed about the surveillance."

"Oh, no. I'm fine. Just sitting in my car most of the time. Get out to stretch my legs every now and then. Listening in and watching remotely. Sooner or later, I'm pretty sure something is going to break. I don't believe that it is only verbally abusive. The dad's got it right. He's beating on her. I know the type."

Kenzie nodded slowly. "Well... I'm sorry to hear that. I mean, good for the dad for pursuing it, and for you to take it on and get the evidence, even if it is painful. But I'm sorry that she's being hurt and that everyone has to take such measures to get her the help she needs. Sorry that you have to listen to the abuse."

Zachary shrugged as if that part didn't matter. Which was just like him. Thinking about other people and seeing justice done, without considering how it affected him. He would put himself in danger or expose himself to his trauma triggers without a second thought.

"it will be worth it when we can get this piece of scum put behind bars. She might not thank her father for it, but he's doing the right thing."

"He's looking out for his little girl."

It was good to have family members who cared about each other. Thinking about Kirk and how unconcerned he had been with his brother's illness and death, Kenzie was saddened. There had been people in Scott Robertson's life who had cared about him. His girlfriend and roommate. She was sure his mother had been concerned about everything that was going on with him, even if she was living in Australia. They had undoubtedly called and emailed each other to keep in touch. Rachel had stayed with him even knowing that he had cheated on her, because she didn't want to abandon him while he was sick. And even though Alex had ignored Scott's allergy to the cat, Kenzie was sure he showed his concern for Robertson in other ways. They had checked in on him, knowing that he hadn't been feeling well. It hadn't been like some cases where the corpse rotted for weeks or months without anyone noticing.

"How about you?" Zachary asked at length. "How did your dinner go with your mom?"

"Oh, it was fine. We had a nice time together."

Zachary eyed her but didn't challenge the statement. He knew Kenzie often found it difficult to engage with her parents socially. They really did live in different worlds. Lisa and Walter wanted Kenzie to be a part of their world, to associate with the people they did, attend the functions, and help run the family foundation. Walter wanted her to be interested in the bills he lobbied for or against, and Lisa wanted her to be involved in her charitable causes.

But what Kenzie wanted to do did not involve parties, functions, or backroom negotiations. What she wanted to do was to get the bodies that came to the morgue to open up to her and to find the truth of what had happened to them. It was grisly, messy work, yet she found the constitution of the human body endlessly intriguing and genuinely enjoyed digging in and solving those mysteries. For her, bringing criminals to justice was far more rewarding than any social or political engagement her parents could offer.

"So that's all it was? Just dinner with your mom? No ulterior motives?"

"I think she wanted to get away from Walter, to tell the truth."

Kenzie opened the fridge and looked for something to eat. Never mind the fact that she had just come back from a long, drawn-out dinner with her mother. Lisa ate like a bird, and Kenzie would have felt judged if she had ordered what she really wanted at the restaurant. When she and Zachary ordered Thai, they always got a number of dishes and shared, and had enough left over for several meals over the following days. The variety and amount of food was satisfying. Tonight, she had ordered a small combo meal, and had felt like a pig in front of Lisa. She'd only eaten a small portion of it, and had not even packed the rest up to take home.

Now, she needed something to really satisfy her hunger. And it couldn't just be ice cream. She'd been eating too much ice cream lately.

"He's driving her crazy being in the house all day?"

Kenzie nodded as she pulled out several plastic dishes, tilting them over to see what was inside. She couldn't help grinning at the thought of Lisa and Walter trying to get along with each other. They were so different in nature. That was, she assumed, why they had divorced in the first place. The forced proximity of Walter living at the mansion during his fictional recovery must be torture for them both, even if there was plenty of space and they didn't even have to see each other if they didn't want to.

"Yeah. I think they're still trying to live separate lives, but they can't ignore the fact that someone else is in the house and they are supposed to get along with each other somehow."

"How bored is Walter?"

"I'm going to see if I can find anything he could do for me. Some background research or case law or something. I don't know. He needs a lot to keep him occupied, or he wanders around the house like a kid on summer holidays."

"Do you have anything for him? I don't know if I have anything right now that would interest him. It's mostly just waiting for the guy to take a misstep. Get video evidence of him crossing the line and assaulting his wife."

"Maybe," Kenzie had been thinking about it all night, but hadn't suggested anything to her mother. She needed to flesh out the idea and consult with Dr. Cook first. She couldn't invite a family member to help with a death investigation without approval. It wouldn't look good. "I need to learn more about this company that my victim was starting up. Maybe I could get Dad to do some research on what exactly it is that he had been planning to do and how much he had developed the ideas. The brother said that he had funding from the dad and some foundations, so it sounds like he was not just in the early stages of planning; he was getting closer to getting it off the ground. Maybe Dad could find out more about it."

"Is it relevant to how he died?" Zachary asked with a frown.

"Well… that's the question. I can't just hire someone to look at it on a whim, if it isn't relevant to the death. I have to show at least some connection between the business and his death, and there really isn't one at this point. It looks like he died from some kind of exposure to a toxin, and I don't think that had anything to do with the start-up company. It was computers or finances, not chemicals."

Kenzie decided on toast and marmalade. Not exactly a decadent evening snack, but comfort food. Something that would hopefully satisfy her need for a treat without adding too many calories. It wasn't like she had consumed a lot at dinner. She put the marmalade on the table and a piece of bread in the toaster. Zachary sat down in his chair.

"Toxic exposure to what?" he asked.

One thing that Kenzie loved about Zachary was his endless curiosity about her job. He relished hearing about her cases, delving into the details of autopsies, strange or startling discoveries, and how she unraveled the truth in particularly challenging situations.

"That's what I need to find out next. It looks like he was exposed to something that affected multiple organs. It could be the medications he was on, only it seemed to start before he was prescribed anything. The medications were an attempt to treat the symptoms of the poisoning, rather than causing it."

"And he didn't work with chemicals, that you know of?"

"No. It sounds like it was mostly computer work. High finance, not chemistry."

"Do you think someone was trying to kill him?"

Zachary had investigated a murder at an investment banking firm, so it wasn't surprising that his mind would go there.

"No, I don't think so. I assume it was an accidental exposure. Something he was taking or was exposed to in his environment."

"Like an herbal remedy?"

"That's a possibility, but there wasn't anything on his bedside table like that. Just a few over-the-counter meds. Again, trying to treat the symptoms of the toxic exposure."

"Can't you test for what the chemical was?"

"We're trying to do that, but you can't test for every substance on earth. You need to have an idea of what you are looking for in order to test for it."

"And it wasn't anything in those over-the-counter meds."

"I don't think so. But it's always possible. If he was taking large doses, and maybe had a preexisting condition, genetic or a virus, something that made him particularly vulnerable... acetaminophen is actually very toxic to the liver."

"I've heard that," Zachary nodded. "And some of the meds in my cocktail can cause damage. I have to get blood tests every few months to make sure... would it be liver enzymes?"

Kenzie nodded. "Right. They probably check kidneys too, checking serum creatinine, blood urea nitrogen, and electrolyte levels."

"That sounds right. But you *don't* think that it was his medications."

"I don't think the timing was right. Maybe they exacerbated whatever caused the initial symptoms. The more things you are taking, the better the chances that there is going to be an interaction or liver damage."

"You don't have any idea what it was?"

Kenzie considered. "We'll have to wait and see what the initial tests show. I have some ideas, but they are not fully developed yet."

He raised his brows, inviting her to tell him more, but Kenzie shook her head. She wasn't at the point where she was willing to share her speculations yet. There were still too many questions.

"I guess both of our cases are moving slowly," Kenzie observed. "You might like something to break faster, but you have to take what you can get."

18

K enzie had to wait until later in the afternoon to go back to the apartment to look around for any environmental toxins that might have affected Robertson and might also affect Alex or his next roommate if the source of the toxin were not found. Alex could be in the earlier stages of being poisoned and not even know it. Kenzie hadn't seen any signs of this, but she couldn't assume.

She put on a pair of gloves and a mask in case there was something in the apartment that could affect her as she investigated. Alex watched her with skepticism plain in his manner.

"I don't understand what you're looking for. Or why you have to protect yourself like that. I live here. Obviously, if there was something here that made Scott sick, I would be sick too. But I'm not. So it wasn't something that is just… in the air here." Alex raised his hands palms-up and looked around as if expecting something to materialize, then shrugged.

"Different people can react to environmental toxins very differently. Think about the cases you've heard of when a huge number of children in the town get a very rare cancer from some toxic chemical plant. Not everybody in the town gets it. Not even every child, or the ones who had the highest exposure. It depends on a lot of things. Each person has an individual physiology that is different from anyone else's. You metabolize chemicals at a different rate. Maybe you have a higher concentration of protective factors than Scott. Or there is something different in your diet. You didn't eat all of the same things, did you?"

"Ha. No, not exactly. We were each supposed to supply our own food, but sometimes we would go in together on something. Or I would leave something in the fridge, and the next time I looked for it, it was gone. Of course he denied ever eating any of my food, said that I just didn't remember when I had finished something, or was sleep-eating!" He laughed mockingly. "Sleep-eating. I never ate in my sleep. The idea is ridiculous. It was just his excuse for when he ate something of mine for a midnight snack and didn't want to admit it."

"And you never ate any of his food."

"No." Alex shrugged. "Okay, I did. Not stealing his food at night while he was asleep. But sometimes he would say he didn't want something, or that I was welcome to help myself, or whatever. He was going through this kick... he said everything was too bland, and he was looking for more interesting experiences. So he would say to go ahead and finish it myself if I wanted it."

"So the two of you did share some of your food."

"Yeah, sometimes. So if something made him sick, it probably wasn't the food. Not that it could be, anyway. He didn't eat the same thing all the time. He was always buying from this store or that restaurant, changing it up. Nothing the same."

Kenzie had hoped it would be easier to identify what might have been part of Robertson's diet. "There wasn't anything that he ate all the time? Some favorite food or treat? A brand of coffee?"

"No, I don't think so. He was experimenting, interested in new things."

"Had he always been like that? How long did you guys know each other?"

"No... not always. When we were in school, he would go on jags where he would just eat one thing all the time. He was big on peanut butter sandwiches. But that changed."

"Just recently?"

"Uh…" Alex considered. "I don't know. I guess so. Like within the last year."

"And he complained that food didn't taste right? That it was too bland?"

"Yeah."

"All food?"

"Well, no. That was why he liked the spicy curries and everything. He had never been big on spicy foods before. But then he decided he really liked them. The spicier, the better. He would eat the super hot stuff that I couldn't even touch, acted like it was nothing."

"It sounds like anosmia or parageusia."

"What does that mean?"

"Loss of smell or altered taste. Maybe one of his medications was changing the way things tasted to him. Or maybe he couldn't smell properly, so he couldn't taste food either. Unless he ate foods with really strong flavors that he could still smell and taste."

"From his meds?" Alex nodded slowly. "I remember when I was on antibiotics once, everything tasted foul. It had this awful metallic taste. Almost everything I ate. But when I stopped taking the antibiotics, it went away."

"Exactly. It isn't that uncommon. It was just within the last year? Do you know if it matched up with when he started one of his medications?"

"I don't know. We didn't really talk about it. The meds, I mean. We knew each other from school, and we never really discussed personal medical stuff. It was kind of a forbidden topic."

"Forbidden?"

"I don't know. Not forbidden, like we weren't allowed to, but just… something we never got into. Personal. Private."

Kenzie nodded her understanding. "Sure. That makes sense. A lot of people don't want to discuss private medical information even if they are close."

He looked away and didn't say anything.

Kenzie started her search of the apartment in the kitchen. She examined each cupboard, one at a time, looking for anything toxic that was too close to the food, anything that looked or smelled contaminated, whatever she could find that was out of place or might have caused Robertson's earliest symptoms.

"When did you notice a change in Scott? He started to act more moody, started eating differently…"

"I really don't know. A few months back, I guess. I thought it was the stress from his business. Trying to get this new company going. To get his ideas out there in the wild and see what happened. It wasn't something I would ever take on. I'm too lazy."

Kenzie chuckled. "I know what you mean. The thought of running my own company or getting all that stuff set up… I just can't imagine ever taking all of that on."

"And the financing! I mean, he wasn't just selling photos out of the trunk of his car or translating documents online. Those are things you can do without any real capital. He was raising hundreds of thousands of dollars to get his start. It was crazy. I would have just shut down. I couldn't do that."

"I understand some of the money came from his father."

Alex nodded. "Start with the people closest to you. He wasn't shy about asking. I could never go to my old man and ask him to give me money to start a business like that. I mean, not that my dad has it. But I can't imagine the guts Scott had to have to go to him and say, 'I want to start up this business. This is what I'm doing and I need you to stake me a hundred thousand dollars to start.'"

Kenzie pictured going to her father with such a proposal. He would have done it without qualms. Approaching her mother would have been a different story. Kenzie would have to prove her case, show that she knew what she was doing and had a good plan and other investors lined up. Lisa was the tough one. Kenzie understood why she was the one in charge of the Kirsch family foundation, and Walter's position in his own foundation was secondary. Lisa was as sweet as sugar but hard as nails.

"What exactly was the business Scott was starting?" Kenzie asked.

"It was…" Alex's eyes narrowed, and he stared into the distance as he thought about how to explain it to her. Kenzie appreciated that he hadn't simply started spouting intricate financial speak that she wouldn't understand. Alex frowned, watching her move from one cupboard to another for a long minute or two while he composed his answer. "You know how when you have a mutual fund or some other financial investment, there are people inside the company who watch the market and consult the opinions of experts and all of that stuff so that they can tell you which fund to move your money into depending on what the economy is doing and what they think will fail or succeed? And since they spend their whole day studying this stuff and the most you do is check what the paper or your favorite stock site says, you just go with whatever they say to do with it?"

Kenzie smiled and nodded, recognizing herself in the description. She *wanted* to understand more about the market and to have more confidence in what actions she would take with her investments, but she spent her day seeking out the mysteries of the human body, not the economy, so she just took the advice of her financial advisor. Or Lisa's financial advisor. Sometimes Lisa herself. But she didn't trust that she knew enough about the market to make those kinds of decisions.

"So those financial advisors, they have their own sources, their own financial gurus. Economists and mathematicians and all kinds of different scientists who make predictions and give them advice as to what trends to look for and what companies, countries, or funds to consider."

"That makes sense. And that's what Scott wanted to do?"

"That was what Scott already did. He wanted to be one of the guys the *gurus* went to."

19

Kenzie turned to look at Alex, abandoning her search for the moment. She looked pointedly around the apartment Robertson and Alex shared; modest, probably the same place they had lived as college students. If Robertson was such a financial guru, why was he living in a place like that? And why did he need money from his father or anyone else? Why didn't he have millions under his control? Why wasn't he living in a mansion in Burlington like Lisa? Or in a fancy apartment in Montpelier as Walter had been before his forced retirement? Or New York or Beijing?

Understanding Kenzie's skepticism, Alex continued, "He was good at what he did, but he didn't have the kind of capital to start his own company. Plus, being good at predicting market trends doesn't automatically translate to personal wealth. It's about leverage, connections, and sometimes just pure luck. Scott was trying to build that foundation."

Kenzie nodded slowly. "He had the expertise but needed backing and the time to make a name for himself, to become a trusted source."

"Exactly," Alex said. "And that's why he was so stressed. He wasn't just managing investments. He would have been brilliant at that and would have made plenty of money. But he was trying to build something new from the ground up."

Kenzie turned back to her search in the kitchen while considering this new information. No wonder the guy had been stressed. She continued her examination of the kitchen but found nothing out of place—no chemicals stored near food items. There were a few dry goods past their best-before dates, but she was sure they were still safe to eat.

Moving on from the kitchen, Kenzie decided to search Robertson's bedroom next.

"What about cleaning supplies?" Kenzie asked as she walked down the hallway. "Anything new or unusual you've started using in the apartment?"

Alex trailed a few steps behind her. He didn't need to stay with her, but apparently wanted to keep an eye on her.

"No. Nothing new. Not that Scott used any cleaning products."

Kenzie looked at him. "What does that mean?"

"Have you ever been sick?" Alex asked. "People don't clean while they're sick. Well, maybe some of them do, but Scott was sick and depressed and he mostly just wanted to sleep the last few days. He wasn't helping with the cleaning. He wasn't taking care of himself. He was just… I hoped that if he got enough rest, he would turn the corner and start to get better again."

Kenzie nodded. "I'm sorry you had to deal with all of this. It must have been very difficult for you."

"What was most difficult was his attitude. The depression, the mood swings, the anger and aggression. I think I could have dealt with it if he was just sick, but the way that he behaved, treated everyone around him. Like we weren't trying to help him! Everyone was doing their best to… accommodate him and help him to make it to appointments, to keep things moving forward with his business dealings or let people know when he couldn't do something. That wasn't my job, but I was trying to help him. And so was Rachel. And for our trouble, we got screamed at. He would slam doors, pound the table, punch a hole through the wall, and yell and swear and insult us for no reason."

Kenzie went through the bedside table drawer again and didn't find any medications she had missed the first time. She found a couple of business cards and looked at them. One was for a Realtor.

"Was Scott planning to move, or was this an investor?" She flashed it at Alex.

He bit his lip. "I don't know. Might have been either one."

"Was he planning to leave? It seems like it wasn't a very good time for that. He was sick, trying to get funding…"

"I… I know that. I put up with it for as long as I could, but in the end…"

"You were kicking him out?"

Alex didn't say anything at first, then he cleared his throat and nodded wordlessly.

Of course it was perfectly logical. Just like it would have made sense for Rachel to dump him for his fooling around, but she had been afraid to because he was sick.

"Things must have gotten pretty bad. It seemed like you guys were pretty close friends."

"We were…" Alex struggled with the words. "To begin with, it was just a convenience. We were going through the same program at school, and it made it easier to rent as roommates and help each other study. But we got closer. So that we were… more than just acquaintances. Friends. As much as we could be when we were so different."

"It must have been tough to tell him he had to find somewhere new. Especially when he wasn't feeling well."

"I just couldn't put up with it anymore."

"No," Kenzie agreed with sympathy. Her mind wandered to her parents. How long would it be before her mother decided it was time for Walter to find a place of his own? He had his own suite in the mansion, but that didn't seem to be working out as well as Lisa had hoped. Walter was still in the way, interfering with her operations. Lisa liked things to be done in a very precise way. Kenzie had always been good at assessing her mother's preferences and then changing her own behavior to accommodate her. Walter wouldn't make the necessary adjustments. Not because he didn't want to please Lisa but because he, too, was set in his ways.

How long would it be before they decided that the charade about Walter having a stroke and needing to be looked after had played out enough that Walter could move out on his own again, with the occasional visit by a doctor or therapist to bolster the deception?

Probably not long.

20

"Do you think it was anything to do with the cat?" Alex asked abruptly.

"What?" Kenzie was startled. "You mean Scott's illness? There is an outside chance that he might have caught a parasite or virus from the cat, but it's very unlikely. I don't think you need to worry."

Alex stared at her in astonishment. "You think he caught something from the cat?"

"I thought that was what you were asking."

"No! I meant the arguing, the yelling. Turning into the Hulk because he saw the cat. Do you think all of the anger was because of the cat? Do you think that's why he changed? Because I brought the cat home? The cat was a constant source of strife. Rachel says I should have just gotten rid of it. Like it would have solved all of the fighting. But you don't think it would have, do you?"

Kenzie considered, and shook her head. "No... Scott was going through a lot of stuff. His health was very bad. I think that's just how it came out. I don't think it was all because of the cat."

Alex nodded, looking relieved. "Yeah, that's what I think too."

"I hope that you can hold on to your good memories of him. It doesn't sound like he was himself the last little while. Blame that on the illness, not him personally."

"He would say he was sorry later on. An hour later, a day later, whatever. He'd eventually apologize. He'd get into a really bad funk, apologizing for how horribly he had been behaving, saying that he should be able to behave better. But it was like he couldn't control himself anymore. He wondered if he was going crazy. If it was early dementia or something. He knew that wasn't how he wanted to be."

"He probably didn't have any idea how sick he was. Especially with the doctor telling him that most of it was just in his head. That he just needed to try harder. Be positive. Go out for a walk and practice some meditation or stress-reduction techniques."

"He knew."

"Do you think so?" Kenzie sat on the edge of the bed, looking at Alex, her search halted for the moment.

"One day last week, he got up to go to the bathroom and I was still up watching TV. He was up a lot at night, going to the bathroom or holding his stomach because it hurt so bad." Alex rubbed his forehead, frowning. "Anyway, one of the times that he was up, he was talking about the future, about something that would happen. Maybe the fight with his brother, I don't remember for sure. He was talking and said, 'When I am dead.' I laughed it off and told him that things were not that bad. His doctor would sort it out, and he'd feel better again. But he just shook his head and said, 'When I am dead...'" Alex choked up. He swallowed and cleared his throat. "I never thought that within a week, I would find him dead."

"That must have been awful. Such a shock."

"It was. Awful. Not a shock. It was and it wasn't. After all, he'd said, 'When I am dead,' so I couldn't say I had no idea it was coming. I didn't know it would be then, that it would be so soon, or that I would see it."

"I'm sorry," Kenzie said again.

"Do you think he killed himself? Did he do this himself because he was in so much pain? Because he couldn't see any other way out of it?"

"We haven't seen anything that points directly to suicide. It's possible that he took more pills than he was prescribed in the hopes that it would bring him some relief, even knowing that it was dangerous, but I don't think he intentionally killed himself."

"There was no note."

"No."

Sometimes, people cleaned up suicide scenes to spare the family. But Kenzie didn't think that had been done in this case. Everything seemed to point to an extended illness due to accidental exposure to a toxin. But what toxin?

A thorough search of the room did not turn up anything suspicious. There were such incidentals as room freshener and mouse bait, but there didn't seem to be any way they could have poisoned Robertson.

"You need to clean up the bait in there," Kenzie told Alex as she closed the closet door and then the bedroom door. "If you have mice that eat the bait, and then your cat eats the poisoned mice."

Alex's eyes widened. "That would be terrible, especially after losing Scott!" He hesitated, his face reflecting the fact that he'd just made the mistake of sounding like the cat was as important to him as the human being that he had lived with for a number of years. "I mean… well, it would be awful. I really like Cuddles. I didn't mean that Scott's death wasn't important. Just that it would be even harder to lose my friend and my pet so close together."

"Of course," Kenzie agreed. "That would be terrible." She stepped into the bathroom to check through the medicine cabinet, which she had already done the day that Scott had died. She checked under the sink, looking through the various cleaning fluids. Nothing unexpected. While they were toxic, using them as directed should not have caused Scott's health issues. If he were drinking them or mixing them in a room with no ventilation, that would be a problem, but a much more acute one than what Scott had suffered. She looked around at the shampoos and other products lining the shower edge and shallow wall shelf. Again, nothing unusual. No industrial chemicals. No sign that Scott had been conducting some weird experiment on himself. The same mild soaps and shampoos she would find in any other bathroom.

She stepped out into the hallway. "I'd like to check the other rooms as well," she told Alex. "Uh… your bedroom? And do you have a guest room as well?"

"My room?"

"I would like to be thorough. Be able to sign off on my report that there wasn't anything in the home that was likely to have caused the signs that we saw in Scott."

It was double talk. Of course she didn't need to sign a statement saying that she had searched the apartment and not found any chemical or medication that might have caused his death. It was not a routine tick box on a list she had to complete.

"I don't think so," Alex said uncomfortably, shaking his head. "You don't need to search my room."

"I would just like to be able to confirm that I searched the entire apartment."

"No. I don't have to let you do that."

"I could get a warrant," Kenzie lied. It wasn't like she was the police. If the police wanted to conduct a search, they could do that, but it wasn't part of Kenzie's job to get a search warrant for anything. If there had been a crime committed, the police would investigate and they could get a warrant to search the entire apartment. Kenzie had been conducting her death investigation with Alex's permission, but it would appear that his goodwill could only be stretched so far.

21

Kenzie knocked on Dr. Cook's office door, even though it was already open. She waited for Dr. Cook to look up and motion her in. His eyes were intent on his computer screen, and it was a minute before he was able to pull his attention from it and focus on Kenzie, sitting in the guest chair on the other side of his desk.

"Dr.—Kenzie. What have we got?"

He was still adjusting to calling her by her given name. He had refused to do so, always addressing her formally as Dr. Kirsch, until he'd realized that Dr. Wiltshire called her by her first name, and then he had tried to make the switch. He and Dr. Wiltshire seemed to have a somewhat adversarial relationship, both competing over the same territory, even though Dr. Wiltshire was too injured to work yet and Dr. Cook would only be there for as long as Dr. Wiltshire was on leave. Logically, neither had to worry about the other infringing on their territory. But that wasn't how they behaved.

"Got some of the lab results back on Robertson."

"Anything that sheds light on his cause of death?"

Kenzie nodded slowly. "As we suspected, the hormone panel was off. He shows very low natural testosterone in the bloodstream. But androgens are high overall."

"Any sign of tumor in the adrenals?"

"None. They looked fine."

"Then we're looking at an exogenous source."

Kenzie agreed. "They are going to run mass spec to identify what anabolic-androgenic steroid was used." She shook her head. "It doesn't make any sense that Robertson would be taking steroids. He did not have any condition in his recent medical history that would have suggested the need for anabolic steroids."

"No, that would be highly unlikely. And if he were being treated with anabolic steroids, they would have known to reduce the dosage when he started to show symptoms of toxicity."

"So he was taking it himself. He wasn't a bodybuilder. It isn't used for anything else."

"Did you find any steroids in his room?"

"No. Nothing in the apartment."

"Then maybe he wasn't taking it himself."

"You think someone else was giving it to him? Why?"

Dr. Cook shrugged. "Why does anyone do anything? We see plenty of weird stuff in autopsies. The result was death. Was that the intent?"

"Oh, boy." Kenzie felt a sudden chill. She tapped her pen on the file folder. "Then we're talking homicide."

"If there was no logical reason for him to be taking it himself, and no sign of it in his room or the common areas of the apartment, then it must have been administered by someone else. Over a period of months. They could see what it was doing to him and continued administering it."

Kenzie shuddered at the thought.

The vast majority of the homicides they dealt with were impulsive, spur-of-the-moment killings, frequently performed in anger. They were not premeditated, carefully calculated executions. They did not require the careful administration of poison over a number of months.

Who could do something like that? What kind of person? It had to be someone close to Robertson, and she had talked to the people who spent the most time with him. Had she already looked into the eyes of Robertson's killer?

"I'd better talk to the police," she said faintly. "Get a detective on to this."

Cook nodded gravely. "Yes. And we're already behind on this case because we didn't immediately identify it as a homicide, so they are going to need to get right on it."

Kenzie swore and rubbed her temples. In the time since Robertson had died, his killer could have destroyed all kinds of evidence of his or her crime. "I'd better pay Sergeant Campbell a visit."

"Okay. I'll let you break the news to him. I'm available for whatever he needs me for, but you're up to speed on the case, so I doubt he'll need me for anything other than sign-off."

Kenzie nodded. She would need to write up her reports and get Cook to sign them as soon as possible. And she would need to go back to the body one more time before it was released to make sure they hadn't missed anything that pointed to a suspect or the manner of death as homicide.

When she called upstairs, Sergeant Campbell was in a team meeting, so Kenzie had to wait a couple of hours until he was ready. She pulled together a preliminary report showing the test results that had come in so far and what they were still waiting for.

When he was ready for her, Kenzie handed Campbell a small sheaf of papers with a brief outline, her draft report, and a few representative pictures.

"Dr. Kirsch," Campbell greeted, taking them from her. "What have we got here?"

He sat down to look at the papers and picked up his cup for a sip of coffee that smelled like it had been sitting on the burner all day.

"Poisoning victim. And unfortunately, we are a few days in at this point. We assumed natural causes at the scene."

"Poisonings can be tricky," Campbell acknowledged. "And they are rare, so you aren't always looking for them."

He opened the folder to look at Robertson's picture. "A young man. Not your usual demographic for a poisoning victim."

Kenzie raised her brows. "Is there a 'usual' demographic?"

"Most of the victims of poisoning are the infants and elderly. Much easier to administer poison to."

"Ah, I guess that makes sense. And is it true that poison is usually a woman's weapon?"

"Statistically, most poisonings—at least the ones we discover—are perpetrated by men. But when you look at the choice of weapons between the two genders, women are far more likely to choose poison when they kill. Men go for guns or blunt objects. Women are, if I remember correctly, about four times more likely to pick poison than men."

"Women are more hands-off."

"Well, I don't know if I would say that. They're also more likely to stab you or throw you out a window."

Kenzie gasped in surprise at his statement and ended up coughing. She covered her mouth and took a minute to recover.

"Sorry," Campbell said, grinning and not looking the least bit sorry. "Need to break down these stereotypes. Women do not just sit at home plotting murder and slipping arsenic into hubby's tea."

"I guess not," Kenzie said with a little laugh, still trying to catch her breath.

"Back to the business at hand…" Campbell looked back down at the papers Kenzie had handed to him. He skimmed through them quickly. "Steroids. An unusual choice for a weapon. I wonder if it has some significance."

"I don't know." Kenzie hadn't thought about the possibility. "I can't think about what it would mean."

"Just something to think about. You're sure he wasn't taking them himself?" He stared at the picture of Robertson. "He was no gym rat or competitive athlete."

"No. Quite sedentary. He is not quite as obese as he looks. A lot of the belly is swelling from his liver. The breast development is a side effect of steroids, and the legs are swollen with edema."

"There wasn't any other reason he would have taken steroids himself?"

"Not that we could think of. And I have searched his room and bedside table and medicine cabinet twice. There were no steroids with the prescriptions and over-the-counter medications he was taking."

"We'll need to do a police search. Our guys might be able to identify some stash spots that you missed. I don't suppose he lived alone?"

"No. Lived with a roommate, old college buddy. I don't know who else had access to the apartment. There was a girlfriend; she had a key. They were the ones who discovered the body."

"Anything going on between them?"

Kenzie considered this. "The roommate and the girlfriend? No... I don't think so. She was actually quite antagonistic toward him."

"And she wasn't overcompensating, hiding a relationship between them?"

"I didn't pick up on any vibes. She was pretty upset about Robertson cheating on her. I don't see her doing the same thing to him."

"You might be surprised at the number of partners who have retaliatory affairs. It isn't an unusual reaction."

"Well... I don't think so. But you'd have to ask them yourself to be sure."

Would Rachel have conspired with Alex to kill her cheating boyfriend? Would she have done it herself, deciding that he deserved to suffer for what he had put her through? Did cheating warrant murder?

It certainly had in other cases.

"The roommate wouldn't let me search his room or their spare room, which was used for storage. Only the other common areas and Robertson's bedroom. I'm afraid... he's had time to dispose of evidence since Robertson's death."

Campbell nodded gravely. "It is what it is. We'll be sure to check the nearby garbage bins and dumpsters. See if he's ever had a prescription or hangs out at the types of places he would be able to pick up steroids." His brow furrowed. "I don't know if I've ever heard of another steroid poisoning case. It's very unusual."

"I don't know if I have either. I'd have to check the literature. But I can say... the steroids did a fantastic job of destroying his heart, liver, and kidneys. The changes in his health from a few months ago until the day he died were astonishing. A few months ago, he was a bit overweight and sedentary, under some stress trying to start a financial advice company, and then everything started to fail. His physician never saw what was happening, and I can't say I blame him. He did his best to treat the symptoms that Robertson reported, but by the time he started to think that something might be seriously wrong, it was too late."

"Did he have any family?"

"A brother he was on the outs with. Mother moved to Australia and hasn't been in touch much. She hasn't called me back. Father died a couple of years ago, and the boys have been scrapping over his money."

Campbell picked up his pen and hovered over his notepad. "You have a name and contact info?"

Kenzie pulled out her phone to look up Kirk's information.

"You don't happen to know whether the money he was fighting over now goes to him, do you?"

"Yes, it does."

Campbell nodded, a glint in his eye.

"But..." Kenzie hated to burst his bubble.

"What?"

"Whoever did this had to have access to his food. To something he was ingesting. For a period of months. He and Robertson had not been speaking, had not seen each other."

"As far as you know."

"Right... as far as I know."

"You wouldn't know if he had sent him a box of chocolates or one-a-day vitamin supplements. Or a tube of toothpaste."

"No," Kenzie admitted. "But I didn't see anything like that at the apartment. Other than toothpaste, of course, but it looked like regular off-the-shelf toothpaste."

"In ninety percent of cases... follow the money. I'm guessing they were in touch more than the brother would have you think. Even if it was only by mail every month or two. That would be enough, wouldn't it?"

"I haven't stopped to figure out the volume of steroids that would have to be consumed. We need to know what steroid it was, first. But... you're right, it wouldn't take a lot. I imagine it could be just a few pills a day. Or some kind of paste or liquid distilled from the pills. These are pretty powerful drugs."

"So you've talked to the roommate, the girlfriend, and the brother. All good suspects. Anyone else?"

"I've talked to his doctor. His contact information is in there."

"Great. I will get a detective on to this, and he will contact you. Anything else you think I should know?"

"We still have other tests we are waiting on, including identifying what steroid it was. All of the damage I saw was consistent with steroids. I also ordered a hair strand test that will show when the administration of the steroids began, along with any recreational drugs and his prescriptions. It will give us a rough timeline."

"But his first symptoms emerged about three months ago."

Kenzie nodded her agreement. "He was complaining of mood swings, fatigue, weight gain; those are all consistent with steroid use. His roommate and girlfriend both commented on his anger."

"Roid rage."

"Yes. He recognized that he was out of control but didn't know why or how to fix it. The doctor told him it was just stress. Encouraged him to walk and relax."

"And these steroids, would they be easy to hide in food? It sounds like he wouldn't need a lot of it."

"As long as he didn't taste it, yes," Kenzie agreed. "although... he had been complaining about everything being too bland or tasting 'off.' He changed his diet, starting to eat spicier foods."

"Is that normal?"

"It can happen. I think it might have been because of his allergies. He was stuffed up and couldn't smell or taste properly, so he started to eat food that he wouldn't have before. Stronger tastes that he could enjoy even though he was congested."

"And it would have been easier to hide the taste of the steroids in the spicy food."

Kenzie nodded. "Exactly. The stronger tasting the food, the more easily they could hide the poison."

22

Kenzie was in a good mood going home. Although it was terrible to learn that Robertson had been targeted and killed by someone close to him, she was relieved they had been able to discover the truth. They hadn't overlooked all the signs and said that it was just because Scott Robertson was living an unhealthy lifestyle or had lost the genetic lottery. She felt like a burden had been lifted from her shoulders as she had passed the case on to the police department.

She had confidence that they would sort it out. They already had three strong suspects. Even though it seemed like Kirk Robertson couldn't possibly have poisoned his brother, Campbell was right. He might have managed to pass food on to Scott as some sort of peace offering and been able to poison him even without being present at the apartment.

Or he might have been visiting Scott in the apartment regularly and lied to Kenzie about it. She had never asked Alex whether Kirk had been to the apartment.

Whoever had poisoned Robertson, Kenzie was sure the police would sort it out and see the culprit brought to justice. She had brought them the information they needed to open an investigation. She would have a hand in bringing Scott's murderer to justice.

She parked the car and let herself into the house through the garage door, humming to herself. Maybe they would have a special treat tonight. Or she would by herself, since Zachary was probably not there. She could order in something he did not like. Or have one of the artisanal soups she enjoyed that were made by a local chef. They were canned in beautiful mason jars with curlicue patterns and rich red and gold labels that were pieces of art by themselves, and were available at the grocery store they frequented.

And Zachary hated them.

He'd never said "hate," but she saw the face he made when he had to slurp his way through a serving of the luscious tomato vegetable soup. He would eat tomato soup—the bland alphabet soup from a can he'd eaten as a kid. But he didn't like the soggy chunks of vegetables in Kenzie's special soups.

Still, Zachary never complained when Kenzie warmed up some of the amazing artisanal soup. Growing up in foster care, he'd been well trained to eat what was put in front of him without complaint. He'd had to eat a lot worse things than tomato vegetable soup, he'd told her. She didn't know any details, but she had seen the way children were sometimes neglected and abused. She didn't need him to tell her the details.

Kenzie kicked off her shoes and went to the cupboard to pull out one of the jars of soup. She also had some whole wheat crackers, the kind she loved to dip into her tomato soup. They were individually wrapped servings so she could take them to work to eat with her lunches, even though she never actually had. Mornings always seemed too stressful to get her lunches together, and she ended up getting crap food from the vending machine or having to go out to a restaurant to pick up something decent.

She turned around to walk through the living room to the bedroom and was startled to see someone there when she had expected Zachary to be out on surveillance. Her startled movement as Zachary looked up from his computer made him jump, and the phone flew out of his hand and landed several feet away.

Kenzie laughed, surprised by his reaction and amused by the

ridiculousness of the phone arcing across the room and the look of alarm on Zachary's face.

He shot to his feet, flushing red and swearing angrily.

"What are you doing sneaking up on me like that?" he demanded.

"I didn't—"

He swooped down to snatch up his phone, bringing it in front of him, cradled in both hands, as if he had caught a baby bird falling out of its nest.

"If it's broken—!"

"Zachary, chill," Kenzie told him firmly, her own heart racing at Zachary's angry reaction. "*You* startled *me!*"

"I didn't do anything wrong. You sneak in here and scare me like that!"

His fingers moved over the phone screen, touching and stroking to make sure that everything was okay. Kenzie couldn't see whether the screen had cracked, but it didn't look like he had discovered anything wrong with it.

"I didn't sneak up on you," Kenzie told him, forcing a light tone as if the whole thing amused her. "I came in, and I got out some soup and crackers for my supper, figuring I would be eating alone, and I was just going to go to the bedroom to change, when I saw you. I was surprised, that's all. *I* didn't do anything wrong either. I wasn't sneaking around. I wasn't trying to scare you."

Zachary slid his phone into his pocket. With both hands in his pockets, he looked down at the floor, embarrassed now instead of angry.

"I'm sorry. Sorry. I just reacted. I didn't mean anything." He swallowed. "I'm glad you're home."

"Yeah, nice welcoming committee." Kenzie couldn't help the dig. "I'm going to change and then we can have dinner together. If you are staying around today. You can get out a can of your soup or something else you would enjoy, since I know you don't like my soup."

He opened his mouth to say that he had never told her that he didn't like her soup, which was true but, at the same time, not true.

When she returned from the bedroom, Zachary had made his way into the kitchen but had not started making anything for himself. He would probably stay out of the way until Kenzie had heated her soup, and then he could make his. Of course, he hadn't bothered to get her out a bowl or silverware or to put her soup in the microwave to warm it up. He could have sped the process along so they could eat sooner.

"I'm sorry," Zachary repeated. "I don't know why it startled me so badly. You didn't do anything wrong. I was just engrossed in what I was doing and didn't hear you come in."

"We were both startled," Kenzie pointed out. "My heart is still going like a train engine. But it was nothing. It's kind of funny, when you think about it."

"Yeah, funny," Zachary agreed. "Such an overreaction."

"I told Dr. Cook he needs to wear bells on his socks so that I can hear him coming and not be startled by him. Nobody likes getting startled like that."

"No," Zachary agreed, his shoulders lowering a little.

Kenzie moved the rest of the way into the kitchen and started to prepare her supper, ignoring Zachary and his awkwardness. They would get over the incident faster if neither of them made a big deal over it. Just one of those things that happened. Dr. B would have told them just to move on.

"So are you off surveillance tonight?"

"No, going later. I just... I needed a breather for a while, so I came home. Thought I would get calmed down and then... I would be able to go out and do the surveillance."

Kenzie tallied up the points she learned from this little speech. Something had happened. Something that had upset Zachary so that he needed time and space to calm down after it. Whatever that thing was, he had not yet fully recovered from it when Kenzie had come into the room and scared him, compounding whatever the problem was and throwing him into a panic. But he hadn't had a meltdown. Not really. He had dropped his phone, shown a burst of anger, and then gotten control of himself.

Since he hadn't explained what had happened to make him

tense in the first place, she didn't ask, letting him choose what he wanted to tell her and when he wanted to do it. He would undoubtedly feel a lot better after he'd had a chance to sit down and eat with her, visiting and talking about other things until the stress had been reduced enough to talk about it.

23

The microwave beeped, and Kenzie pulled out her soup and put it on the table. She picked up the package of crackers and sat down to open them while Zachary made his own meal.

He didn't go to the cupboard, but sat down across from her without anything to eat. Kenzie searched for the tear notch on her crackers packet, then ripped it open. The wrapper crackled as she tore it and pulled the crackers out, wrestling each one out of the sleeve.

Zachary's face transformed into a grimace of pain.

His misophonia. A painful or emotional reaction to a noise, like some people had to fingernails on the blackboard or other scraping, scratching sounds. Typically, people had misophonia to sounds like chewing, breathing, or sniffling. Zachary's reaction was a recent development that had probably been triggered or exacerbated by something in his current med cocktail, and the biggest trigger was the rustling and crackling of wrappers. The wrapper on his granola bars, her crackers, or a bag of chips.

Kenzie had made suggestions to help with the troubling new symptom. Making a slight adjustment to his medication, using scissors on the wrapper instead of tearing it, and letting Kenzie repackage offending items in non-crinkly baggies. But he wouldn't hear of it. He believed that if he just put up with it, his brain would eventually stop overreacting, and the misophonia would disappear.

"Oh, good grief!" she snapped when she saw his grimace at the noise. "Get over it already! I can't even open a package of crackers?"

Which, of course, was unfair. Zachary didn't choose to react that way and *would* have gotten over it if he could. He was doing the best he could to manage all of his symptoms. But every change to his medication protocol caused new symptoms, and all they could do was to find the protocol that worked the best, with the fewest serious symptoms, and stick with that.

Which was exactly what Zachary had done. His problem with noises was minor compared to the side effects that he experienced on other drugs, and he was willing to put up with the painful reaction to noises instead of constant nausea or obsessive thoughts.

Kenzie put down the crackers and reached for Zachary's hand, but he pulled back. Kenzie put her hands over her face, trying to wipe away all of the emotions and anxiety and just communicate clearly and not trigger Zachary further.

"I'm sorry. That was uncalled for. You can't help your reaction and I know that. I guess I'm still wound up from being startled. I was in such a good space, really feeling great, and now... I've screwed everything up."

She actually meant that *he* had screwed everything up, ruining her good vibe with his overreaction and unjustified anger, but she couldn't say that. She couldn't blame his mental illness for her unjustified comment.

"Can we just start over?" Kenzie suggested. "Like, a do-over from the time I walked in the door?"

"Okay," Zachary said evenly. "Let's do that." But his voice was completely flat. Disconnected from his emotions. She had pushed him too far and he had withdrawn from her. She might not get him back all night.

"Do you want me to get you some soup? Some of *your* soup?" Kenzie offered.

"No. Not hungry."

"Are you sure? Have you eaten today?"

He was better about eating now that he was no longer nauseated all the time from his medications, but sometimes he still forgot to eat, getting so wrapped up in his work that hours went by without his realizing he had missed meals or other appointments.

"Sure, breakfast with you and lunch. And I'll grab something when I'm on surveillance tonight. Gives me something to do while I'm watching."

"What, like popcorn at the movies?"

"Popcorn would be good," he agreed. But there was no smile or laugh at her suggestion.

Kenzie sighed and started eating her soup. She forced herself to go slowly and savor it rather than wolfing it down and disappearing into her bedroom, which was what she felt like doing. She dipped her crackers in the soup and ate them, crunching them as quietly as possible, not wanting to aggravate his sound sensitivity any more than she already had. She swallowed.

"What have you been working on today? Just computer stuff?"

"No, I was out earlier."

He didn't give her any more information.

"Yeah? On the same case? Or something else?"

"Same one. Just checking out a few leads. People who know them. His history. Digging down deeper."

Kenzie studied Zachary whenever he wasn't looking in her direction, searching his dark eyes for emotion and warmth. But he had checked out.

"Did something happen that bothered you? Earlier today, I mean, not me coming home and scaring the pants off you."

"You didn't do anything. How did your day go? You said something good happened."

"Well…" Kenzie figured he was just asking by rote or because he didn't want to answer her questions, but if there was a chance she could get him back by talking about her work, she would take it. "I wouldn't exactly say that something good happened, but we made an important discovery. Went to Campbell with a murder case."

"Murder?" He couldn't resist showing his curiosity about what she might have found. "Was it something interesting?"

"I didn't know it was murder from the beginning. We thought it was natural causes. Some environmental toxin. But as it turned out..."

"Not an environmental toxin?"

"No." Kenzie smiled and sipped her soup. "Deliberate poisoning."

Zachary waited for her to go on, but Kenzie waited for him to press her further. She would make him engage with her fully. She would pull him back from the dark place he had retreated to.

"How do you know it was deliberate poisoning?" Zachary asked finally.

"Because there were not any anabolic steroids in his environment."

"Steroids? Like what bodybuilders use? Not the ones that hospitals give you?"

"Yeah. Like bodybuilders use. But he wasn't a bodybuilder, even before they started to poison him."

"So did he get really big? How do steroids kill you? I know that there have been stories about athletes who were on steroids killing themselves and their families in a psychotic breakdown." Zachary leaned forward, looking her in the face at last. "Or crashing their car or committing suicide. Is that what happened?"

"No. Multiple organ failure from steroid toxicity."

"That sounds bad."

"It was. He suffered a lot in the last few months, and it would have been very painful in the end. A pretty cruel way to die."

"Do you think the person who poisoned him knew how bad it would get? Or that it would kill him?"

"We'll have to ask him that when we can pin down who did it."

"You don't have anyone yet?"

"There are several good suspects. I don't know if any of them knew what kind of a death it would mean, but two of the three of them were close enough to watch him suffer."

"And they didn't stop."

Kenzie thought about that. What if the poisoner had withdrawn the steroids when they saw how much it was hurting Robertson? At what point had it been too late, and stopping the administration of the poison would have done no good? Once his heart or liver was failing, his death had been assured, whether they kept up the poisoning or not.

But the answer to Zachary's question was in the blood test.

"There was a very large concentration of synthetic testosterone in his blood. So, no. They didn't stop. They kept administering it right up until the time he died."

24

It was Detective Cameron who called Kenzie to get the scoop on the steroid poisoning, asking her a number of questions about how the poison might have been administered and what they should be looking for at the apartment.

The answer was pretty straightforward. He was looking for pills. There were no injection marks on Robertson's body, so there was no point in looking for needles. Whatever food the steroids had ended up in, they had started as tablets or capsules at some point.

"Do you want to come with us for the search?" Cameron asked. "Then, if we have any questions about what we have found, you'll be right on hand to answer them."

Kenzie realized that he didn't actually need her there. He was just offering her the opportunity to be there if she wanted it. She didn't have any reason to go when she had already been to the apartment twice and wasn't the one who would be performing the search. But she was really hoping that they would find something and wanted to be there when they did, so she took him up on his offer.

"I'd like to be there, if you don't mind another person hanging around," she admitted.

"I wouldn't have asked you if I minded. You want to meet me over there, or to hitch a ride with me?"

"I'll take my own car. Then, if we have to leave at different times, we can."

"Sounds like a plan. We'll be there to serve the warrant in an hour."

Alex and Rachel were both at the apartment when Kenzie arrived. The warrant had been served, and the police were gloving up and getting ready to begin the search.

"You were already here," Alex protested in frustration. "How many more times are you going to violate my civil rights? You can't keep coming here and searching my apartment. Do I have to just sit back and take it whenever the mood strikes?"

"If you have a complaint, here is the number to call," Cameron told him, handing over a business card. "There's a file number on the warrant, which you can refer to. But as you can see, it was granted by the court, so they're just going to tell you that you need to put up with it. They've already decided that the circumstances are suspicious enough to warrant a search of the property. If you want to stay, you can sit on the couch, but you have to stay there. If you can't do that, then please leave, and someone will call you when we are done. It may take a few hours, so you'll have to be prepared to sit and wait that entire time."

Alex's eyes went to Kenzie. He scowled. "This is your fault. You are incompetent! I don't know what you think happened to Scott, but you're wrong. He was sick. Something was wrong with him. That wasn't caused by anything in this apartment. We're clean. There are no drugs here. Whatever you think you're looking for, you won't find it here."

Kenzie nodded and didn't say anything. He ran out of steam when he couldn't get a rise out of her, and eventually sat on the couch like Cameron told him to. Cameron kept Rachel talking for longer, not wanting her to go directly to the couch to sit down with

Alex. Rachel folded her arms and shook her head, insistent that she didn't know what he was talking about. There had only been Scott's prescriptions. Maybe they had been filled with the wrong substance. There had never been any other drugs around the apartment.

Kenzie wondered, given the way that Alex was protesting, if they were going to find any steroids in his room. He could still claim they were his and had not been used to poison his roommate. But it would be a hard argument to make.

Rachel didn't seem worried they would find anything, just bemused that they thought there was anything to find.

The police conducted a full search of the apartment, checking not only the places she had already searched, but also various potential stash sites like the electrical outlets, toilet tank, and backs of drawers, and, of course, the two rooms Kenzie had been unable to search.

But there was no sign of any steroids.

Kenzie walked out to her car, frowning to herself. It shouldn't have surprised her that they hadn't found any steroids in Alex's possession. He wasn't a bodybuilder or gym rat as far as she could tell, and he'd had plenty of time to get rid of the evidence if he was the killer. He would have been stupid not to realize he needed to get rid of it after Robertson died and, even if he didn't realize it then, he would have when Kenzie asked to search his room.

She shouldn't have done that. She should have told Cameron about it and let him get a search warrant without giving Alex a heads-up. She had been too eager to do the search herself and had not known yet that it was murder. She had thought she had been looking for an environmental contaminant or prescription.

A man in a worn school football jacket stood near Kenzie's car smoking. He watched her approach it.

"That's a pretty sweet ride for a cop," he told her.

Kenzie smiled politely. "I'm a medical examiner, not a cop. And you're right; it didn't come out of my government salary."

It wasn't unusual for her to be approached by men with comments or questions about her car. Some of them thought it was sexy for her to be driving it. Others were far more interested in the car than they were in her. She waited to see which type this man was. She suspected he fell into the first category.

"I've seen it here before; this isn't the first time you've been here."

"No. I've been here a couple of times before."

"So," he raised his eyes toward the apartment Kenzie had been visiting. "What happened over there? One of those guys died?"

"Yes, Scott Robertson. Did you know him?"

He looked surprised. "Scott. Yeah, I knew him. I mean, I didn't *know* know him, but I knew who he was. You know, to see him around. Worked on their plumbing a few times, replaced some wiring. I can't believe he's dead."

Kenzie evaluated him and his statement. "You work for the building?" she guessed.

"Yeah. Contract for the landlord. There are always things around here that need fixing." He took a drag on his cigarette. "Same as any building, I'm not saying it isn't well-maintained. Mr. Harris, he looks after the place. Not a slumlord."

"No, I can see that," Kenzie agreed.

"Matt Johnson," the handyman introduced himself. "If you need anything, I'm sure Mr. Harris would want me to help you out."

Kenzie thought about it. "You've done a lot of work on Alex and Scott's apartment?"

"A lot? I didn't say that. No more than any other apartment."

"No, I didn't mean that they've done anything wrong or that there was a problem with it. I just thought... we might have some questions for someone who has been in and out of the apartment."

He spread his arms. "I'd be happy to help. Not sure I can tell you anything helpful, but I can try to answer any questions you might have."

Detective Cameron was talking with his men as they all went back to their cars. Kenzie motioned that she wanted to speak with him. He walked over.

"Sorry we weren't able to find anything," he told her. "But we didn't really expect to find anything too incriminating. They had time to destroy any evidence. We will search the girlfriend's place too. You never know; they might have figured she was safe."

"You think they were in on it together?"

"Why was she over there?" Cameron asked. "If she was involved with Robertson and not Collins, then why was she over here today? She wasn't in his room, packing up his personal things or retrieving her own items."

"You think they are romantically involved?"

"I don't know. It is suspicious her just hanging out here, don't you think? Has either of them told you that they were all friends with each other?"

"No," Kenzie admitted. "They were fighting the first time I came here."

"Might have just been a ruse. Or they might just be the type of couple that fights."

25

Kenzie motioned to the handyman. "This is Matt Johnson, the handyman for the building. He has done some work in the apartment and wondered whether we had any questions for him."

Cameron nodded, looking the handyman over. "What kind of work have you done?"

Matt shrugged. "Just regular maintenance like you see in any apartment. Clogged drains, some wiring that needs to be replaced. Stuff like that."

"You ever see any pills there?"

"Pills? No, I can't say I have."

"In the bathroom or one of the bedrooms? A stash in an unusual place? If you've been poking around under sinks and around pipes, you might have seen something you thought was unusual?"

"I've seen all kinds of things under sinks," Matt laughed. "Nothing in there. Just cleaning fluids, as far as I can remember." He looked at Kenzie and Cameron. "Do you think there was foul play? It wasn't natural causes?"

"We can't tell you anything about it," Cameron pointed out.

"Well, no, I guess not. You wouldn't want to tip people off. But it's pretty obvious that you're looking for something."

"Sudden deaths are investigated. You can't read anything into that."

"Oh. Okay. Well... I never really saw anything suspicious there. They seemed like nice enough people."

"You ever hear any fights or get any complaints about them?" Cameron asked.

"Well... I've heard them argue," Matt admitted. "Neighbor complaints wouldn't have come to me. They'd go to Mr. Harris, the owner. People might mention stuff to me, but if they wanted to make an actual complaint, they'd have to talk to him."

"What's the best way for us to reach Mr. Harris?" Cameron asked. "Does he live in the building?"

"Sure, he's in the penthouse." Matt chuckled. "That's a joke. His apartment isn't any different than any of the others, but it's on the top floor and he's the owner, so we joke about it being the penthouse suite."

Cameron nodded. "It might be helpful for us to talk to him while we're here. You know Robertson's girlfriend? Rachel Evans?"

"The blonde, right? Yeah, I know who she is."

"How often was she here?"

"Pretty often. She didn't live here, so she wasn't here all the time. But I saw her enough."

"Always with Scott Robertson? Or was she ever by herself or with Alex?"

"Maybe. I didn't really monitor who was there or whether Scott was always home when Rachel was there. But I don't think they were a threesome. Alex had his own girlfriend, though she wasn't here as often. He probably went to her place some of the time."

"And Rachel wasn't sneaking around behind Scott's back?"

"Not that I could tell. But..." He shrugged. "I don't know. I wasn't monitoring anyone."

"You said you had heard them argue?" Kenzie asked.

"Yeah. Sometimes pretty loud," he admitted.

"What did they argue about?"

"I don't know... you know how couples are. They recycle old arguments, and you don't necessarily know what it's all about."

"You didn't have a sense?"

"She wants to go out, and he doesn't... she thinks he should get out more. He works hard and just wants to relax. She complains that he's working too much."

"So it was Rachel who was unhappy with Scott?"

Matt gave her a look. "She complained the loudest. I'm sure he had issues with her too."

"Probably," Kenzie agreed. She thought about the way she and Zachary had different natures. She would snap at him. He would withdraw and get quiet. Neither of them was the type to shout and throw things, but Kenzie was the louder of them. And, of course, Bridget had been too. Kenzie's occasional shots were nothing compared to how Bridget had screamed at Zachary like a harpy, even in front of other people. Kenzie could only imagine how bad things had been behind closed doors.

Matt had stubbed his cigarette out while they were talking, rather than blowing smoke in their faces. He put his hands in his pockets and looked at the building.

"Is he moving out now? Alex? I don't know if he'll want to get another roommate. Now that he's working and not a student, he'll want to get a nicer place. Without a roommate. Maybe move in with his girlfriend or find a place together."

"I don't know," Kenzie shook her head. "I don't think he would confide in me. He's not exactly happy with me at the moment."

Matt frowned. "Because you're investigating his friend's death? Why wouldn't he be happy with you?"

Kenzie glanced at Cameron and decided she'd better not blab anything to an outsider about what reason Alex had to be upset with her.

"Oh..." Understanding flooded over Matt's face. "Are you telling me this was a suspicious death and Alex is a suspect?"

"I'm not saying anything," Kenzie said firmly. "We can't disclose anything about an active investigation."

"Oh, yeah, I get it. I'm sorry, I never even thought about it...

and that's why you're asking about pills? You think Scott was taking pills? Alex?" he shook his head. "I know, I know, you can't tell me."

He stared up at the window pensively. Kenzie had a feeling that he wanted to tell them something about Alex, so she wasn't in a hurry to end the conversation with him. She could initially have just said hello to him and then walked away but, from the start, it had seemed to her that he might know something and was still trying to decide whether to tell them about it.

"Do *you* think he'll move out now?" she asked him, since it had seemed for a moment like that was where he was going with it. "Has he been talking about moving?"

"Well..." Matt looked back and forth, an almost cartoonish portrayal of someone being furtive. "To be honest... Mr. Harris wants him out."

"Mr. Harris does? The owner of the building? Why?"

"I really couldn't say." Matt patted his pockets to locate his half-smoked cigarette and lighter. "It really isn't any of my business. Forget I said anything."

Cameron stepped up the pressure, seeing that Matt wasn't inclined to spill his guts to Kenzie even though it had seemed to begin with like that was what he was going to do.

"Mr. Johnson, you need to tell us what you know. Withholding information from the police that may impact an investigation is very serious. It could land you in a lot of trouble."

"Well, so could ratting out my boss. I need this job. I'm good at it, and I didn't get to be here by talking to the police when I should keep my mouth shut."

"Why did Mr. Harris want Alex out of the building? Has there been some kind of trouble between them? Is Alex involved in something suspicious?"

"No, no. I'm sure Alex is a good guy and hasn't done anything wrong. But Mr. Harris wants to convert the space. He has big plans for redeveloping the building, bringing in a higher class of tenants. He doesn't want starving college students and paycheck-to-paycheck employees. He wanted Alex and Scott out of there. But Alex signed a long-term lease in the beginning. It was supposed to force him to stay, so that Mr. Harris knew that he would be stable and not just dump the place and move out after a month or two."

"But it ended up working the other way around," Cameron guessed. "Now he wants Alex out, but he can't break the lease."

Matt nodded. "Exactly." He fidgeted, twirling the cigarette around his fingers. "They've always paid on time, so he can't evict them. Not allowed to kick him out just because he wants to redevelop the building." He shrugged. "So he's stuck with them."

"They're not the only ones refusing to move out, are they?" Kenzie asked. "You can't tell me that everyone else in the building has agreed to leave."

"Not everyone has to. Some of them, Mr. Harris is going to leave as lower-rent apartments. But he wants to convert Alex's floor. Bigger suites, hot tubs, walk-in closets, like luxury suites."

"And Alex won't leave."

"No. He likes it here, says it's a good lease."

"Why doesn't Mr. Harris just offer him money to leave? There's nothing illegal about that, is there?" she looked at Cameron, unsure if she had missed something. Maybe there was some kind of law protecting people from being bought out of their homes.

"Happens all the time," Cameron informed her. "Cash for keys."

"Why doesn't he do that, then? I'm sure if he offered Alex a good price to leave, so he had the money to put into a down payment on a nicer apartment or a house, he'd do that."

Matt shrugged. "I don't know all of the details," he admitted. "I'm just the help around here; he doesn't talk strategy with me. I just know what's going on because he wants me to help with the new work, and because most of the others are gone, those other apartments are empty so we can get started on the work soon."

Cameron rubbed the whiskers on his chin. "I think we'd better go have a chat with Mr. Harris."

26

K enzie probably should have just gone back to the morgue. The police investigation wasn't within her purview. She had plenty of work of her own to do.

But Cameron said he didn't mind her tagging along with him if she wanted to hear what was going on directly from the horse's mouth. It wouldn't hurt her to know all of the circumstances surrounding Robertson's death. Maybe she would see or hear something that Cameron did not.

Kenzie somehow doubted that. She doubted that Harris had anything at all to do with Robertson's death. They weren't about to find a stash of steroids in full view in his apartment. If he did have suspicious prescriptions in full view, Cameron would spot them just as easily as Kenzie.

But she went up with him anyway.

If she had been expecting a big, bullying, flamboyant character for the part of the landlord-turned-developer, she was disappointed by the pale, nondescript Mr. Harris.

He opened the door and peered out at them through a two-inch crack, and she thought at first that they had gone to the wrong apartment. He looked like a reclusive tenant, not the owner of the building. "Yes?" he whispered, "Who are you?"

"Detective Cameron, Mr. Harris. We'd like to ask you a few questions."

Harris stood in the doorway, uncertain, thinking through his options, before he finally opened the door the rest of the way to let them in. "Do you have identification?" he asked. "Or is there someone I could call to confirm you are who you say you are?"

Cameron handed him a business card and flipped open his wallet to show Harris his shield and ID card. "You're welcome to look up the main number for the Roxboro Police Department and call them for confirmation that I am an employee there," he advised.

Harris squinted at the identification, looked at Cameron's face, and retreated to sit in a chair on the other side of the living room.

"What is this about, Detective? I haven't done anything wrong; I can assure you of that. I have always been very careful to abide by the laws of the land. I don't have as much as a speeding ticket. I've never had a problem with building code enforcement, and any disputes with tenants have been quickly resolved. I've never had the police cite me for anything."

"That's admirable, Mr. Harris. I don't think many people could say the same thing," Cameron complimented him. "And I am not here to accuse you of anything. I am wondering whether you can help me out with some information about one of your tenants. Or two of your tenants, actually. One of them has passed away. Mr. Scott Robertson."

"Mr. Robertson?" Harris sounded shocked. "I heard a rumor that he had passed, but I can't believe it. Is it really true?"

"I'm afraid it is."

"He was such a young man!"

Kenzie appreciated that he didn't say "I just saw him last week!" which was how many people responded to such news. Right after the initial disbelieving "Are you kidding?" or "Are you sure?"

"He was young," Kenzie confirmed. "It is a real tragedy. That is why we are following up on his death."

Harris's eyes went to Kenzie and he examined her, eyes going up and down her. "And who are you, young lady?"

She probably wasn't very much younger than he was. She doubted there was even ten years between them.

"I am Dr. Kenzie Kirsch. Assistant Medical Examiner."

"Oh. Medical Examiner. Oh. Really. Then… there really was something wrong with Mr. Robertson's death. How tragic. How absolutely tragic."

"Yes. It was a terrible thing," Kenzie said. "I have not yet made my final report, but I will be doing that shortly. I'm sure his family wants to claim his remains as soon as possible," Kenzie lied, knowing that Kirk wasn't even planning to hold a funeral. He probably would be happy to have her handle the cremation and disposition of Scott Robertson's remains in a pauper's grave.

"Well, if there is anything I can help you with, I am happy to do it. But I don't know what I can do. You have talked to his roommate? If Alex can't help you, I don't know how I can help. I didn't know them personally. And I only dealt with Alex on the rent. He was the designated representative. I like to just have one person that I deal with in an apartment, so there is no miscommunication."

"Did you ever have complaints about them from the other tenants?" Cameron asked. "Maybe noise complaints? Maybe they were having a loud argument or there was a lot of noise coming from their apartment?"

"No, no, I don't remember there ever being anything like that. They were quite well-mannered boys. I'm always leery of dealing with college students, you know. They can be so immature, wanting to get out of the lease and leaving you in the lurch. But Alex has always been very stable."

"Have there been any complaints about them at all?"

"I really don't think so. Well, maybe another tenant complaining about people coming and going at all hours of the day. But I really don't think that was a problem. They weren't too noisy; I think it was just the two young men and their girlfriends. Some people just don't like to see other people having a nice time."

Harris apparently did not share the viewpoint and was fine with visitors at all hours, as long as they kept the noise down. And with a cat. Most apartment dwellers were not allowed pets, but Harris had either allowed it or looked the other way.

"What did you think of Scott?" she asked Harris.

"I told you, I didn't have much to do with him. He was a quiet young man, came and went, had his girlfriend here some of the time. Went to work."

"How about drugs?" Cameron asked. "Did you ever see either of them with a pill of any kind? Even a bottle of Tylenol?"

Harris's pale brows bunched together in consternation. To his credit, he didn't immediately protest that he had never seen any such thing, but thought about it for a full minute.

"No," he said finally. "I don't think I ever saw either of them with pills. Or anything else that might be drugs. There are some unsavory elements around the neighborhood. We have managed to get rid of most of them. A very active neighborhood watch, everyone reporting what they see to the police. I have been very proud of everyone for working together and getting that riffraff out of the area. Mostly. But Alex and Scott, they were never that type. They weren't involved in any drug dealing."

"What about personal use?"

"Well, I guess I wouldn't know anything about it, would I? What they do in their apartment when no one else was around, I wouldn't know about that. I can't imagine that they were junkies." He shook his head at the image. "Maybe... Adderall to help them study for an important test. But recreational drugs... opiates or rave drugs... I can't see it. They're just not that type."

"You've never seen anything that concerned you in their apartment?"

"No, of course not. I haven't had a lot of opportunity to be in there, but the very idea of them having illegal drugs... it seems ridiculous. Are you sure someone isn't pulling your leg?"

"We're just exploring all of the possibilities," Cameron told him neutrally. "I didn't say that they were involved in drugs. Or not involved in drugs. I just asked you what you had seen."

"I stay away from it. I would not know illegal drugs if I saw them. I know the type who deal drugs around here and the people who buy from them. That just isn't something those boys were up to."

"And they didn't take anything else? For an illness, maybe?"

Harris shrugged. "I'm sure I don't know."

"Did they ever have a water leak in their apartment that you had to go in to check on? Or some wiring that wasn't working properly?"

"Yes, on occasion. I can tell you I did not go into their apartment unless I had to. I am very careful of my tenants' right to privacy. I am not one of those landlords who goes snooping through people's things, sneaking into apartments while they are gone. I could never do such a thing."

Cameron nodded and looked inclined to believe it. The landlord's shoulders relaxed and his next words were not so forceful.

"I am very sorry about whatever happened to Mr. Robertson. And very sorry for Mr. Collins for losing his friend. It is a terrible loss."

"Yes, it is. It was very tragic and, between the police and Dr. Kirsch, we will find out what happened and see that justice is served." Cameron leaned forward, arms folded, elbows on knees. He met Harris's eyes. "I understand you wanted them out of here."

Harris blinked. His eyes got wide. "I wanted them out of here? No! That's not true. Someone is giving you false information."

"Why don't you set me straight, then? Are you telling me you were not trying to get them to give up their lease? You were not offering cash for keys?"

"Well, yes, but… it wasn't like that. I didn't want them out. I just needed the apartment they were in. I needed them to free it up so I could renovate. They were great tenants, but I was hoping… to create something better. Something that would service a different part of the community. To scale this building up a little. It can only be good to improve it, right?"

"But for you to do what you wanted to, you needed them to take the cash. And they wouldn't. They were going to make you wait until their lease was up."

"It's not that big a deal," Harris assured him. "I could live with that. They were abiding by the terms of their lease. How could I fault them for that? I would have waited."

"You *would have* waited?" Kenzie repeated. "Does that mean Collins has agreed to go?"

"Mmm... yes. He wouldn't have to split the money that I offered them previously. And I added a bonus. So... he's agreed to be out of here in a week."

Cameron and Kenzie looked at each other.

27

C ameron looked at Kenzie as they left the building and were about to go their separate directions.

"We don't have any proof that the landlord had anything to do with it. In fact, quite the opposite. He might have had a motive to get Robertson and Collins out of the apartment, but I don't think it rises to the level of a good motive to kill him. First of all, Robertson was not the one making the decisions or the one designated to talk to Harris. That was Collins. I question how he would poison one without poisoning the other, even if we could prove he was accessing the apartment while they were away. Collins is not sick—can we agree about that?"

Kenzie raised her hands to stop him. "I never suggested it was Harris. I agree; he might have had limited access and a bit of a motive, but I don't think it was very much. I think it was more likely that he would increase the cash offer or try to find another pressure point or way to motivate them to move. Maybe find them a nicer place in another apartment. One with a pool or sauna. Some other amenity that meant something to them. Maybe one closer to work. Or closer to one of their girlfriends."

Cameron raised his brows. "Yeah. I think there were still a lot of methods that he could try to get them out of there. Collins seems like a reasonable kid. I imagine they would have eventually come to an understanding. He obviously was not prepared to fight to the bitter end."

"I still think the brother is the most likely suspect. Even if he wasn't meeting with Robertson in person, he might have sent chocolates or something we haven't identified as being a contamination source."

"Chocolates?"

"It was Sergeant Campbell's suggestion, and he's right. He could have been sending something to his brother every few days or weeks. Something that he ate or used regularly. But it was enough to build up enough to cause his death."

"And his motive was the money from the father's estate."

Kenzie nodded. "Simple greed. He's the one with the most obvious, simple motive. From the sounds of it, the father's estate is quite large. The only obstacle is Kirk's alibi."

"We'll do what we can to prove it. We will see if we can get a warrant to search his house as well as the girlfriend's."

"The court isn't going to get tired of you requesting search warrants? They won't say that you're just fishing?"

"You let me worry about that."

Kenzie shrugged. "Okay. I will. Let me know if you need anything else from the ME's office. I'll issue my final report soon."

———

Kenzie slowed as she approached the ramp for the police underground parking. A car parked on the street had attracted her attention. A very familiar-looking car. Slowing down, she checked the license plate and saw that it was the car she had thought it was.

After parking her own car, Kenzie took the elevator up to the main floor where the police department reception desk could be found, and she walked in, looking around for Zachary. The duty officer nodded, recognizing her.

"Can I help you with something, Doctor?"

"Did you see my partner in here? Zachary Goldman? I saw his

car outside on the street and can't think of where else he might have gone."

"Oh, yeah, he is here." the officer looked down at his logbook. "He is filing a witness statement on a DV."

A Domestic Violence case.

Kenzie swore. That was not what she wanted to hear. She would much rather have been told he was there to pay off his parking tickets. Or even that he was being obstructive in a police investigation. She did not want to hear that he had witnessed a domestic violence incident.

She remembered how jumpy and anxious he had been the previous night. What had happened to set him off? She had known from the start that it wasn't just his being startled by her walking in. She knew there was something else bothering him, something that already had him on edge.

"Can I join him?"

The duty officer shook his head slowly. "I'm not sure that's a good idea. He needs to file this witness statement without being distracted or influenced by what someone else says. I'm sure he'll be done in a few minutes, and then you can talk to him."

"I wouldn't interfere. Just be there for moral support."

"We really prefer the witness to be the only one in the room whenever possible. Memory is a changeable thing. We need to make sure that no one is influencing it."

Kenzie understood they wanted to ensure their evidence was as unshakable as possible and would stand up in court. But she still wished that the duty officer hadn't been quite as well-versed and as firm as he was about it. She sighed and walked over to a chair to sit down. The duty officer looked alarmed that she was going to stay there.

"I can call you when he comes out. Or have him call you or see you downstairs."

"I'm going to wait here for him."

The man swallowed. He seemed to have paled since she came in. Not that everyone in Vermont wasn't already pale from the long winter. "You don't need to do that. I'm happy to accommodate you."

"But not by letting me in to see him."

"No, not at this point."

"Then I'm going to sit here and wait." She smiled tolerantly. "You're not wrong. I understand your reasoning. But I want to see him as soon as he is finished. Before he sees or talks to anyone else. I don't want to have to call him or for him to have to call me. I will be right here waiting for him."

The duty officer shook his head and slumped over his desk. "Fine."

Kenzie smiled at his reaction and settled in to wait. The officer didn't think it would take Zachary long, and he had a better idea than Kenzie.

After a few minutes, she pulled out her phone and worked her way through her email inbox. It was much more challenging to do on the phone than it was on the computer sitting at her desk, but she wasn't sitting at her desk. She left anything that needed to be printed or specially filed in the inbox. She went through the rest as rapidly as possible, deleting or archiving each.

She skimmed through some of the reports as they came in. Others she knew would be formatted in such a way as to make them difficult or impossible to read on her phone.

Time passed more slowly than she had hoped, but she was stubborn. She wouldn't give in and go downstairs to wait at her desk until Zachary was finished and the duty officer forgot to call to tell her. Zachary might be home before she discovered he was out. She didn't want that.

Eventually, there was a murmur of voices as a couple of men made their way from the inner offices to the public area. Kenzie recognized Zachary's intonations, even though she could not hear exactly what he was saying. She slid her phone into her pocket and stood up.

The duty officer tried to warn Zachary that Kenzie was there to see him, but failed to get his attention before Kenzie did. He looked surprised, stopping in place for a moment, frozen like the proverbial deer in the headlights.

But it was only for an instant, and then he was moving again. He forced a smile and walked toward her.

"Kenzie, what are you doing here?"

"I saw your car when I got back from my... from... I was out, and I saw your car on the street." She reached her arms out for him, and he hesitated only for a split second before giving her a brief hug and then letting her go. "Are you okay?" Kenzie asked, looking into Zachary's dark, perpetually tired eyes.

"I'm fi—" He cut himself off before finishing the word "fine." One of the rules they had adopted with their couple's therapy was that brushing the other person off with an "I'm fine" was not allowed. They had to express how they were actually feeling after sufficient consideration. No waving a hand or arm and thinking that would pass for a response.

Zachary swallowed, looking into Kenzie's face. He turned back and looked at the law enforcement officer who had been walking him out. Someone junior, not a detective or sergeant that Kenzie recognized.

"I was just making a report on a domestic violence situation."

"I know. The one you have been doing the surveillance on?"

He nodded briefly. "It wasn't unexpected. But... that doesn't make it much easier to file it."

"No, I guess not," Kenzie agreed. "How are you holding up?"

He took a deep breath and blew it out. "This is why I am a private investigator. So that I can use my skills to help other people who are stuck in situations that they don't know how to get out of. So that I can bring justice to people who otherwise might be overlooked or disregarded."

"Yeah."

Still not an answer. She knew how important it was for him to help those who were less fortunate. To help victims of abuse. To try to pay for the mistakes he felt he had made years before when his own family had dissolved, and he had lost everything he knew and entered the foster care system.

Kenzie grasped his arm and held it firmly. Not hard, she didn't want him to feel threatened. But firmly, calmly, waiting for him to actually answer the question she had asked.

Zachary swallowed again. He looked at Kenzie's feet.

"It's hard," he admitted. "I don't want… to keep seeing it."

"What you saw today or something that happened to you?"

"Both."

"Do you want to talk to Dr. B?"

"No. I don't need anything. Just… time. I had to do this—" Zachary motioned back toward the inner offices of the police department he had just come back from. "Now that I have, I can put it behind me."

"I assume you have to write a report for the father."

"I got a copy of the report, and I have the pictures. I'll send those to him. Then I'm done. I don't need to do anything else."

"Do you want to hang out with me until I'm done? Or do you want me to leave early and come home with you?"

"No, no. You don't need to do anything special. Best if I just behave like nothing happened. Just go on as normal."

"I think that is just bottling up your feelings. How you felt when you were… at home." She didn't want to say, "Being abused" in front of the cop. That was not her information to share. "How you felt seeing someone else hurt. Not being able to do anything about it. You don't want to bury those feelings."

"Well," he gave a teasing grin. "Actually, I do."

"If you bury them, they'll just pop up again at the most inconvenient time."

He nodded his agreement and let out a hard sigh. "We'll talk when you get home later. Let me just chill until then."

"Okay. Call me if you change your mind, and I'll close up shop early today. I can do that, you know. I'm allowed to set my own hours and I put in more time than I'm required to under my contract. I can take off early today if I need to."

He patted her on the arm and turned away from her.

"I'll see you at home."

28

Zachary hadn't wanted to talk about what happened that night, though Kenzie had provided him with lots of opportunities to open up and had given him a couple of gentle nudges to do so. He was, under the rules they had established in couple's therapy, allowed to say that he did not want to talk about something if he wasn't ready. That was to help prevent lies and deception from creeping into their relationship over issues they found too difficult or personal to discuss. It was frustrating, but Kenzie had to admit that Dr. B had prevented a lot of needless arguments by helping them set the boundaries she had.

So, they did not discuss the domestic abuse that Zachary had witnessed. Kenzie comforted herself with the knowledge that he was finished with the case and could now go on with other things and not be stressed by it. There would be no more evening surveillance while Zachary waited for the man to hit his wife.

Kenzie didn't join Detective Cameron's interview with Kirk Robertson, but he sent her a link to the recording of the discussion that had taken place in one of the interrogation rooms upstairs in case Kenzie wanted to watch it, which she did. She put on her headphones and watched the image on the screen.

Cameron leaned forward, studying the big, red-faced man closely.

"So, tell me about your relationship with your brother. From what I have heard, you were not on the best terms with Scott."

"Well…" Kirk spread his hands apart. "A lot of siblings do not get along together. Just being born to the same parents doesn't mean you have anything else in common. We were… very different. Scott was always the one Mom and Dad favored."

"And you resented that."

"I was used to that. I dealt with it all my life. It didn't mean anything."

"How we are treated as children can greatly affect how we function as adults."

"I'm not some traumatized kid. We were both raised with everything we needed. I wasn't abused. I just didn't have all of the opportunities and praise that he did. He was the one who was so bright and had such a promising future. I was just kind of… an afterthought. People were always surprised to find out they had two kids, you know? Oh, Kirk. The other kid."

"And that was why you didn't have anything to do with Scott the last couple of years."

"I didn't have anything to do with him because he was a spoiled brat and had already taken half of my father's money, and then he figured he was entitled to another half after he died. He was greedy. After all the money he got for his company, he shouldn't have been looking for any more."

"You saw it as an early payout of his part of the estate."

"That's what it was. I wasn't trying to color it as something it wasn't. That was exactly what it was, and Dad intended right from the start that it would count against the amount he would get under the will."

"He told you that?"

"Sure. He said that I would still get my portion. That what he was giving Scotty was his portion. I just had to wait longer for mine. Then he died, and Mom and Scott tried to say that he was entitled to another half of *my* money."

"Your mom even picked sides?"

"She didn't want to pick. She went away to Australia and, even when I call her, she usually doesn't bother to answer or call me back." Kirk shook his head. "She thinks she can just stay out of it, and not say anything, and then after it is all sorted out, we'll be able to all be a family again and we'll all get along."

"But that won't be happening now."

Kirk tried to put on a sad face, but couldn't pull it off. He looked smug and self-satisfied. "I don't have to keep fighting anymore. It doesn't matter what Mom or anyone else thinks. God has set everything right."

"God has?" Cameron asked skeptically.

Kirk shrugged. "He knows the way things were supposed to be. He knows what it was that Dad intended, and now... everything is lined up the way it was supposed to be again." He took a deep breath through his nose and let it out slowly, his shoulders lowering. "And you don't need to feel sorry for Scotty," he advised. "He's with Dad. He and Dad always got along well, so he's happy where he is. And I'm here with Mom. Everything is... balanced. The scales are balanced."

"Is that how you see it?"

Kirk nodded. "That's how it is," he agreed.

"Where did you get the steroids?"

Kirk blinked at him, his pouchy, watery eyes looking slightly confused.

"What steroids? What are you talking about?"

"The steroids for Scott. The pills that made everything right again."

"I didn't give him steroids or anything else. You're crazy. I hadn't even seen him in the past two years; how would I have given him steroids? And why would he take them if they were making him so sick? It isn't like he was a musclehead. He was always more interested in math stuff than in his body. I didn't do too bad in gym, and I was on the high school football team." Kirk thrust out his chest and paused for Cameron to admire him. "But Scott wasn't interested in any of that. He was all about the schoolwork and moneymaking schemes."

"You didn't think much of him."

"He was the golden boy. Everyone thought he was the greatest. He won all kinds of academic awards and everyone thought he was destined to become this brilliant financial wizard. What was he going to do with all of this talent? Was he going to solve the world's problems? World poverty and homelessness? A more balanced distribution of wealth? All he was going to do was make more money. What exactly excited people about that? They wanted him to be a millionaire? A billionaire? Why? Did they think that he would give them some of his money?"

Cameron nodded. "That is kind of weird, isn't it? But maybe they did. Maybe your parents thought he would take care of them if he made a lot of money. Friends thought… maybe he would fund their ideas and be a resource for them to get their new ventures off the ground."

"And the teachers and principal and his university professors? What made them so excited to have this brilliant kid in his class? Just because they could say that they had known him? Like knowing Steve Jobs or Elon Musk back in the day? I don't know. All of this hero worship for someone who… was never going to do anything heroic."

Kenzie wondered how he saw himself. Did he see his job or his position on his high school football team as heroic? Or was he still planning something heroic later in life? Or maybe he didn't care about being heroic at all; he just didn't want people to worship his brother.

"And when did you decide to do something about it?" Cameron asked gently. "When did you decide that going through the courts was not the most effective way to get the money that was rightfully yours? Did your lawyer tell you that he didn't think you would win? You could see all that money that was rightfully yours slipping away from you…"

"My lawyer still thought we could win. It wasn't over yet. I had no reason to do anything to Scott and I *didn't*. I never did anything to hurt him. It doesn't matter how many different ways you try to ask it. I didn't do anything. I never saw him, and I never told him to take steroids."

"That's interesting."

Kirk frowned. "What is that supposed to mean?"

"You never reached out to Scott in any way?"

"No."

"Never called him? Emailed him? Took one step to try to reconcile?"

"No. What was stopping him from doing any of those things? Why should it fall on me to take the first step?"

"Someone had to."

Kirk shrugged. "Well, no one did. And now it is too late."

"Yes, it is."

"That coroner lady that I talked to about claiming his remains said that he had a roommate and a girlfriend. Why don't you talk to them? They'll tell you that I never went to see Scott. I was never there!"

"What about sending him something? Didn't he get a package from you? You sent him a box of chocolates, was it?"

"What are you talking about? I never sent him anything."

His response sounded genuine to Kenzie's ear. Surprised and confused. If he had sent something that had been poisoned to his brother, he was a very good actor.

"I will find out, you know. I will get the details from his roommate. There will be something left lying around. A receipt or delivery slip. People remember who came into the building, packages left in front of apartment doors. You think you can avoid all the cameras and witnesses, but you can't. They are everywhere."

"You're crazy." Kirk shook his head. "You ask his roommate. Ask if I was ever there or sent anything to him. I never did."

29

At Cameron's request, Kenzie went with him to question Rachel, Scott's girlfriend, to see if he could find any inconsistencies in the stories of the witnesses.

"Rachel is comfortable with you," Cameron told Kenzie as they drove to her house. "I think it's important to see her away from Alex. Up until this point, I have only ever seen her with Alex. I want her away from his influence. Whether they are rivals or lovers or just acquaintances. It is important to hear what she has to say without him in the room."

Kenzie nodded.

"I talked with her at the morgue the one day after he died. I told you about that."

She didn't know what, if anything, Rachel might still have to tell, but she didn't mind tagging along with Detective Cameron. It got her away from her computer for a few minutes, and then she could go back to her report with a clear head and put the final touches on it. Dr. Cook would review it for completeness, sign off, and then she would be finished with the Robertson case. Cameron would tell her if they ever gathered enough evidence to charge anyone. She would go on and deal with the next body. And the next, and the next. Solving the puzzles each body presented and trying to get justice for those who had met with foul play.

"Long thoughts?" Cameron asked, looking sideways at her.

"Oh, no. Just thinking about... the rest of the files I have to work on. Now or in the next few weeks."

"Sounds like pretty long thoughts to me."

"Well, maybe in a way, but it's work that I enjoy. I like uncovering clues about what happened to someone and being part of the effort to bring them justice. And sometimes, I get to come out with someone like you on an interview or part of the investigation I'm not normally involved with. It's interesting."

"In a small town and police department like Roxboro, we can get away with taking some liberties. But it's within your purview to ask questions of friends and family about the deceased and their history, so it's not that much of a stretch."

Kenzie felt fortunate to work with a small-town police department that afforded some opportunities for boots-on-the-ground investigations a big city medical examiner's office might not have.

The young blonde must have been watching for them to arrive. She was standing at the door and opened it for them before they had the chance to knock or ring the doorbell. She had dark circles under her eyes, not hidden by concealer.

At first, Kenzie thought it odd that a nurse of Rachel's age would be able to afford the pretty little bungalow in an older neighborhood but, when she looked around the living room that Rachel led her into, it was obvious it was not her house, but her parents'. Big family photos showcased a younger Rachel at various ages and stages, some with the rest of the family and some by herself for special occasions like her graduation. The furniture was in good condition, but not new. The room was comfortable and had the feeling of being well lived in. The smell of coffee hung in the air.

Rachel looked around and gave a little shrug. "I know, I'm too old to still be living at home. But with student loans and working shift..."

"I think it's great," Kenzie told her. "It's so hard to make a living these days. A lot of adults are still living in their childhood homes. And there are a lot of benefits to both generations."

"I wish that Scott and I could have had a place of our own. But I guess if we had, I'd have to move out now, because I wouldn't be able to afford it on my own."

"Did you ever talk about it?" Kenzie asked, settling into a comfy upholstered chair. "Finding a place of your own?"

"We did, but… to begin with, Scott wanted to wait until he got his business off the ground so that he knew he had a stable place even if things took longer and didn't become profitable as quickly as he hoped. And then… he was sick, and I wanted him to get out of there in case there was something in the apartment that was making him sicker. Gas or toxic mold or radon or something. But he said it took too much mental energy to think about it. He needed to wait until he felt better before he could start planning a move."

Kenzie had dealt with that inability to plan anything with Zachary as he entered a depressive cycle. Even answering questions about his preferences for Christmas food or decorations or when he wanted to see his family were just too difficult. He could not move forward until he was past the critical point.

"That makes it really hard," she acknowledged.

"You know we're here to ask more questions about Scott and what happened to him," Detective Cameron told Rachel in a compassionate tone. "I know this is really difficult, and you are probably ready for us to just let it go, but if you'll bear with me for a little longer…"

Rachel nodded and rubbed her forehead as if she might have a headache coming on. "I know. I want to know why he died too, although…" she shrugged, "you don't always get satisfactory answers in medicine. You give it your best guess based on what you see, but sometimes you don't get it right. Sometimes, there is no good answer, and you can't explain why someone died."

"You know we were looking for more evidence at Alex's apartment yesterday."

"Yes, of course."

"Well, we were hoping to find some sign of the medications that poisoned Scott."

Rachel looked at Kenzie for verification, as if she didn't trust Cameron. "Poisoned?" she repeated, "He was on a few different prescriptions as well as the over-the-counter medicines. You already have all of those, and you don't say 'poisoned' when someone has a drug interaction or allergy, or ends up taking too much of something. You asked me before if he might have intentionally taken an overdose."

Kenzie nodded. "I know. But it doesn't look like it was an accidental drug interaction or overdose. It wasn't a fatal overdose of Tylenol or anything else that was in his bedside table."

"What, then? Your search warrant said that you were looking for pills or medications, but it didn't say what kind."

"Steroids."

30

R achel looked blank. "He wasn't taking steroids."

"He took so many steroids that it completely destroyed his heart, liver, and kidneys," Kenzie told her.

"But Scott wasn't on steroids. I would have known. He wasn't the type. He wouldn't have taken them."

"That is why we are saying poisoning," Cameron explained.

Rachel's brow furrowed. She shook her head. "I don't understand. Why would someone poison him? And why would they use steroids?"

"It's an interesting question, isn't it?"

"You think it was Alex?" Rachel demanded. "Is that it?"

"I didn't say that."

"Well, he was the one who lived with Scott. He was the one who had access to his food."

"Do *you* think he put steroids into Scott's food?"

"Alex couldn't have done that to Scott. How could he?"

"Doesn't he seem like the most likely suspect?"

"Well, him or me, yeah. And I know *I* didn't do it."

"But why would Alex want to poison him?" Cameron pressed. "We are pursuing this as far as we can, but the 'why' is still an open question. Was there a problem between them?"

"They were good friends," Rachel said, hesitant. "They had been friends since college. They shared an apartment all that time, so you know they got along well. If they hadn't, Scott would have left."

"Did they have a written agreement between them? Was Scott committed for a certain length of time? I understand there was quite a lengthy term on the lease. Alex had probably wanted Scott committed too, so he wasn't left with the full rent himself."

"No. They had a one-year agreement to start with, when Scott initially moved in with him. After that... it was just month-to-month. He could have given notice and left whenever he wanted to."

"So he wanted to stay, and Alex wanted him to stay," Cameron stated.

"Yeah, of course."

"Then why would Alex poison him?"

Rachel shook her head. "He wouldn't." She closed her eyes, thinking about it.

"Did they always get along together?" Kenzie asked. "They must have had some friction points. Like the cat."

"Oh, the cat." Rachel rolled her eyes. "I can't understand why Alex got the cat. He knew that Scott was allergic. You don't think Alex got the cat just to drive Scott out, do you? Was that his plan?"

"He could have just asked Scott to leave, couldn't he?"

Rachel nodded. "They were both working. Either one could probably have afforded the rent by themselves now. Not like when they were students. Scott was making pretty good money, and I don't think Alex is doing too badly. He would make comments sometimes, kind of complaining about the fact that Scott made so much more money than he did."

"Do you think there was some real resentment behind it? Not *just* teasing," Kenzie asked, "but hiding his real jealousy over money behind a joke?"

Rachel nodded. "Sure. I got the feeling that he did kind of resent the fact that Scott was so much more successful. I mean, he was doing this start-up company, and had thousands and thousands of dollars raised for it before even starting."

"Who gets that money now that Scott is dead?" Cameron asked.

"I guess no one," Rachel said, shaking her head. "I mean, it was in escrow, but Scott didn't actually have access to it yet. Now that the project won't be going forward… I guess it all gets returned and the investors can spend it on the next big thing."

"There wasn't any contingency plan for someone else to carry it forward if something happened to him?"

Rachel shook her head slowly. "I don't think so…" She got up from her chair and started to pace. "There was, though!" She whirled around to face Cameron again. "Yes, there was. I remember! He had to have something in his business plan, or one of the big investors would not step up. He said that they had to have a plan for what would happen if something happened to Scott!"

Cameron and Kenzie just sat there looking at each other and Rachel. Rachel drilled knuckles into her temples, trying to remember everything that had been said.

"There weren't a lot of people who could take over something like that. Scott said that if something happened to him, there wasn't really anyone who could have covered for him, but they had to name someone anyway."

"Who did he name?"

"Alex and Scott went to school together. They went through the same program. So Alex had the right background. But he didn't have the same level of skill as Scott. Scott had a knack for it from the time he was a kid. He was really smart. A genius or phenom or whatever you want to call it."

"And he named Alex?" Kenzie asked.

"Yeah… he said it would never happen. But he had to put someone down."

"So Kirk and Alex both benefited from Scott's death. To the tune of thousands of dollars for each of them," Cameron pointed out.

Kenzie nodded. She was thinking through everything that Kirk and Alex had said. Alex was Kirk's alibi. He was the one person who could say that Kirk had never been close to the apartment or sent anything to Scott.

What if they had been in on it together?

But if Alex successfully launched the start-up company, Kirk would lose all the money his father had put into Scott's start-up. If the company could not be started, it would go back to his estate, and therefore to Kirk.

"Have you ever seen steroids or any unidentified medication at the apartment?" Cameron asked. "You are the person most likely to have seen something."

Rachel shook her head slowly. But her words were in opposition to her actions. "I know that when they first started out in college, Alex was really athletic. He was involved in sports and spent a lot of time at the gym. I didn't know them back then, but I've seen pictures of them at the bar together and that kind of thing. Alex was really cut."

"Like maybe he was taking steroids?" Kenzie asked.

"Yeah. It's hard to get definition like that unless you are."

"But he eventually gave up on the bodybuilding? It got to be too much to do with his studies?" Cameron suggested.

"He was injured," Rachel said. "Pectoralis Major tendon rupture." She put her hand over the outside portion of her chest where it connected to her shoulder. "Here. It's really painful. When guys use steroids, their muscles can grow too fast for the connective tissues to keep up. Ligaments and tendons can tear because there is too much stress on them. That kind of tear is really unusual in anyone but weightlifters. Sometimes, it happens to someone who falls and catches himself; that sudden force on their shoulder can cause a pec tear. But other than that, it is almost always athletes, and usually only those who are juicing."

"And it is a career-ending injury," Kenzie said.

Rachel nodded. "You can't come back from that. And Alex didn't. I don't know if he would ever have been a competitive body-builder. I don't know how good he was. But after that, there wasn't any way he could compete. He had surgery to repair it, and I guess then he had to get serious about his studies, because he sure wasn't going to make money lifting."

31

Cameron checked his phone after getting back into the car. Kenzie waited for him to put it away, but he tapped, scrolled, and sent out a few messages. Before putting it back in his pocket, he turned and smiled at Kenzie. His eyes were hard and calculating.

"Good thing we decided to do a search of the dumpsters close to the apartment building."

Kenzie's jaw dropped. "Really? You found something?"

"We found packets of steroids. Everything has to be finger-printed and chemically tested, but it looks like we might have caught a break."

"That's fantastic. You think you can connect it back to Alex?"

"That's our hope. It will lead where it leads, but we're assuming that Alex decided we were getting too close and he'd better ditch them before we got a warrant to search the apartment that included his room."

"Wow. It would be great to connect it up and be able to tie him to the poisoning."

"A couple of days for all of the testing to be done. Fingers crossed that it all comes out like we expect it to and that Alex assumes he got away with it and doesn't run."

"No reason why he should think we're on to him, unless your cops went back to his apartment afterward to tell him what they had found."

Cameron chuckled. "Well, I believe they are trained a bit better than that. I sure hope so."

Kenzie was up to her elbows in an autopsy when her phone started to ring. She ignored the vibration of the phone, as she always did during a postmortem. No one needed to get ahold of her that badly. They could wait until she was finished.

After the phone stopped vibrating, it started again. Dr. Cook paused in his work and looked at it. "Do you want to get that?"

"No. It's fine. Sometimes people think they need to reach me right away, but it is rarely that urgent."

He nodded and went back to working on some microscope slides.

The phone beeped a notification of a voicemail received. Kenzie found that she rarely received voicemails on her cellphone anymore. People either decided to call back another time or sent her an email or text follow up. Kenzie glanced toward it, wondering if she should take a break to listen to it.

"Do you want me to check it for you?" Dr. Cook asked.

If he checked, she might not have to remove her gloves and wash up again. He could see whether it was just an annoying marketing call or something really important. A call from her father, maybe. She needed to call him to see how he was doing and figure out whether there was any work she could pass on to him. Or to urge Zachary to find something for him to do.

"Uh… if you can see who the caller is…?" she suggested tentatively.

Dr. Cook nodded and took a couple of steps down the counter, where he pulled out her phone and looked at it.

"Zachary."

Zachary?

Kenzie tried to decide whether that meant it was important or not. Sometimes, he just left her messages about unimportant things so she would know she didn't need to call him back. Or he had butt-dialed her, and the voicemail was just five minutes of background noise. Though the voicemail had arrived faster than that, so maybe it was just a single sentence telling her he would call her back later and not to worry about it.

But it could also be urgent. He had been out of sorts lately, triggered by little things, worrying about things that didn't normally bother him.

"Dang. Maybe I'd better see what that is. Thanks."

Kenzie started to strip off her gloves.

"Do you want me to play it for you on speaker?" Dr. Cook offered.

"Uh… better not. Never know what Zachary might say on voicemail." Kenzie laughed awkwardly.

Let Dr. Cook think she meant he might say something sexy or embarrassing on voicemail, rather than some mental health concern or random message that wasn't even intended for her.

She continued to pull off her gloves, wadded them up, and threw them out in the appropriate bin, then retrieved her phone from Dr. Cook. She touched the fingerprint recognition and went to her voicemail, where she tapped on the new voicemail message to see what was up with Zachary.

"This is Officer Winslow of the Roxboro Police Department…"

Kenzie gripped the phone more tightly, suddenly unable to breathe. Her first thought was that he'd been in an accident. He was notifying her that Zachary was critically injured or dead. But there hadn't been a callout for the medical examiner's office, so he couldn't be dead.

"Zachary Goldman has been arrested for disorderly conduct and is being held at the police station. I understand that you may be in the building. He's currently being held in Booking. If you are not able to get here soon, he will be moved to Holding."

Kenzie put down the phone and started to remove the rest of her protective clothing.

"Is everything okay?" Dr. Cook asked, looking concerned.

"No... Yes, he's okay, but... at least I hope he is. Sheesh, what did he get himself into now?"

"Is Zachary in trouble? Do you need anything?"

"No. I don't need anything. He's not hurt. I don't think he's hurt."

Of course, he could have sustained minor injuries during the arrest. Or in whatever disturbance had preceded the arrest. If he was guilty of disorderly conduct, it might be because he'd had a meltdown. Or it might have something to do with a case.

But if he was fine, then why had it been the arresting officer who had placed the call rather than Zachary himself? He had the right to make the call if he could, which made her wonder if he might not be able to.

She swore under her breath, ripping off the flimsy outer clothing and jamming it into the bin.

"I'm sure it's all fine," she told Dr. Cook. "I... I'm off for the day."

There was no point in telling him she would be back if she could. She would not be coming back. She would not be bailing Zachary out, sending him home, and then returning to finish the postmortem. She looked back at the body she had left on the table without regard to tidying up and putting it back into storage until she could return to it.

"Go ahead," Cook told her. "I'll put him away."

"Thanks." Kenzie hurried out of the morgue, her lips pressed tightly together, trying not to let her brain go wild on everything that might have happened to precipitate Zachary getting arrested.

She would find out soon enough.

32

U pstairs, she went directly to Booking. The officer had *just* left the voicemail message, so she had no worries that Zachary would have been processed through to Holding yet.

She stopped at the intake desk and looked around. Zachary was sitting chained to a bench. He held his hands over his face and was rocking back and forth.

What had happened?

The officer at the desk looked at Kenzie with a scowl. "Can I help you? This area is not open to the public."

"My partner, Zachary, he's over there. I was called by Officer Winslow?"

She looked around and flagged down a big cop with a belly. "Winslow? This one is for you."

He looked at Kenzie. "Are you Dr. Kirsch, then? You must have been close by to get here so fast."

"Yes, just down in the morgue. Only an elevator ride away. What's going on? What happened?"

"He was arrested for causing a disturbance in the grocery store parking lot. He was quite emotionally distraught and, as you can see," Winslow cast a glance toward him, "he is having a difficult time. I was going to call it in as an EDP and get a medical team here, but he said you were here, and I thought that if you could get things under control…"

"Yeah, okay, I'll try." Kenzie agreed. "Do you know what happened? Why he made this disturbance?"

"Possible child abuse case. We are looking into it. But he needs to… back off and disengage. Just let us do our job."

Kenzie nodded. "Okay. I got it. Sometimes… that can be a challenge."

"I hope you can help us. I'd rather send him home than to a cell or a psychiatric hold."

He directed her around the counter to a hinged portion that could be folded back, allowing her through a swinging gate into the restricted area. A number of people were being processed and the smell of sweat and unwashed bodies was potent. Winslow walked with her over to Zachary. He took a breath, looking like he was going to start in on a lecture, telling Zachary that his ride was here and that if he wanted to be able to go home, he'd better shape up quickly.

Kenzie put up her hand to stop Winslow from proceeding. "If you'll just let me?"

He shrugged and folded his arms. Kenzie bent down so she was closer to Zachary's level.

"Zachary. Zachary." She touched his shoulder gently. "Hey, Zach, talk to me. Tell me what's going on."

He moaned and didn't remove his hands from his face. Kenzie wondered how he had managed to communicate to Winslow that she was there in the building. He must have been verbal enough to get that across.

"Zachary. Come on." She put a little pressure on his wrist, encouraging him to move his hands away from his face. "You want to go home, don't you? If you want me to get you out of here, you will have to talk to me."

After a little more encouragement, she managed to get Zachary to lower his hands part of the way. His eyes were swollen and he had a few bruises—whether from the arrest or what had happened prior to that she didn't know.

"Yeah," Kenzie smiled reassuringly. "You want to go home, don't you?"

"Yes," he agreed in a choked voice. "Home."

"Do you know what happened? Can you tell me?"

"She hit him. I had to stop her. Get the police."

"Okay," Kenzie nodded her agreement. "That sounds about right. Officer Winslow said that it was a possible child abuse case. You saw someone hit a child?"

Zachary nodded. His eyes were still far away, not seeing her even though he was reacting to her, trying to follow what she said. He might be experiencing flashbacks or might be in a dissociative state.

"What did you do?" Kenzie asked, keeping her voice neutral. Zachary's reaction must have been extreme for him to be arrested for disorderly conduct.

"I… told her not to hit him, and I… she was yelling at me, and she was going to hit him again…"

Kenzie winced at the thought of the two trauma triggers hitting at the same time; Zachary feeling like he was under attack and a child was being hurt. It probably pulled him right back to his child-hood, trying to protect himself and his siblings from their abusive parents.

"So you called the police?" she prompted, knowing this was not the case. If he were calm and reasonable, he would certainly have called the police. But in the midst of a traumatic event, he had not been calm and sensible.

"I protected him. Took him away from her."

Kenzie could see the escalation in her mind's eye. A mother who was angry or at the end of her rope, smacking and berating her child. Attacking Zachary verbally when he tried to stop her. He moved in, getting between the mother and child and separating them, not letting her get close to him again. The mother freaking out that this strange, scruffy man was kidnapping her child, keeping him from her. Hitting Zachary because he put himself between them or because she was angry with him for interfering. Bystanders calling 9-1-1 because of the ruckus, possibly under the impression that Zachary was the aggressor or that he had tried to kidnap the child.

"But you didn't hit her, right?" Kenzie asked. Zachary shook his head. She looked at Winslow, who also shook his head.

"No. Witnesses agree he never threatened or attacked her. She was violent, possibly intoxicated. The child does not have any visible injuries, but we are investigating the report that she hit him. DCF will put him into emergency care until they are convinced that it is a safe environment."

"You heard that?" Kenzie patted Zachary's arm. "He's not going back to her today. They're going to make sure he is safe."

"People think it's okay, that they can do whatever they want because it's their kid."

"I know. But it isn't. They'll make sure she doesn't hurt him."

Zachary shook his head slightly. "They'll put him right back in the home. Or somewhere else he'll be hurt."

He knew the foster care system too well. Some kids were safe there. Some kids, like his siblings Vince and Mindy, stayed with one family and were even adopted and protected from further abuse. Others, like Zachary, never settled permanently in one home and, as they went from one foster home or care facility to another, experienced serial abuse.

"He'll be okay," she told Zachary anyway. "They'll look after him."

Zachary moved his hands up to rub his eyes and seemed startled by the chains on his handcuffs. He stared at them for a minute as if he didn't know what he was looking at. Then he cupped his palms over his eyes, ignoring the shackles.

"Are we going home?"

"Yes. Once Officer Winslow is convinced you've calmed down and don't need professional help."

"I'm fine," Zachary said, "and I'm not hurting anyone. I don't need to be monitored."

"He was pretty wound up at the scene," Winslow told Kenzie,

defending his choices, "I thought he was going to have a break-down right there."

"I've seen him like that before," Kenzie assured him. She put her hand on Zachary's bowed, short-cropped head. "It can be pretty worrisome. But I can see he is through the worst of it. He'll probably just want to sleep when we get home. You don't need to worry about him causing any trouble. He won't be out tonight. He doesn't know where this woman lives."

"There's a video," Zachary said.

33

W hat?" Winslow demanded, his head swiveling to look back at Zachary.

"On my camera. I took a video as proof."

"Do you have his possessions?" Kenzie asked.

"Yeah. He had a camera around his neck at the scene, but..." Winslow retreated, muttering something to himself as he retrieved Zachary's personal possessions, which he would need to give back to him if he was releasing Zachary to Kenzie anyway. Kenzie was glad that he'd had the presence of mind to remember the video before they had left. It saved having to make another trip back and to prove that the video had been taken where and when he said.

Winslow returned a few minutes later. He had the sealed envelope in which Zachary's possessions were stored.

"Do I have your permission to open this?"

Zachary peeked through his fingers and nodded. Winslow looked at Kenzie, and she nodded, agreeing that he had Zachary's permission. He ripped the envelope open and pulled out the camera.

"I'm going to access your camera and give the rest of this to Dr. Kirsch. Does it have a passcode?"

"No."

Winslow handed the envelope to Kenzie so he had two free hands to access the camera. He pressed a few buttons and brought up the last video. Kenzie leaned over to watch the small LCD screen.

In the distance, a woman and child came into focus. Zachary spoke the date, time, and location. The camera changed focus as he moved it to the car license plate and zoomed in so that the numbers became clear. Then it returned to the woman and child, zooming out so they were framed within the viewfinder again. The woman was shouting and the child defiant, giving her loads of preteen attitude.

She shoved him once and he fell into the car. Not a hard blow; he was not obviously injured. He bounced back toward her, crying out in protest. The framing of the video changed as Kenzie thought Zachary let the camera drop to his chest, held in position by the neck strap to keep his hands free, and he strode toward the mother and child.

The mother hauled off and gave the child a slap across the ear and side of the head that made Kenzie wince. She could easily burst his eardrum. The boy's high shriek confirmed that this blow had hurt more than just his dignity.

"Hey! Leave him alone!" the camera picked up Zachary's shout.

She turned to face him and, just as Kenzie had pictured when he told his story, the mother immediately started to berate Zachary and swear at him for interfering in her God-given right to discipline her own child. Zachary got closer, ignoring her vitriol.

"You can't hit him. Leave him alone."

The mother shoved the boy back, farther away from Zachary, slamming him into the vehicle much harder this time. Kenzie saw his head snap back and impact the side of the car. She winced in sympathy.

Zachary got too close for the camera to take in the woman's face, centered chest-high and catching a whirl of bodies, arms, and the boy's face as Zachary moved to physically prevent her from hurting the child again. A number of blows hit Zachary's body and face, making the camera bounce around wildly, but it was clear what was going on.

Zachary managed to put himself between the woman and the child, blocking her from reaching him but not restraining her or hitting her. The boy was out of sight, apparently sheltering behind Zachary rather than going around him to return to his mother.

There was little action after that, with Zachary staying in position until the arrival of the police, when the video stopped abruptly. Kenzie gulped, trying to swallow the emotion that welled up at hearing both the child's sobs and Zachary's own on the video. She had no doubt he had been fighting through a serious flashback to his own childhood abuse. Until the police had arrived to take over, relieving him of the responsibility of controlling the situation.

At that point, he had succumbed to the pull of the past and, as Winslow had observed, had obviously been in a great deal of distress, and they had thought the EDP team would be required.

"Can I copy this from the memory card?" Winslow asked.

"It has wireless email capabilities," Kenzie told him. She leaned over to look at the controls and the icons on the screen and pointed to the envelope. "Try that."

Navigating the onscreen keyboard with the D-pad, Winslow managed to enter an email address to forward the video to himself or their forensic evidence department. He pulled out his phone and watched the screen for a while until an alert sounded and he gave a nod. He tapped the screen a few times to make sure the video was playable.

"Got it. Do you want me to delete it from the camera so you don't have to see it again?" Winslow asked Zachary.

Zachary nodded, swallowing. "Yeah."

Kenzie rubbed his shoulder comfortingly. He was not doing as badly as she would have predicted. He was over the peak of the panic attack and recovering.

"Is that everything you need?" she asked Winslow. "He can come in and sign a statement tomorrow if you need something in writing."

"I'll need an affidavit as to the authenticity of the video, but yes, he can come in and do that another time. Give me a few minutes to talk to my sergeant about the charges. I'll be back."

Kenzie nodded. He left them and went to talk to his superior.

"Can I sit with you?" Kenzie asked.

Zachary lowered his hands and looked around him. "You don't want to sit here like a criminal," he said, cheeks flushing.

Kenzie didn't care what anyone thought of her sitting down with her partner in the booking room. Since that was his only objection, she sat beside him and put her arm around him. They leaned toward each other, touching heads gently.

"You did good," she murmured.

"I did?" his tone was surprised. "I thought you would be mad."

"I'm not. You helped a child who needed someone to intervene on his behalf. You know I would never stop you from doing that."

Despite her words, she knew that she had gotten after him in the past for neglecting his own welfare to protect a child or other vulnerable individual. Zachary was small and lightweight and didn't carry a weapon like a TV private investigator. He was vulnerable, especially when he put himself into a highly volatile situation like the one he had stepped into. But she couldn't fault him for what he had done. She would probably have reacted similarly.

She rubbed Zachary's back. "You did good," she repeated. "That video will ensure that boy gets the help he needs. Even if he has no visible injuries and denies that she hurt him, the police and DCF can see what happened and how volatile she is."

Zachary nodded slightly.

They were silent, just giving Zachary recovery time until Winslow returned. The background of ringing phones and other conversations continued. Eventually, Winslow stood before Zachary again, his thumbs in his duty belt.

"The disorderly conduct charge is being dropped," he told Zachary. "That means you are free to go."

Kenzie smiled her appreciation. Zachary looked at the hand-cuffs. Winslow bent down and unlocked them.

"Thank you for doing what you did."

Since Zachary didn't have his car, which Kenzie presumed was still in the grocery store parking lot, there was no discussion over whose car they would take home, and Zachary just melted into the passenger seat and closed his eyes for the short trip home. Kenzie didn't try to engage him in conversation. He would be exhausted by his ordeal and would probably go to sleep as soon as he got home. It was the one time when sleeping was not a problem for him.

Entering the kitchen through the garage door, Kenzie asked, "Do you need anything? Water? Soft drink?"

Zachary paused, thinking about it. "Water, yeah."

His medications tended to give him dry mouth, and she imagined that after the confrontation with the woman, the arrest, sweating, and crying, he was probably dehydrated too. A bottle of water might stave off the headache and grouchiness that were bound to accompany it. Kenzie got him a bottle and cracked the top, following Zachary to the bedroom.

He lay on the bed and pried off his shoes, which he hadn't done at the door, dropping them onto the floor beside the bed. While normally, this would have irritated Kenzie, and she would have immediately started into a lecture on picking up after himself and helping her to keep the house tidy, she didn't this time. He could take care of them when he got up later. She wouldn't even pick them up now, fearing it would just make him feel guilty for being so wiped out. It wasn't his fault his brain and body were shutting down.

Zachary curled up on his side. Kenzie sat on the edge of the bed and held the water bottle in front of his face.

"Oh, yeah." Zachary sat up to take a few swallows, then put it on the bedside table. "Thanks."

"Do you want a pill?"

"No."

She should have known. An anti-anxiety pill earlier in the day before the incident at the grocery store might have helped prevent a meltdown but, since it was over, there was no point in taking it now.

"Anything else? Do you want to talk to Dr. B?"

"I'm just going to go to sleep."

"Okay." Kenzie gave his shoulder one pat and backed off. He knew what he needed, and her hovering over him asking more questions wouldn't do either of them any good.

He could sleep and, since she wasn't going back to the morgue but was still within her usual working hours, she would connect to her email from home and see what she could process from there.

34

Cameron took the elevator to Alex Collins's floor with a deep sense of satisfaction.

It was a weird case, but they had sorted everything out. They had figured out that not only was Collins one of the only people with reliable access to Robertson's food to poison it, but that he also had a history of steroid use and had reason to want Robertson out of the way. Finding the steroids in the dumpster was the icing on the cake. They had him now. He would not slip between their fingers.

He walked down the hall to the apartment door and rapped on it loudly. He stood to the side, as he always did, training that had become second nature over the years, and he waited for Alex to come to the door, listening for any suspicious sounds from within.

On TV, the suspect always ran. Even if it were in an apartment building like this, where there was no good escape route.

There was no old-fashioned fire escape. How many of those buildings did Hollywood think were still around? There were so few of them, yet one would think from watching TV that every building in New York had them.

Maybe in New York, they did. But not in Roxboro, Vermont. The other thing that they had in the big city, if one were to believe

Hollywood, was buildings built so close together that a suspect could jump from one roof to the other several buildings in a row until they were able to escape through the building or to make a jump that their pursuer did not have the guts to try.

But they were on the third floor of a four-floor building, and in Roxboro, that was as tall as the buildings got. And buildings of that size were not butted up against each other, but were blocks apart. Good luck to Alex if he tried to go through the window or up onto the roof. He would break at least a few bones if he tried to jump.

There was no sound from within. He'd had an officer watching the building for the last few hours and they had not seen Alex leave it.

Cameron pounded on the door again. His knocks echoed through the building. "Police, Mr. Collins. Open up."

There was still no sound. Was it possible that he was out?

Luckily, Cameron knew where to find the landlord, assuming he wasn't out doing his grocery shopping. He took the elevator one more floor up to Harris's apartment and had him come down with his keys.

"I don't know about this," Harris said worriedly. "Do you have a search warrant?"

"I have a warrant for the arrest of Alex Collins. Unlock it, please, and then stand to the side."

Harris started to fuss about it again, and Cameron gave him his sternest cop look. Harris quailed and turned to the door to do what he had been told. He unlocked it with shaking fingers and then stood to the side. Cameron turned the handle and pushed the door open.

"Mr. Collins? Are you home? This is Detective Cameron. I'm coming in."

Even with the door standing open, he couldn't hear anything. He felt a little silly. Clearly, Alex Collins was not home.

He went in anyway. A short walk through the apartment showed that it was, in fact, empty.

A tricolor cat wormed its way around his ankles, yowling plaintively. Cameron walked into the kitchen and looked down at the cat's dishes. Both were empty. Not just with crumbs left at the bottom, but completely clean. Both the food and the water bowl.

Cameron picked up one bowl and filled it with water. The cat jumped up on the counter to watch the process and, when he turned the tap off, started licking water out of the sink. Cameron put the bowl of water down on the floor and picked up the food bowl. There was dry food in a nearby cupboard, and he filled the second bowl and put it down. The cat jumped down from the counter and started to eat immediately. Cameron watched it for a moment, then checked the fridge.

There was a carton of milk past the best-before date, but it didn't yet smell sour, so there was no reason to throw it. There were some restaurant takeout boxes. The garbage nearby was smelling quite rank. It had only been two days since they had searched the apartment. Collins had been there with no indication that he planned to go anywhere. He had accepted the landlord's offer of cash for keys, but there was no sign he was packing to move.

Cameron checked Collins's bedroom and bathroom, but there was no sign that Collins had packed an overnight bag.

There was the sound of voices and then footsteps. Cameron walked back out to the main door of the apartment and found himself facing a young woman with dark hair.

She looked at him, a scowl on her face. "What are you doing here?"

"Looking for Mr. Collins. Are you…?"

She sniffed. "His girlfriend. Anna. The landlord let you in there? I don't think he's allowed to do that. You shouldn't be here without anyone to supervise you. I know how things like this turn out. It wouldn't be the first time a cop planted the evidence he needed to make an arrest."

"I fed the cat."

She looked startled and stopped her lecture. "What?"

"Has Alex been gone for long? Would he leave without leaving food for the cat?"

Anna looked uncertain as to how to proceed. She looked around, glancing in through the kitchen doorway to see Cuddles still eating his kibble. "No, he wouldn't do that. She didn't have any food?"

"Both bowls were licked clean. No food, no water."

"That doesn't make sense."

"Do you have the number for his work? Can you find out whether he was at work today or yesterday?"

"Do you think something is wrong?" Anna looked around uneasily, hugging herself like she was cold. "Nothing is wrong, is it?"

"When did you talk to him last?"

"It's been... a couple of days. I've been at this conference. We've talked a couple of times, but cell coverage was spotty and I was really busy."

"You've talked to him a couple of times in the last two days?"

"No, I mean a couple of times during the conference. Not... not today or yesterday. The day before, maybe. I think. It's hard to keep track when you're traveling."

"It would be good if we could find out whether he has been at work."

"Okay, yeah." Anna took Cameron's measure, but obviously still did not trust him. She turned away from him and found a seat in the living room. She put down her heavy handbag and pulled out her phone. She had to search to find the number she was looking for. Obviously, she did not typically call the office number where Alex worked.

Rather than giving it to Cameron, Anna called it herself. She had to deal with several transfers before getting someone willing to talk to her. Cameron tried to listen to her without being obvious about it. She had chosen not to tell the person on the other end of the phone that she was talking to the police, but instead relied upon her very real concern to get the sympathy of the boss or HR person at Alex's office to get the information she was looking for.

"No," she said finally, her voice a little faint. "You don't need to call the police. I'll deal with it." She tapped the screen of her phone and looked at Cameron.

"Well… who are you, exactly?" she asked. "Do I talk to you, or should I be talking to someone else?"

"I'll take your initial statement. I'm not sure whether I'll stay on it or if it will be assigned to someone else."

"They said he hasn't been in the last two days. He took the day before off as a mental health day and no one talked to him during the day."

"I saw him here that day. So sometime between then and now…"

"He left," Anna said. "He wasn't planning to go anywhere. And we were going to spend the evening together tonight. I was planning a little candlelight dinner…"

"And it doesn't look like he had started packing for his move."

"His move?" Anna repeated blankly. "What move?"

"His move out of this apartment. Did he have a new place lined up, or was he still looking?"

"He wasn't moving out of this apartment."

"He accepted the landlord's offer to buy him out of his lease early."

"No, he didn't."

Cameron glanced toward the hall, where the landlord was probably still standing waiting for him.

"The landlord said that he did."

"I don't think so. He would have told me that. We talked about it when Mr. Harris started to push for him to move out, but he wanted to stay here and so did Scott, for the time being. We talked about what we could do with the money, get a nicer place with a bigger down payment… but we would have to be able to afford the monthly rent, and we weren't sure we would be able to."

"The two of you both working couldn't afford a place together?"

"It's really tough out there, detective. Rents are crazy high. A lot of people our age are moving back in with their parents. A person should be able to afford an apartment on a full-time salary, especially since we've both been working for a few years, but it isn't that easy."

Cameron had, of course, heard the same thing from a lot of

young people. He had managed to buy a house before the economy had tanked. If he were renting now instead of paying a mortgage, he wasn't sure how he would have managed to support a family.

"So he either lied to the landlord or he changed his mind again. Or he didn't have a chance to tell you yet that he had changed his mind and decided to take what the landlord was offering."

She looked at him, calculating, thinking about the three possibilities. Eventually, she nodded.

"I'm sure he didn't decide to leave. We had already been through all of that. We'd discussed it to death. He didn't want to move out of here; he was going to stay until the lease expired. He was hoping that by that time, he would have a promotion or a better job, or the rents would go down and we would be able to afford a place more easily."

"Did he talk to you about Scott's company?"

"What about Scott's company?" she shook her head.

"That Scott had named Alex as his successor. If anything happened to Scott, Alex would be in charge of the start-up and getting it off the ground."

"Oh, that… I remember him joking about it a few weeks ago. Asking me how I would like to be married to a billionaire CEO when it all worked out." She blushed. "We aren't married; we didn't even talk about it seriously. It was just a joke. You know…" she shrugged. "Just one of those unattainable dreams. Not something that was actually going to happen."

"But he was named as Scott's successor, and now Scott is dead."

"But you don't mean that… he has to take over the business now, do you?"

"*Has* to?"

"Gets to, I guess." Anna shrugged, and then she shook her head. "No, I don't think he actually would have wanted it. I mean, it's fun to talk about making that kind of money sometimes, but I don't think Alex would like the work. He is… he is a lot more fun than that. Down to earth. He isn't the kind of financial planner who always has his head in the clouds and dreams about annuity tables or whatever it is that they do. He likes to help people to plan for the future and meet their goals, but he isn't a shark like Scott. He isn't stupid; I'm not saying that. Just that… it isn't how he wants to spend his life. With Scott, that *was* his life. Every moment of every day, he was thinking about it, trying to figure out how he was going to make all of it happen. But not Alex. He wants to have fun, marry, have a family. He wants to have leisure time to go boating or skiing or travel around the world."

"And if he accepts the position of CEO of the start-up, that won't happen."

"No. He'd be locked into that for twenty years. Building the company out. For Scott, that was heaven. Bringing it all to fruition. But it wouldn't be like that for Alex."

"He would turn it down."

"Yeah. I'm sure he will."

"Then the money that would have gone into the start-up will revert to the trust."

"I don't know what you're talking about."

"Did you know Scott's brother, Kirk?"

She looked blank. "No. I don't think I even knew he had a brother. Oh, wait a minute, he… no, that wasn't him. No, I'm sure I never met any Kirk."

"And no one mentioned him? Not Scott? Not Alex?"

"No."

"You don't think he'd ever been to the apartment?"

"There were people who stopped by for visits sometimes. Scott didn't usually introduce them. He just took them to his room for a private visit. I don't know who any of them were."

35

K enzie saw Cameron's name on the caller ID on the desk phone and answered.

"Detective Cameron."

"Hi, Dr. Kirsch. How is your day going?"

"Oh, it's going along. How about yours?"

"Zachary doing okay?"

Kenzie sighed. "You heard?"

"You know cops. They gossip worse than… er, something that isn't sexist."

Kenzie laughed. "Word does get around pretty quickly around here," she agreed. "Yes, Zachary is fine. He slept more than usual, which means he got about five minutes. Today, he says he is fine, everything is back to normal, and he's working on his cases like usual."

"And how is he really?"

"Maybe a bit more distracted than usual. But he'll be fine. He'll use work to take his mind off of what happened yesterday and, in a few days, it will be less raw."

"Good. He's a good guy."

"He is," Kenzie agreed. Zachary was always trying to do the right thing. Many people were just looking out for number one, and didn't put much thought into what happened to anyone else. But with Zachary, it was the opposite. He was always worrying about everyone around him and whether they would be okay. He was a good person, thoughtful and loyal, right down to his core, and people sensed that.

"So, what were you calling about? Not just to ask about Zachary, I assume."

"No. We've had some interesting developments on the Robertson murder and I thought you might want to hear the highlights."

"Of course."

"Or lowlights."

"Hmm?" Kenzie was a little confused by the comment.

"I'm not sure I'd call them highlights."

"Oh, got it. Right. What's the news, then?"

"Alex Collins has disappeared."

"He ran?"

"He is officially a missing person. I think we will be lucky to ever see him again."

"Wow. I guess he was spooked by the search of the apartment, even if you didn't find anything there. Maybe he suspected you would be searching dumpsters, too, and he should have disposed of the pills farther away."

"It wasn't hard for him to guess that we would focus on him as a suspect the deeper we got into the investigation. He had the best access to Robertson. Could access his food and monitor his symptoms. He had a motive: all of the money he would have his hands on as the CEO of the company. He had the means; he knew how to get his hands on enough steroids to kill Robertson and the temerity to keep feeding them to him until he was dead."

"Do you have any leads on him? Where he might have gone?"

"Left without a trace. Nothing on his computer indicating where he was off to. Checked his browser history for anything to do with travel, and there wasn't anything. Maybe he did some searches on his phone. We don't have that."

"Does he have it with him or did he dump it?"

"If he has it with him, we'll know about it the next time he uses it. Have a flag on his credit cards as well. It's not as easy for a novice to disappear as it used to be."

"But if he ditches the phone and just works for cash…"

"Then he won't be able to work in his chosen profession. He's going to be a blue-collar worker. Under the table. Possibly for the rest of his life. And even then, maybe we'll get a hit on his finger-prints or DNA sometime."

"So that's it, just waiting for him to mess up?"

"We're still working the case. Waiting for the forensic test back. Reviewing your report. Tying up any loose ends."

"And then waiting."

"And then waiting," Cameron agreed.

"Well, thanks for letting me know. I guess I won't expect to see anyone arrested for Robertson's murder in the next little while."

"We'll do what we can. We've got a pretty good solve rate. But I wouldn't hold my breath."

Kenzie took a break at lunchtime to get herself something from the closest sandwich shop rather than the vending machine. She patted herself on the back for looking after herself in two ways, both by taking a break and by getting a sandwich that was reasonably healthy for her. After unwrapping the sandwich and taking the first few bites, she tapped her phone to call Zachary. He sometimes needed a reminder to stop and get himself lunch. While Kenzie tended to get too busy, Zachary got too distracted or had no idea how much time had passed since he had last eaten or come up for air.

He didn't answer his phone. That was not of immediate concern. There were a lot of reasons he might not answer his phone. He was talking to someone else, working on something important, too distracted to notice his phone ringing, had accidentally left it in another room, or was in a meeting. Rather than leaving him a voicemail, she texted him to call or text her back when he was free. She reread the message she had sent for any auto-correct errors, just to be sure. She ate her sandwich and browsed through her social networks for anything of interest.

It was a couple of hours later that her phone rang, and she reached for it and answered, thinking it would be Zachary, without looking at the caller ID.

"It's about time."

There was a laugh at the other end of the line that was not Zachary. Kenzie looked at the name, but she had already recognized the voice before she processed it. Heather, one of Zachary's older sisters. She helped him with some of the administration for his PI work and did some computer investigations from home.

"Oh, sorry. Hi, Heather."

"I guess that means you haven't heard from Zachary for a while."

"No." Kenzie sat back in her chair and thought about it. Zachary should have called her back by now. But it wasn't particularly alarming that he hadn't. She wasn't really worried about him.

But maybe he had been more traumatized by the encounter with the abusive mother than Kenzie had realized, and had crawled back into bed to shut out the flashbacks and emotion it had stirred up. She had seen him react like that before, spending all his time sleeping until he had been able to start processing the trauma.

She should get him in to see Dr. Boyle as soon as possible. She didn't want him reverting back to that kind of existence.

"No. I wonder if he's sleeping. He had something happen yesterday. I don't know whether he told you about it…"

"No, he didn't say anything. But I don't think he's sleeping."

Kenzie frowned at the phone. "Oh?"

"I was checking his location to see if he was home."

"And he isn't?" Kenzie switched to the map on her tracking app to verify this. Zachary's location did not pop up on the map. She entered his name and waited for it to locate him.

No location found

Kenzie stared at the screen. "That's weird. I can't track him. Are you seeing a location?"

"No. I'm not getting a location."

"Me neither. Maybe he forgot to charge it."

"Could be," Heather agreed. "But he hasn't checked his email either, so I don't think he's on his computer."

"What are the odds he isn't on his phone or his computer?"

"He could be out in the field," Heather said. "If he's on surveillance or something like that. He might be actively tracking someone and is focused on that. Or he could be…" Heather trailed off. "Doing something else," she finished eventually.

"He might have turned off his location tracking," Kenzie said, staring at the map on her screen.

"I guess so. It's probably just something going on with his phone. Maybe he's out of range. That's happened before."

And if he were out of range for long enough, the phone would stop looking for a cell tower to conserve battery power. If Zachary didn't realize that it was out of range, he could go hours without realizing there was a problem. He might not realize no calls or texts were coming in because he was busy with something else.

There was no reason to panic.

"I guess we just wait and see," Kenzie said in a slow, measured voice. "This has happened before, and he was just fine."

"Yeah. Okay, well, let me know if you hear from him. It isn't anything urgent. I was just going to touch base," Heather said lightly.

"Sure. No problem."

"Kenzie…?"

"Yeah?"

"What happened yesterday?"

Kenzie sighed. While she didn't like to share private information about Zachary, Heather was family, and she was sure Zachary would have said it was fine to talk to her about it. She gave Heather the bare bones of the confrontation and police response the day before.

"But he was okay this morning," she told Heather. "He seemed perfectly fine."

"I'm sure he still is," Heather assured her. "Thanks for letting me know."

After Heather disconnected the call, Kenzie sat staring at her phone, but Zachary's location didn't suddenly pop up on the app.

There was nothing to indicate that anything had happened to Zachary.

He had been kidnapped once. But he wasn't working on any files that were dangerous. Everything was fairly routine, as far as she knew. And Heather would know if he were working on a file that was dangerous or might attract the attention of bad actors. She would have told Kenzie if that were the case.

The other thing Kenzie worried about was Zachary's obsessive stalking of Bridget, his ex-wife.

He had seemed to have been cured of that behavior following the kidnapping, which had occurred on Bridget's street. Zachary had developed a strong aversion to the place, which had suited Kenzie just fine. She and Dr. Boyle had both been relieved that Zachary now avoided the area as assiduously as he had once been drawn to it.

Had the encounter with the abusive mother destabilized Zachary, impelling him back toward Bridget? It had been pretty clear to Kenzie that Bridget had been a substitute for the abusive mother Zachary had grown up with, who had eventually abandoned him, telling him he was incorrigible and that the dissolution of the entire family was his fault.

It made perfect sense that an encounter with an abusive mother who reminded him of his own mother could drive him back toward Bridget.

But what was Kenzie to do about that?

She was sure that Bridget or Gordon would have called her if they had seen Zachary camped outside their home. But they might not have noticed, since it had been months since Zachary had last been there.

She could drive by and see whether Zachary was parked nearby.

Kenzie wanted to call him to find out what was going on in his head, but she couldn't very well do that if his phone was turned off or he refused to answer it.

36

Kenzie reluctantly returned to her work. Chances were, Zachary was just fine and had simply turned off his phone or accidentally let it run out of juice. After his incident of the day before, he would most likely stay home for at least a day of recovery. He was probably sleeping. Panicking wouldn't help anything. She would return home at the end of the day, and he would be there waiting for her, working on his laptop or sleeping. No amount of worrying or imagining the worst was going to help things.

It was challenging to focus on her work, and she knew she would have to double-check anything important the next day. She might ask Dr. Cook to check her work for silly errors. Or she might not. She wasn't sure she wanted him to know she was susceptible to an emotional reaction or distraction.

After looking at the clock ten times in as many minutes, she decided she was finished for the day. She would head home an hour early but make it up the next day. Or on the weekend, when she usually came in to work a few hours on Saturday, even though she technically had weekends off unless she had a callout. She let Dr. Cook know she was leaving early, but didn't give him any explanation as to why. He had never required her to account for her time.

On the contrary, he had told her that he knew she put in extra hours and she could set her own schedule.

Most medical examiner work was not rush. Even getting to a callout. They would wait for her. Occasionally, they used technology and had a cop with an iPad walk them through the crime scene and show them the body in situ.

It wasn't like they were going to get any deader.

Death could be declared by another professional at the scene, and the crime scene techs and the ME's transport crew were perfectly capable of collecting any trace evidence on or around the body.

"Have a good evening," Dr. Cook told her, unconcerned by Kenzie's abrupt decision to leave early. "Do you and Zachary have something nice planned?"

"I'm not sure what we're doing tonight," Kenzie told him honestly.

He nodded, eyes on the file in front of him. "Well, have a nice time whatever you do."

Kenzie nodded and took her leave.

She might have been a bit lead-footed on the way home, maybe had run one yellow light that she could easily have stopped for, but she hadn't technically broken any law. Except for maybe speeding a little.

Kenzie drove past the front of the house on the way to the garage, and her heart sank.

Zachary's car was not parked in its usual place at the curb. He was not home. She pulled over and took out her phone, again looking for his location. She had resisted doing so again since talking to Heather, reasoning that looking at it more often would not make Zachary come online any faster and she would just make herself crazy with worry until he did. If she just ignored the fact that she couldn't track him, everything would be fine.

No location found

Kenzie could just sit in the empty house waiting for him to come home. Sooner or later, he would.

But she had sat around for long enough, being calm and

reasonable and patient. Now, she was starting to get worried and angry.

Worried something had happened to him.

Angry he was not there and might be stalking Bridget or doing something similarly stupid or dangerous that he didn't want her to know about. Why else shut off his location tracking?

She pulled out again and headed for Bridget's house. Roxboro was a small town and it only took a few minutes to get there. Kenzie didn't see Zachary's car on the street in front of the mansion. But he wouldn't necessarily have parked somewhere so obvious. She drove around the block, eyes peeled for his car parked on any adjoining street. His white compact was meant to blend in, and it did just that. She had to slow down and check every single white compact on the street to see whether it was his.

It was time to buy him an eye-catching bumper sticker so his car was easier to spot.

But, of course, that would defeat the purpose of having such a nondescript car, and he would never use it.

She drove around the house twice, then parked her car and got out to walk around looking for any sign of Zachary.

Still nothing.

She didn't like to stay out too long, making herself visible. She didn't want to attract the attention of Bridget or Gordon. They had both always been cordial to Kenzie, but she did not want to make them think that Zachary might be stalking Bridget again when he was not. They all needed to give Zachary the benefit of the doubt and not assume he was doing something he should not.

Kenzie heard sirens in the distance. Her stomach clenched. There was trouble somewhere nearby. She didn't want to associate it with Zachary's disappearance, but she couldn't help it.

The sirens got louder. She could hear the loud horns of fire engines honking for traffic to get out of their way.

A fire?

37

Kenzie climbed back into her "baby" and started the engine. With the window down, she could hear the sirens well enough to guess their direction and did her best to follow at a distance. It was ridiculous to associate Zachary's disappearance with a fire, but she couldn't help it. She knew how much Zachary was affected by fire. He had grown and progressed a lot since they had first met, but that didn't mean that he liked fire or wanted to be close to one. He could be around a fire now without being thrown into a flashback. At least usually. The way that he had been triggered lately by abuse scenarios, she couldn't make any assumptions. Something that would not normally set him off might anyway.

The fire engines might not even be going to a fire. They might be going to a medical emergency. She might even be wrong about the sirens being fire engines. Maybe she had just assumed they were fire engines because she was thinking of Zachary, and she had failed to recognize the slightly different sound of a police car or ambulance.

Trying to put everything else out of her mind and not to speculate on what she might find, she just focused on following the sound of the sirens.

Her phone vibrated in her pocket, but Kenzie ignored it. She was driving, and it would be dangerous to try to dig it out and see who it was. The caller would have to wait until she had reached her destination.

It would be ironic if Zachary were trying to reach her, realizing that his phone had been off half the day. She had left him several messages, so he should call as soon as he turned the phone on, got back into cell range, or rebooted it.

She reached Main Street in time to see the last fire engine in the convoy turn off and disappear from sight. She stepped on the gas and sped up to reach the turn it had taken.

Up into a residential area. Kenzie might lose them if she couldn't keep the fire engine in sight and they all turned off their sirens when they reached their destination. She would have to drive around looking for the flashing lights and big red trucks.

They slowed down on the residential side streets and cul-de-sacs. No matter how bad the call they were going to was, they didn't want to hit a child running out into the street after a ball or excited by the sight and sound of the flashy emergency vehicles. Kenzie closed the distance between herself and the last fire engine.

She breathed a sigh of relief. She wasn't going to lose them. She would see their destination, and it would have nothing to do with Zachary. She knew now that he wasn't stalking Bridget again, and that made it less likely in her mind that he was doing anything dangerous. She would tell him later how she had chased the fire engines in case it was something he was involved in. He would think it was funny. Did she actually think he would be running toward a fire?

The fire engine took another turn, slowing to a crawl, and then pulled up behind another firetruck.

The street was jammed with emergency vehicles. There was no way Kenzie was getting any closer than she already was.

She backed up until she found a parking space she could get into. She unbuckled her seatbelt so she could get her phone back out of her pocket.

When she saw the caller ID, her heart started to race. She had hoped it would be Zachary, and he would put all of her fears to rest with a story of how he had goofed up again, or his phone had run down, fallen into the toilet, or something silly.

But the caller was Mario Bowman. And one thing that she knew about Zachary's friend Mario was that he knew everything that went on at the police station and, if there were a case or rumor that involved Zachary in some way, he would call Kenzie to give her a heads-up.

Cold sweat trickled down her back.

Looking at the fire engines with their flashing lights up the street, Kenzie tried to swallow the lump in her throat and tapped the recent call log to call him back.

"Kenzie, glad you called back," Mario greeted. "Listen, there's nothing to worry about, but—"

If there wasn't anything to worry about, then why had he called her in the first place? He knew that it was something she *would* be worried about or needed to know about.

"Where is he?" she cut Mario off.

"There's a situation in the heights—"

"Is there a fire?"

Zachary could *not* be involved in a house fire. He was already experiencing the negative effects of witnessing domestic and child abuse.

But there was no smoke in the air. Kenzie had to believe that the firetrucks were there for something other than a residential fire.

"No fire yet," Mario said, his tone cautious, as if he were afraid of saying the wrong thing. "Zachary was concerned about the *possibility* of a fire."

Well, he would be, wouldn't he? Zachary was always concerned about the possibility of a fire. And it made perfect sense after what he had been through lately that he would be more concerned about a fire than ever. He was probably having flashbacks about it almost constantly.

"Is he here?" Kenzie asked. "On… Goldenrod Road?"

There was a silent pause from Mario before he answered. "How did you get there so fast? I didn't even tell you where he was. Did he call you?"

"No, he didn't. I've been trying to reach him, but he hasn't answered, and his location tracking is blocked."

"Then how did you get there?"

"I followed the firetrucks."

"Oh. Well, okay. He is there. You might be able to talk your way in to see him."

"I will. Can you give me the background? Did he say why he thinks there is going to be a fire?"

"Everything I got was garbled. At least secondhand. There is... a situation. A standoff."

"Not with Zachary," Kenzie said, trying not to sound shocked. He might have been destabilized by the multiple trauma triggers, but he would never use a gun and he would never hold someone hostage.

"No. He called it in. An assault in progress. Police showed up. The guy is still holed up inside with his wife. Then Zachary starts going off about a fire. So... fire brigade was called in... and now you're caught up."

"Okay." Kenzie swallowed and kept her voice calm and steady. "Great, thanks for the background."

She disconnected the call and headed toward the command center for the standoff, a quickly assembled white canopy where a number of officials were gathered in a beehive of activity.

Before Kenzie reached the perimeter tape, an officer moved in to stop her.

"Ma'am, you need to stay back, please. Go back to your house and let us handle things here."

"My name is Dr. Kenzie Kirsch. I'm the assistant medical examiner. My partner, Zachary Goldman, is here with the police. I need to get in there. Who is in charge?"

"Dr. Kirsch." The cop's voice grew deferential. "I don't think we need you here. Not yet, anyway. If you want to stick around, you could just stay here and wait until—"

"I didn't ask you that. I asked who is in charge," Kenzie told him, putting as much steel into her voice as possible.

He looked startled by her response and straightened his spine immediately.

"Sergeant Campbell is in charge, ma'am. He—"

"Please tell him Dr. Kirsch is here."

He opened his mouth to argue. Kenzie raised her brows and folded her arms over her chest, waiting. The officer looked around for a higher authority. He flagged down another uniformed officer and spoke to him in a low voice, motioning to Kenzie. The other officer nodded and retreated to the command center. Within a few minutes, Kenzie was being escorted into the tent, where Campbell and Zachary were at the center of the hive of activity.

38

Zachary was not looking particularly good. He was pale, with dark bags under his eyes and a sheen of sweat glistening on the surface of his skin despite the chill in the air as the sun got lower in the sky.

"Kenzie? What are you doing here?"

Kenzie shrugged. "There seemed to be a lot of activity around here. I thought you were going to take a quiet day today."

Zachary was unable to hide a slight grimace at the suggestion. "The day... didn't go quite like I'd hoped."

"What happened? What brought you out here? Is this the couple you've been surveilling?"

"Yeah."

"I thought you were finished with the file."

"So did I. But... then I knew it wasn't over. I couldn't just leave things the way they were."

Kenzie nodded slowly. "You had proof that he was abusive. You filed a police report and gave your final report to your client, but then..."

"Then... he wasn't going to stop. Even if my client talked her into breaking up with him, he wasn't going to stay away. The detectives would look into my report and evidence, but if he wasn't arrested right away, he was going to come right back here…"

Zachary turned and looked at the house. Kenzie looked at it, but couldn't see anything. Zachary had been watching them closely for a few days so, when he looked at the house, he saw a lot of things in his mind's eye that Kenzie could not. Each room and its layout. Where they spent their time. Where the husband sat when he drank. All of those little things. But all Kenzie could see were the curtains pulled across the windows.

"So he's in there now?" Kenzie asked. "You were right, and he came back again? Did the wife allow him back or tell him to stay away? It's so hard to get women out of abusive situations. If they're not ready…"

"Her dad talked her into filing a Restraint from Abuse order against him," Sergeant Campbell told Kenzie with a friendly nod. "Temporary RFA was granted. And as you may gather, he immediately violated it."

"So you came back here and saw him," Kenzie addressed Zachary. "And got the police out."

"Did anyone think he was going to stay away?" Zachary asked heavily. "They all knew he would come back here, didn't they?"

"Unfortunately, we can't arrest people for what we *think* they are going to do," Campbell responded.

"You could keep violent offenders in jail until their hearings."

"I wish we could. Unfortunately, even when the crime is witnessed or recorded, we still can't always keep them in custody. They get bailed out, often by the very person they are charged with assaulting. They go home, and…" Sergeant Campbell gestured toward the house.

"Well," Kenzie kept her voice carefully neutral. "Now that the police are here and have a handle on things, maybe we could go home."

Sergeant Campbell gave her an amused look, his face turned away from Zachary so he couldn't see it.

Zachary immediately shook his head. "I need to stay here and see this through," he insisted.

"I'm not sure there is anything else you can do."

Zachary pointed to a few TV screens showing the interior of the house. None of them, as far as Kenzie could see, showed the occupants of the house at the moment.

"These are my spycams," he pointed out. "They wouldn't have eyes in the house if I hadn't set those up."

"But now that they are set up, they don't need you here. I'm sure they'll return them to you when everything is over."

Kenzie wasn't "sure" of any such thing. Were the spy cameras even legal? The police might just as easily confiscate them.

Zachary shook his head. He wiped his sweaty forehead. "I'm not leaving. Not until he's out of there and she is safe."

"That could be a while. Do they have some kind of hostage negotiator? Are they trying to talk him out?"

"He's trapped. You never know how someone will behave when backed into a corner. Animals are dangerous when you corner them."

"I know. But they must have trained professionals…"

"He doesn't think he has anything left to live for," Zachary said. He ran his fingers through his stubbly hair in a gesture that would have messed it up and made it stand on end if it hadn't been just a quarter inch long. Zachary walked up to the monitors and scrutinized everything he could see on the screen. Kenzie could see that other monitors were not blank as she had first thought, but were picking up cameras pointed at closed curtains. Zachary leaned close to them to see if he could see through the crack between two curtain panels or worn moth holes.

"What do you think happens when you take away the thing someone loves the most in the world?" he asked, staring at the monitors.

Kenzie swallowed. "Is that why the fire engines are here?" she asked. "You think he's going to hurt her or himself?"

"If this place goes up, they'll only have seconds to get in there to save her."

"Why do you think he's going to set it on fire?"

Zachary paced, not able to get very far without bumping into anyone in the enclosed space. But he needed to keep moving to keep his thoughts flowing. Kenzie knew how agitated he would get if he had to sit quietly instead of being allowed movement.

"The place is full of highly flammable material," Zachary told her. He jabbed his fingers at the screens, which showed windows obscured by curtains. "Bundles of newspapers and magazines. Bales of clothing. I thought they were sorting them for a charity drive or something. But they weren't. He was bringing them in because he wants instant ignition. He wants an inferno."

"You don't know that," Campbell told Zachary reassuringly. "You are guessing at his motives. I'd be more inclined to believe the theory of a charity drive than a bonfire."

"You're just letting your fears take over," Kenzie agreed.

But the firetrucks were already there. On some level, Campbell must believe that Zachary could be right, or he wouldn't have called them.

"I'm not. He had gasoline in the back of the truck." Zachary pointed at an outside camera shot of a black F-150 with an empty bed. "He had at least three gas cans."

Kenzie couldn't deny the anxiety that crept into her chest at the thought of three gas cans disappearing into the house filled with tinder where an angry, cornered abuser held his wife, knowing he was never going to be able to get out without being arrested. She glanced at Campbell, who gave her a slight nod. Signaling, she thought, that he trusted Zachary's observations well enough to make sure that there were firetrucks lining the street outside the house.

Kenzie wondered if the operations center might be a bit too close to the house, given the fact that at least three gas cans could go off in a blazing inferno without further warning. She bet each can would become a pretty good fireball.

Would the husband pour the gasoline all over the piles of newspapers and clothes before setting it alight? Or would he run fuses into the cans and try to explode them that way? She'd heard it was harder than Hollywood would have everyone think to set off a gasoline explosion. She crossed her fingers and hoped that was true.

"But they have a negotiator, right?" she asked again. "They have a trained hostage negotiator talking to them?"

"They're trying to find someone," Campbell said. "To get someone here from the city."

Burlington was a couple of hours away.

"He's not answering the phone anyway," Campbell added philosophically. "So there's no one to negotiate with."

Kenzie looked anxiously toward the house. "So we're just standing around here waiting for him to set fire to the place?"

"We're hoping that won't happen. If he's left alone, hopefully, he will de-escalate and give up peacefully."

That wasn't the way it happened on TV. Was that the way it happened in real life? He would just throw in the towel and not go out in a blaze of glory?

Some patrol cops were setting up rows of chairs so everyone didn't have to keep standing.

"Can we sit down and talk?" Kenzie suggested. "I'm a little anxious standing around here."

Zachary looked at the chairs and clearly did not want to, but he wanted to take care of her. Zachary's role as a nurturer was always close to the surface. He would sacrifice himself for someone he loved.

"I'm tired," Kenzie said, leveraging that instinct. "It's been a long day. It must have been for you, too. How long have you been here?"

"I don't know." He looked around, as if uncertain what time of day it was or how much time had passed since he had arrived. Given his problems with time blindness and distortion, she was sure that was probably exactly the case. At times like this, he lived in a world without time.

"I was trying to get you at noon and you didn't answer, and your location was turned off."

"Uh…" Zachary shifted uncomfortably. "I didn't want you to worry."

"Well, if you don't want me to worry, you should probably not ignore my calls and shut off your location. Because I was going through all kinds of scenarios." Kenzie looked around. "And this was not one of them."

"The fire engines just got here. It hasn't been like this all day. For the first few hours, I was just here by myself, watching. She was by herself in the house."

"But you didn't think it would stay that way."

Zachary nodded. "I knew it wouldn't."

39

Zachary sat down with Kenzie to visit for a few minutes but was too restless to sit down for long. He got up to "stretch his legs," and she could see as he walked back and forth that he was dictating notes or messages into his phone.

Kenzie was trying to stay out of the way and take as much responsibility as she could for Zachary. Campbell had enough to worry about without being concerned about what Zachary was doing. Considering his impulsivity and protective nature, someone had to make sure he didn't just walk up to the house and open the door, thinking he could straighten everything out himself.

Kenzie's stomach was growling, and she was trying to figure out what to do about it when one of the patrol cops entered the tent and approached Campbell.

"The father is here."

"The father?" Campbell repeated. "Whose father?"

"The woman's father."

Campbell put one hand over his face. "You've got to be kidding me."

"No, sir. What do you want me to do with him?"

"What kind of mood is he in?"

"Well… not good."

Campbell shook his head. "No, I would imagine not! But how bad is he? Is he raging? Hysterical?"

"No, sir. He seems… reasonable."

"Okay." Campbell sighed. "Bring him in here."

Kenzie felt sorry for the man who was escorted in. He was looking rumpled in a dark raincoat but, when Kenzie looked at him closely, she could tell that he was someone who normally cared about his appearance, and the brands of the clothing he wore were not cheap. The cop walked him toward Sergeant Campbell, but his eyes went to Zachary, and he hurried to him.

Kenzie rose to her feet, not sure how this man would feel about coming face to face with the private investigator he had hoped would help him get rid of the son-in-law he suspected of abusing his daughter. Unable to do anything to the man inside, he might go straight for Zachary's throat.

But when the man reached for Zachary, it was not to throttle the life out of him. He gave Zachary a tight hug, then released him to talk to him, completely ignoring Campbell.

"Zachary. Thank you for keeping me apprised."

Zachary nodded. He met Kenzie's eye and gestured toward his client.

"Kenzie, this is Mr. Kymchuk, my client in this case. Lydia's father."

Kenzie nodded. "I'm so sorry, Mr. Kymchuk. This is a terrible thing to have to go through. I'm sure you must be very worried about your daughter."

He nodded. "Yes, of course I am," he agreed. "I was hoping to avoid something like this. But I was worried. I had a sense about Jason."

Everyone in the command center was listening in, but pretending not to.

Zachary motioned to the bank of monitors showing the inside of the house or the closed curtains. No sign of any movement.

Mr. Kymchuk looked them over. "Not much to see, is there?"

"Unfortunately not," Zachary agreed. "I had a good view of the inside until he decided to pull the curtains. If the police would let me get close to the house, I could move this camera over a couple of inches so that it was between the two panels, and we might be able to get a good view inside."

He looked at Campbell, who shook his head. Of course. They had probably already had a lengthy conversation about it, and Campbell had kept Zachary from going any closer to the house only by threatening to have him kicked off the scene altogether, with a trip to the municipal jail if he wouldn't stay back, well out of the way.

"And you haven't been able to make contact with him?" Kymchuk asked Campbell.

"I'm afraid not. We've tried both of their cells. There is no land-line. We left a phone on the doorstep, too, but no luck. He is incommunicado."

"I thought Mr. Kymchuk might have more luck," Zachary said.

"You did, did you? You are the reason Mr. Kymchuk is here?"

Zachary nodded. "Can we try it?"

"I don't think it's a good idea. We should wait for a trained negotiator."

"That could still be hours away. Days, even."

Campbell rubbed his forehead. "Fine," he said eventually. "I appreciate you coming all the way here and asking permission rather than just calling. This needs to be handled very carefully. The consequences of one wrong step could be… tragic."

"You don't have to tell me that, Sergeant," Kymchuk agreed.

"There's every chance he might surrender before the negotiator even gets here."

"Why don't we see if we can move things along?" Kymchuk urged. "I'm sure you don't want to be here for a week while he goes back and forth on whether he's going to cooperate."

"We need to sit down and discuss the situation and strategy. Unless you've negotiated a situation like this before, you have a lot to learn in a short period of time."

Kymchuk agreed, and they all sat down together, pulling chairs out of the rows to sit in a rough circle.

"Well… here goes nothing," Kymchuk said, holding the phone in front of him like an unexploded bomb.

Campbell gave him a nod. "It's up to you. If you want to wait for the negotiator, no one is going to blame you for that. In fact, it would be a wise move."

"I have to try to talk to my little girl. I need to hear her voice and know that she is okay."

Kenzie hoped that Lydia was, in fact, okay. Despite the bugs inside the house and the laser listening devices pointed at the windows, they had not caught any conversations between Lydia and her husband, Jason. Kenzie worried about who might be on her table the next day. Was Lydia already dead? Was that why they had not heard her voice?

No objections were raised, and Kymchuk took the plunge, tapping his daughter's number on his phone screen. He set it to speaker, and they all waited, listening to it ring. Would she answer? Would she be allowed to?

Two rings… three… Kenzie had noticed that cell phones went to voicemail a lot faster now than they had a few years before, when they would ring six or eight times before the automated voice answered. Sometimes, even more than ten times.

There was the faint static of background noise, then a loud male voice.

"Mark?"

Kymchuk gave a little nod. "Jason. I'm glad you answered. Is everything okay?"

Vitriol flowed from the phone. "You did this!" Jason accused. "You had to go poking your nose into something that was not any of your business. You had to stir things up. You had to get other people involved, to make up stories. Going to the police! How could you go to the police and tell them your lies? Why are you trying to break us up?"

"I'm sorry," Kymchuk's voice was sincere, profoundly apologetic. "I screwed everything up. I should have just stayed out of it and minded my own business."

There was a shocked silence from Jason for a moment; then he came back just as forcefully. "You need to tell them that! Tell them you lied. That there is nothing to the report you made. No one has any proof of anything. You're just trying to ruin our marriage."

"I'll tell them whatever you want me to. I'm so sorry, Jason. I never meant for it to go this far. I just wanted to protect my daughter. I love Lydia. You don't know how devastated I was when her mother died. Now it's just me and Lydia, and I felt like you were taking her away from me."

"I wasn't taking her away from you."

"I know, I know. I'm just a silly old man, imagining things because I miss my daughter and don't want to be alone. I overreacted."

"I love her too," Jason declared. "I don't know what I would do without her. When I thought of you taking her away from me, I went a little crazy."

"I don't blame you. I know what it's like to love someone so much."

Kymchuk was doing a good job of doing exactly what they had told him. Telling Jason that he was not a bad guy, that he just loved his wife and it had all been a mistake. Validating his feelings and giving him nothing to argue or get riled up about. And Kymchuk made it sound sincere. He didn't sound like he was just pouring on flattery.

"She's my wife," Jason said. "I would never do anything to hurt her. You messed everything up."

"Jason…" Kymchuk reproached.

"I would never hurt her."

"But there is video. You hit her. My daughter. The most important thing in my life."

"No, that was a mistake. I know what it looks like, but that's not how it happened. She just… I only… I reacted. It was an accident. It will never happen again. I just slipped up. You can't judge my whole life by one mistake. You can't take away the thing I love most."

"I think... you need help."

"I do," Jason said. "I just lost control, but it wasn't intentional. I will take care of her. Nothing is going to happen to her again."

Kenzie's skin crawled at his turn of phrase. Was Lydia already dead? Had he already ensured that she was beyond any more pain, that he would never be able to "accidentally" hurt her again?

"I know you don't want to ever hurt her again," Kymchuk agreed, reinforcing the statement. "That's the last thing you want. I want to protect her, too. Both of us... we only want the best for her."

"Yes, that's right."

"I'm glad we understand each other."

"I love her," Jason repeated, tears in his voice.

"Let's get her the help she needs," Kymchuk suggested, keeping his own voice steady and calm. "She must be scared with all of this drama. Let's make sure she can get a good sleep tonight and not have to worry about whether you are okay. She needs to know that you're safe and this is all over."

There was a period of silence from Jason. Kenzie took comfort in the fact that he was not raging and had not shown any anger since the beginning of the call. Was he looking at his wife now? Deciding he didn't want her to have to suffer anymore? That it was time to let her go and not be scared? Or was it too late, and all they could do now was avoid his taking half a city block down with him? When she thought about all of the first responders who could be hurt if he decided to go ahead with his plan, she choked up. She dealt with dead bodies all the time, but that didn't mean she was immune to the tragedy of death and loss. Maybe she was more aware of it than most people, who went through their lives not really thinking about the tragedy that was always happening around them. They could shut it out. Kenzie could not.

"What do you want me to do?" Jason asked.

40

Everyone watched with bated breath as Kymchuk walked Jason through the instructions that Campbell whispered to him, having him come to the door unarmed, hands in the air, to walk down the steps and away from the house, and then to lie down with his arms outstretched. Kenzie didn't imagine it was any too comfortable to be lying down on the concrete and mud in the chilly April weather, but they didn't hear any complaints from Jason, who seemed to be tired and defeated.

He did not come out of the house with a lighter held aloft or ignite an inferno rather than stepping out the door to face the police.

The police hurried in to handcuff Jason and pat him down, and everyone in the command tent let out a sigh of relief at the same time.

That was the first step. Zachary patted Kymchuk on the back. No one said anything about the fact that Jason hadn't spoken to Lydia or said whether she was okay or not. They hadn't heard her call out or make any sound while he had been on the phone or when he opened the door.

"You can't send your men in there blind," Zachary told Campbell.

"What?" Campbell shook his head. "Jason is secured. We need to go in to find Lydia and see whether she needs any medical attention. We don't know yet…" His gaze flicked to Kymchuk's face, "If she's had anything to eat or drink. She might be dehydrated or in need of other treatment."

"Let me reposition the cameras so you can see into each room. You don't know what he's done inside while the curtains were closed. He might have set up booby traps. Just because he's out, that doesn't mean it's safe."

"You aren't going to be able to see past the curtains anyway. We will see what we can from outside and go in carefully. My men are trained. I'll remind them to watch for any tripwires or other hazards."

"There are gaps and holes in the curtains. I can get you a view inside if you'll let me reposition the spycams."

Campbell considered this. He looked at Zachary, then at Kenzie.

Kenzie didn't see any reason not to allow it. If Zachary couldn't get them a clear view inside the house, they would be no worse off than they were now. If he could get the cameras into a better position to allow Campbell and his men to evaluate the hazards before setting foot inside the house, it could be a great benefit. Low risk, high reward.

"I think you should try it," she told him.

Campbell was apparently thinking through the same possibilities and nodded reluctantly.

"I want you to take two men with you." Looking around, he picked out two cops to approach the house with Zachary. "As far as we know, there are no traps set up outside the house, but even though you didn't see him set anything up outside the house, we can't assume that it is safe. He could have set something up days ago, even before you made your report. He might have sensed that someone was watching him or just been paranoid enough to want to protect his woman and his castle by any means necessary. You don't approach a window until Gene and Harry tell you it is clear.

And then you watch your footing, and you don't touch anything but your cameras."

Zachary nodded several times throughout the discussion. Kenzie didn't bother to tell Campbell that he had nothing on Zachary as far as paranoia about booby traps and incendiary devices went. After twice being the target of an attempted bombing, Zachary was more aware than anyone else of his surroundings and the possibility of explosives or other hazards.

"I'll need to use my phone to position them properly."

Campbell nodded his agreement.

Even though the hostage taker was in custody and Zachary was under the protection of two capable-looking officers, he was outfitted with a tactical vest before being allowed to approach the house. Kenzie watched as he first approached the big window of the living room, then waited until the officers had carefully searched the ground in front of it before allowing Zachary to cover the last few feet and reach to reposition the tiny camera.

Kenzie had seen some of the devices that Zachary was equipped with, which sometimes reminded her of the outlandish devices in old spy movies. She had seen the nickel-sized wireless cameras that adhered to a window and allowed him a view inside of the house he was surveilling. Carefully positioned along an edge or in the corner of the window, they were unobtrusive, practically invisible unless someone was looking for them.

Watching Zachary from that distance, she could not see the camera Zachary was repositioning, but she could see the picture on one of the monitors changing as Zachary moved it around, looking for just the right crack or hole in the curtains to afford the best view. He held his phone in one hand, watching the video feed, and moved the camera with his other hand. Eventually, he found the position he liked best and pressed the camera back into place, re-adhering it to the window. He stayed there for a moment, making sure it would stay in place before nodding at his escorts to move on to the next window.

Kenzie studied the monitor showing the living room. She

wasn't the only one. Campbell and several of his men leaned in and pointed out the various dim shapes in the room, evaluating the hazards carefully. Kenzie was relieved that they would have some idea of what they were walking into. Even if Jason hadn't intentionally set up any booby traps, he had filled the house with highly flammable materials, and Kenzie didn't relish the thought of any burned bodies on her autopsy table.

Zachary moved quickly from one window to the next and managed to find some peephole or angle at each one that afforded some view of the room. In some cases, it was only a small portion of the room but, in the majority, they had a good view of most of the room. Another group of technicians was setting up big spotlights to shine in the windows, banishing the twilight the curtains had brought. They were not blackout curtains and allowed enough of the light in to be useful.

Kymchuk made a choked noise when one of the cameras showed Lydia stretched out on the bed in the master bedroom. They could not see her whole body, only her waist down. Zachary tried several times to readjust the camera to give them a better view of her but couldn't find a better angle. Lydia lay very still. There was not a twitch to show whether she was still alive.

Kenzie put her hand on Kymchuk's arm in sympathy, but didn't know what to say to him. She couldn't assure him that Lydia would be okay. Even a medical examiner could not tell from the pair of legs what kind of condition the woman was in. There was not even a patch of skin showing for Kenzie to evaluate Lydia's coloring.

Kymchuk gave her a grateful look. No one said anything. Zachary returned to the tent, where he would watch the next step of the police action from the same vantage point as everyone else.

"Good job," Campbell told Zachary. "Thanks for that." He turned his attention to his men, who ran through various entry procedures until they had hammered out an approach that everyone agreed on.

Kenzie tried to be calm and breathe normally as they watched the entry team. Her heart pumped hard in anticipation, and she tried to slow her breathing and relax her muscles. Everything would be fine. The hostage taker had been arrested, and the law enforcement officers were prepared for what they would face inside the house.

It took a few minutes, but then the word went out that the house was cleared, and the first responders could enter to treat Lydia. Campbell looked Kymchuk in the eye. "She's alive."

He breathed out shakily. "Thank you."

"Much of the thanks goes to you for looking out for her and hiring Zachary, and Zachary for investigating *and* coming back when everything should have been fine, but he didn't feel right."

They both looked at Zachary, who turned bright red and shrugged, looking away from Campbell. "I just... I knew something was wrong. I couldn't leave her alone until I knew she was safe."

"Jason was right about one thing," Kymchuk said, rubbing the fatigue lines across his forehead. "This wouldn't have happened if I hadn't interfered in the first place. If I hadn't hired Zachary and then convinced Lydia to take out the restraining order, there wouldn't have been any standoff."

They all looked at each other. Kenzie could see Kymchuk's point, but not finding out whether his son-in-law was abusive and simply leaving his daughter in that situation wasn't the answer.

"If you hadn't done anything, she might be dead," Zachary told him. "Or she might be in an abusive relationship for another twenty years and then dead. You just don't know. But pretending you didn't know something was going on and just leaving her to deal with it on her own wouldn't have solved anything. It wouldn't have protected her."

"There must have been something I could have done differently."

"There are a lot of things you could have done differently," Campbell acknowledged. "But none of them would have guaranteed a better outcome than this. There are a lot of choices that would have gotten her dead." He looked at Kenzie.

"I don't know if you know who I am," Kenzie said. "I am an assistant medical examiner. I am one of the people who sees what happens when something like this goes bad."

Kymchuk looked toward the house. "That must be hard."

"It is. I can tell you… getting Lydia out of there alive is the best possible scenario. Other women are not so lucky."

Zachary stopped for burgers on the way home. Kenzie couldn't even think of making supper for them. Even warming up a frozen dinner was too much. Even going to a restaurant where she had to look at the menu and wait for their dinners to be brought to the table. She headed straight for home. Zachary, driving his own car, went through the drive-through and ordered their usual favorites so Kenzie didn't have to think about it.

She was amazed that he could function after the ordeal he had been through. Kenzie had only been there for the tail end of the drama; he had been at the house almost all day and had been dealing with the situation between Lydia and Jason for days, as well as the parking lot confrontation. She felt like a boneless blob of jelly and expected him to feel the same way, but he didn't seem to be experiencing the same shut-down as Kenzie was. He arrived home only a few minutes after she did, and he busied himself by unpacking the fast food and serving it to them both.

"How do you still have any energy?"

Zachary shrugged. "I'll probably crash later. Right now… I'm wired. I'm hyped up about being able to get her out of there alive. About being able to stop Jason from sending the whole place up in an inferno."

Lydia had been bound and gagged when they found her, but she had walked out of the house under her own power once they released her. Kenzie choked up when Lydia and her father embraced. Kenzie fanned her eyes as she thought about it now, trying to keep the tears from overflowing. Zachary laughed.

"It's all okay," he told her. "She is okay. A bit beaten up and traumatized, but she'll heal quickly. She's got fire in her eyes."

That was the kind of fire that Zachary could appreciate.

Kenzie dug into her burger. They would eat, crash in front of the TV, and maybe she would be able to drag herself from the couch to bed at some point. She wasn't sure about that part.

41

D
r. Cook had already heard about the standoff the evening before and Zachary's and Kenzie's attendance at the scene. As Mario had said, cops were notorious gossips. Cook understood Kenzie's decision to start late so that she could sleep in and recover after the ordeal, and encouraged her to take the day off if she needed to. But Kenzie didn't want to be bouncing around the house all day and didn't have the motivation to go shopping or do any of the other errands that she should on a day off. At the office, she could work mindlessly on filing, catch up on some of the tests that needed to be reviewed, and not be distracted by Zachary's restlessness.

Zachary had not exactly crashed as predicted. He'd been physically tired, sleeping more than usual, but he hadn't experienced the emotional letdown and inertia that Kenzie did. Instead, he obsessed over every detail of what had happened, analyzing each choice and whether it had been the right or wrong one. Not just his own choices, but Kymchuk's, the judge's, Lydia's, Jason's, Campbell's, and everyone else at the scene he had interfaced with. He paced and tried to discuss the stand-off in minute detail with Kenzie when she just wanted to put it behind her.

The medical examiner's office was an oasis of calm. Kenzie's files and desk were all arranged the way she wanted them to be. She could choose what she wanted to do first and impose order on all the emails, voicemails, postal mail, and deliveries that arrived at the medical examiner's office. When she was ready, she could complete the smaller pathology jobs that required her attention. There were no new bodies requiring autopsy, just some tissue samples and slides that needed to be processed.

There was a messenger packet from the forensic lab with the results of a number of samples they had sent over to be tested in the past few weeks. A backlog had built up because the mass spectrometer had been offline due to a system upgrade that it had needed. Stan at the lab had told Kenzie the details, but she couldn't recall the specifics. It wasn't anything she needed to do; it was just a bottleneck at the lab that they would eventually straighten out, and then she would be able to get the results of the various tests they had ordered.

It would appear that it was back online again, and a number of tests they had been waiting for had been completed and returned. They were probably in her email inbox as well. She usually liked to take care of email first, but today she wanted to handle the physical tests and reports first. She wanted to be physically engaged with her work and to push everything else aside for a while.

She sorted results into piles according to which files they related to, then went through the results one at a time and updated the control sheets on the files. Sometimes, it took months to get tests back, and they needed to track what they were still waiting for.

After reviewing the physical results and evidence, Kenzie went on to what was on her computer. She stared at the results Detective Cameron had sent her from the lab tests on the evidence that the police had requested. She reached for the phone.

Luckily, Cameron was at his desk, so Kenzie didn't have to wait for a callback or to try to track him down.

"Detective, I have the results you sent me for the steroids your men found in the dumpster near the apartment."

"Yes," Cameron agreed heartily. "Steroids, as we had hoped. That wraps it all up pretty neatly."

"Uh… no, it doesn't."

"What? Why do you say that? They were methandrostenolone."

"Yeah. And there was no methandrostenolone in Robertson's blood."

"That can't be right. Maybe it had already been absorbed. What about the liver or kidneys? There must have been some trace of them."

"No. It's the wrong steroid. He was poisoned with oxymetholone."

"Could there be a mistake? Or maybe Collins had just received a new shipment. He'd run out of whatever he had before, and he was *going to* give the methandrostenolone to Robertson."

"Maybe," Kenzie couldn't argue against the possibility. "But we can't prove that in court. We can only draw a line from what he was given, the oxymetholone that killed him, to… some source. But we can't establish Collins as the source if we can't show that he ever had oxymetholone."

"Well, this is a problem. We might not be able to prove anything with the dumped pills. But we can use them as leverage against Collins. Get a confession out of him. Say we have proof that the pills were in his possession in the form of his fingerprints were identified on the packaging. Attack that angle and why he would have steroids in his apartment. Demand to know why he was in possession of steroids without a prescription for them and tell him we know he was going to give them to Robertson, just like he gave the rest to him. Just like he put into Robertson's food in the weeks leading up to his death."

"Do you know where he is? I don't know if you're going to be able to get a confession from him when the steroids you found don't even match. Did they really have his fingerprints on the packaging?"

"Did you get a report from me about fingerprints identified on the packaging?" Cameron countered.

"I haven't been through everything yet." Kenzie typed his name into the search bar, but no such email came up in the results.

"Well, don't expect to find one, because no, there were no

fingerprints of known parties on the packaging, either Robertson or any other person involved in this case. Or anyone else in AFIS."

"Wouldn't he know that he hadn't left any fingerprints on it?"

"Criminals make mistakes. It isn't beyond the bounds of belief. They forget to wear gloves once or miss one corner when wiping down a package. Easy mistake to make, and he wouldn't know he had made it until we told him so."

Kenzie shook her head. Alex was a pretty smart guy. She wasn't sure Cameron would be able to squeeze a confession out of him, claiming that his fingerprints had been on the steroid packaging when they hadn't been.

It bothered her that the steroids did not match. Of course, Alex could have changed his source or decided to change the type of steroid for some reason, but it didn't make a lot of sense. Why would he change after months of administering oxymetholone?

"Do you have a line on Alex? Any chance you're going to be able to find him?"

Maybe it was all academic anyway. If there was no one to question or charge, then it didn't really matter what drugs they had found and whose fingerprints had or had not been on them. They had to find Collins before they could charge him and take him to trial.

"His phone has been used a few times in the Montpelier area, so we are working with Montpelier police to make inquiries and see if we can track him down. We've requested more detailed location records from his provider."

Maybe Alex wasn't that bright after all. Why would he still be using his phone when anyone who watched any cop shows on TV knew they could be tracked? Dumping his phone should have been one of the first things he did.

"Well, I hope you find him."

"I think we will… sooner or later."

42

Kenzie had just returned from her lunch break and was getting settled at her desk when Dr. Cook came looking for her.

"Don't get too comfortable. Got a callout."

"Oh, okay." Kenzie straightened, pulling her handbag back out of the drawer where she had just been putting it away. "Where do I go?"

"Lakeshore Drive. Police are at the scene. They can direct you once you get out there. This side of the lake."

Kenzie nodded. She pulled off her shoes and left them under her desk. A water dump would require boots, especially during mud season. They kept a good stock of protective gear in the room beside the loading dock for just such occasions.

"Is Carlos coming out with me?"

"Yeah, you can take the van with him and not worry about messing up the paint job on your pretty car."

"Great. Do we know anything about the location or the remains?"

It was always nice to know what to expect. Bodies that had been out of doors or in the water for a long time were not as easy to load as a more recent death.

"Sounds like a couple of days in the water. Bloated but intact."

Kenzie headed toward the loading dock. "Thanks. Shouldn't take us too long to have it back here."

Carlos was unusually chatty, eager to know all the details about the stand-off from the previous day. Kenzie answered a few questions, but focused on her phone, pretending that she needed to deal with some emails, not wanting to spend the whole drive answering questions or dredging up details for Carlos.

When they pulled onto Lakeshore Drive, it was not difficult to spot the emergency vehicles, including an ambulance, that had arrived ahead of them. What was an ambulance doing there? If the body was bloated up, they should not even have been called. Anyone could tell the difference between someone who had just gone into the water and a body that had been soaking for a few days.

Carlos navigated as close to the dump site as possible, guided by one cop's gestures. When he was stopped, Kenzie climbed out for a look.

There wasn't a lot to be done since the body had already been pulled from the water. There were footprints in the mud all around the body, as well as drag marks from the legs and heels of the corpse. A blue tarp had been discarded to the side, which Kenzie suspected the body had been wrapped up in at some point.

"Who secured the scene?" she demanded.

The cops and paramedics looked around at each other.

"It was pulled out of the water by a couple of local residents," one of the cops advised. "The scene was already compromised when we got here."

"Who pulled it out?"

They again looked at each other. The same cop scratched the back of his neck.

"We sent them on their way. To keep them from further contaminating the scene," he explained.

Kenzie shook her head. "You got their names and phone numbers? Their statements? Footprints? Fingerprints? DNA samples?"

He swallowed. "Why would you need all of that?"

"So we can sort their trace evidence out from the rest of the trace we might find."

"I have their names and phone numbers."

Kenzie nodded to Carlos. "Would you collect whatever they have, please?" She approached the body, irritated with the lack of concern over proper procedure. They would be lucky to be able to find out anything from the scene. Or the witnesses.

She crouched down, evaluating the body. Male. Young adult. Fully clothed. Nice clothes, no gang signs. She studied the clothes and the bloated face. It would not be easy to identify him based on his current appearance.

"There was a wallet," the cop said, his face red.

Kenzie turned and looked at him. He held out the wallet that one of them had removed from the body. Kenzie didn't take it from him. "Put it in an evidence bag. Is there a name?"

The cop flipped it open, though he had undoubtedly looked at it previously.

"Alex Collins."

43

Kenzie had told Detective Cameron there was no point in coming to the dump site. Still, he asked her to hold everything as it was so that he could see it with his own eyes, which would, hopefully, help in figuring out just what had happened to derail their investigation. Kenzie's head whirled with the contradictions as she waited for Cameron to get to the site.

They found the steroids, but they were the wrong steroids. Alex was one of their prime suspects and, when he disappeared, it was tantamount to a confession that he was, in fact, the one responsible for Robertson's death. But he was dead, and not by his own hand. Cameron had placed him in Montpelier, where his phone had been used, yet Kenzie had turned up the body in Roxboro.

Or at least, the corpse's ID said he was Alex. It was hard to recognize him with the level of disfigurement. He was about the right height and had the right hair coloring. His clothes were similar to what Kenzie had seen him wear. His face was unrecognizable, and with the bloating from soaking in the water and decomposing for a couple of days, his original body shape could no longer be discerned.

The damp air clung to them as they waited. The afternoon sun was not providing much heat.

Cameron used lights and siren, so it didn't take him long to get there. Faster than Kenzie in the transport van, with Carlos driving sedately below the speed limit. Cameron clambered out of the car and picked his way over to where Kenzie stood. He had not thought to change into boots before he left, so he was trying not to get his nice shoes caked with mud. He looked around the scene and glared at the cops standing around it.

"Does no one here know how to preserve a scene?"

They looked at each other uncomfortably.

"That is a serious question," Cameron snapped. "Not a rhetorical one. Who here knows how to preserve a scene?"

They all raised their hands partway. Cameron pointed to one.

"Where is the perimeter tape?"

"There wasn't really anything to tape off. The body was obviously just dumped, not killed here. There is nothing to attach the tape to over there," he pointed to where the cars were grouped. "There wasn't anyone around. It didn't seem like we needed to do anything before the medical examiner arrived. She was on the way, so why waste our time putting up tape until she got here and then taking it down after she removed the body?"

"Whose footprints are over here?"

He glared and waited until a few hands went up.

"Why?"

"Checking for signs of life," one offered.

"You couldn't tell that a body that had been in the water for a few days was dead?"

"Well, I wasn't sure of anything until I got close..."

"Did you touch the body?"

The cop shook his head, making a face. "No."

"So you checked for signs of life just by getting close?"

"Close enough to see that he... was dead."

"Were you the one who pulled him out of the water?"

"No, there were a couple of witnesses. The guys who called us in."

"They had already pulled the body out of the water when you got here?"

"Yes."

"So you detained them and got all their information and samples?"

He looked at Kenzie. "She already told us that we should have."

"Did you *miss that class?*"

"We don't get a lot of body dumps," another complained, "I haven't ever had anyone move a body before."

"It happens. You have to know what to do when it does."

"Yes, sir."

Cameron looked around. "This is where the body came out of the water," he observed. "Where did the body go into the water?"

They just looked at him blankly. Cameron raised his brows.

"Is this where it was dumped?"

There were a few hesitant nods. Cameron shook his head, and everyone followed suit. *No, sir. Not here.*

"If it wasn't dumped here, where was it dumped?"

They looked at the river and, eventually, their heads turned upstream. Cameron nodded. "Go find out where it went into the water."

"How are we supposed to figure that out?"

"Do you think someone walked up to the river and dropped him in?"

They all looked back at the body.

"Maybe somewhere they could drive a car closer to the edge of the water?" one of them eventually asked.

"Yeah. Exactly. Bodies are heavy. They are hard to carry. They are awkward. You don't want to carry one any farther than you have to. Once you try it, you'll quickly adjust your thinking and either use something to carry it, or adjust your plan so you don't have to carry it far. Dragging it is better, but only marginally. Dollies, wheelbarrows, wheelchairs, and wheeled coolers are all helpful. Cars are better. Trucks. SUVs. At least a car with a roomy trunk, or you will be strapping the guy into the seat next to you in the car, and that's creepy. And risky. Someone might see. So go find my dump site."

The cops murmured among themselves to make a plan to

search for the disposition site upriver. After casting a few glances at Cameron to make sure he was serious and wanted them to find it now, they went to look for it.

Cameron, Carlos, and Kenzie were left with the body.

"Did you want to see anything else?" Kenzie asked. "Like I said, the site has been disturbed, so there isn't much for us to get from it."

"There will be more at the scene of the crime and the dump site, if we can find them. What can you tell me about the cause of death?"

"Lots of head and facial trauma. Several blows with a blunt object. I don't see any other signs of violence on the body, but I won't be able to until we get him on the table and remove his clothing. It could be covering up a lot of other trauma. Hands are intact, and I don't see any marks on them to suggest he fought off his assailant. The water is still quite cold, so there hasn't been a lot of predation. It shouldn't take much time to give you a full report. I don't think this body holds too many secrets."

"Except that he was our suspect in Robertson's death. And if he has now been killed, then that begs the question… was he killed because of what he did? Because of something else? Or was he not our killer at all, and he was killed by Robertson's killer?"

Kenzie nodded. She had been thinking about the same thing.

"And if he was killed a couple of days ago, probably the day he didn't show up at work, then who has been playing with us? Who has been using his phone in Montpelier?" she asked.

"Clever killer. Or not so clever. We won't know until we find that phone whether it was somebody intentionally trying to mislead us into thinking that Collins was still alive and had fled town. Or is his killer stupid and doesn't realize that if he continues to use Collins's phone, we can trace its location."

Kenzie nodded. Bluff? Double bluff? Or stupid?

Cameron studied the ground but, like Kenzie, could make no sense of the mess of footprints. Kenzie and Carlos took a few pictures to preserve what they could, knowing there wasn't much point, and then Carlos was in charge of the removal of the body. Cameron insisted on helping rather than letting Kenzie do it.

"I am experienced in moving bodies," Kenzie pointed out.

"Of course you are. But I'm playing my 'too old to change my outdated sexist ideas' card and insisting upon it."

Kenzie shrugged and motioned to the body. "Have at it."

He and Carlos got the body properly contained in the body bags and loaded it onto the gurney and into the van. When they were finished, the other cops returned from their mission and pointed Cameron to a dock that extended out onto the water upriver.

"You can take a car or truck right out to the end of the dock and just dump the body into the river that way. No need to carry it through the mud and the weeds and push it out to the middle."

Cameron nodded. "Gold star. Any evidence out there?"

"Nothing obvious. Maybe should look for tire tracks. And... I don't know... any blood on the dock. An alternative light source might help us to find it."

Cameron shrugged. "The body was wrapped in a tarp," he pointed out, motioning to the blue tarp Kenzie still had to fold up and take with them. "So I doubt there is any blood on the dock. And people clean their fish out there, so there is probably plenty of contamination from fish blood and guts."

"Oh. Right."

"Any tire tracks leading up to the dock?"

"We'll check."

Cameron sent them off again and grimaced at Kenzie. "So that covers the dump site and the retrieval site. We still need the kill site."

Kenzie nodded slowly. "I'll let you know whatever I can find that points to the location of the murder once I've completed my examination. In the meantime, you should probably go back over to his apartment and make sure he wasn't killed there."

Cameron sighed. "Will do," he agreed. "I'll get the crime techs to see if there is any blood evidence."

"There were multiple blows," Kenzie reminded him. "There

should be quite a bit of spatter. It's very hard to clean up every drop, especially without a light source and all of the proper chemicals. I don't remember smelling bleach while I was there. Do you remember any smells?"

"Just the cat and the cat box. Ammonia. Maybe an air freshener."

Kenzie nodded her agreement. "See what you can find. I'll let you know what I can contribute."

44

Kenzie was nearly finished with the postmortem examination of Alex Collins when Detective Cameron showed up in the observation room adjacent the autopsy. He turned on the mic and leaned in to talk to Kenzie.

"Good afternoon, Dr. Kirsch. I'm afraid I don't have much news for you at this point. I did a thorough review of the apartment with an eye to discovering any blood evidence or anything else that pointed to it being the site of Alex Collins's murder, but was unable to find anything of significance. The crime scene boys are going to go through it and see if they can find anything I might have missed, but I don't think they will. There was no smell of blood, decomp, bleach, or other cleaners. Just the cat, which I think the girlfriend has taken now. It wasn't there as far as I could tell. I don't think the apartment is our scene."

Kenzie nodded. "Okay. Well, hopefully, we will find it, and that will reveal the identity of the killer."

"I think you and I probably already know who did this."

Kenzie looked up from her work. "Kirk Robertson?"

"I keep going back to him. We refocused our investigation on Alex when it appeared that Kirk had not had any contact with his brother and that he had a motive of his own for wanting Robertson dead. And he had the best access to Robertson's food."

"But now we know that Alex was not the one who killed Robertson."

"Not for sure. It could be that he killed Robertson, and then someone killed him. Either as retaliation for killing Robertson or for profit or another reason. But I'm inclined to think that the same person killed both of them. The simplest solution is that we have one killer who killed both."

Kenzie nodded. She looked back down at her work.

She had not done a full dissection of Collins's body. The trauma was isolated to the head. There was no other sign of violence on the body and, from what she could tell of her observations before his death, he had been a pretty healthy man. There was no sign that he had been poisoned like Robertson had. He had no jaundice, no swelling of the internal organs, no acne or breast development that might indicate an imbalance of his hormones. Kenzie had taken a number of blood samples and would run both the standard tox panels and also specific tests for anabolic steroids. If he had been using steroids or was being poisoned by them as Robertson had been, they would know it pretty quickly.

She took samples of vitreous fluid and other fluid and tissue samples just in case, but she didn't see anything that warranted opening the body up.

The head, of course, was another story.

The head and the face had been badly damaged by the killer. It was Kenzie's job to uncover as many clues as possible about the killer and method of killing from the wounds.

"What have you been able to find so far?" Cameron asked cautiously. He could see that Kenzie was not finished, and she might not appreciate his pushing her to answer questions before she was ready.

"Several blows to the back of the head and to the face," Kenzie told him. "They all appear to have been inflicted by the same object. All of the wounds are consistent in size and shape. The blows to the back of the head are deeper and bloodier. I would say that was where he was hit first. A blow—multiple blows—from behind."

"So he was taken by surprise. He either didn't know the killer was there or did not have reason to believe that person would be dangerous to him when he turned his back."

"That would be my guess," Kenzie agreed. "He literally never saw it coming."

"Hopefully, that will be a comfort to his family. It won't be open casket, though, will it?"

Kenzie shook her head. "The blows to the face were not as hard. Maybe the killer was squeamish about hitting him in the face. Maybe whatever rage or other emotion had prompted the attack was spent once he was dead. The blows to the face may have been intended just to obscure identification for a time."

"If he intended to hide his identity, he should have taken his wallet," Cameron said dryly.

Kenzie chuckled. "Yeah, I guess you're right. Maybe he forgot. There are a lot of things to remember when you are disposing of a body. People don't really think it through ahead of time. They don't know how difficult it is going to be until they get into it. TV always makes it look easy, but hauling around a dead weight and getting rid of it in a way that escapes detection is complicated."

"If there is anyone who knows how difficult moving dead bodies around can be, it would be you."

"Exactly," Kenzie agreed. "Anyway, I have mapped out the injuries for you, taken plenty of pictures and x-rays during my examination of the head."

"Mmm-hmm."

Kenzie looked down at her handiwork. While she was very precise in her work, and the head before her was the very picture of a textbook head, face, and brain dissection, it was probably pretty gory and distracting to the uninitiated. Luckily, Cameron was an experienced cop who had seen a number of postmortems and would not be shocked by what he could see on the monitors.

"Do you have any guess as to the weapon?" Cameron asked.

"There are two separate profiles, but I think the same weapon.

In the back, round, about an inch in diameter, probably metal since there is no trace in the wound. The facial wounds are different: a double track, something sharper, possibly chisel-shaped, and also metal."

She paused, giving Cameron time to think about this and to form a picture in his mind. She put pictures up on the screens that showed the two different shapes she was talking about more clearly.

Cameron blew out his breath, nodding. "A clawed hammer," he suggested.

"That would be my guess. Hit in the back of the head using the face of the hammer, and the face mutilated using the clawed side."

Cameron wrote a few notes in his notepad and put it back in his pocket.

"Any other injuries I should know about? You couldn't be sure at the scene."

"No, I haven't found anything else. No defensive wounds, which bears out the idea that he was surprised by a blow from behind that immediately incapacitated him. Either he was knocked out by the first blow and killed by one of the ones that followed, or he was killed by the first one and everything else was postmortem. Whichever way it happened, it was very quick. I wouldn't say the killer was frenzied, but he seemed to be... motivated."

"Anything you can tell about the killer physically? Height, build, handedness?"

"Sorry, no. I'm not qualified to make that judgment. I can have Dr. Cook look and see whether he has any other insights. Otherwise, we would need an expert to estimate those factors. And it will depend on what position the victim was in when he died. Was he standing straight up? Bending over? Kneeling? What could look like a blow from a tall man if he was standing could be from a short woman if he was kneeling or sitting on the floor. If we find the crime scene, we might be able to work some of that out. The position Collins was in, directionality of blood spatter, that kind of thing."

"Certainly nothing that would rule Kirk Robertson out."

"No."

"Okay. I'm going to call him in for a further discussion. Tell him that he no longer has an alibi witness. There is no proof now that he didn't contact his brother in the months before his death."

Kenzie smiled and shook her head. "That's dirty."

Cameron nodded pleasantly. He didn't seem at all conscience-stricken. "If Kirk killed his brother because of the money that had been left in the trust, then there was only one reason for him to kill Collins, and that is because Collins decided he wasn't going to provide Kirk with an alibi anymore. Maybe he was blackmailing him. Maybe he was going to tell me that he'd been covering for Kirk. He did something that made Kirk believe he was no longer protected by Collins's testimony."

Kenzie rested her hands and looked across the room at Cameron. "What about the others?"

Cameron opened his mouth to ask Kenzie who she was talking about, then caught on.

"The girlfriends?"

"What if one of them saw Kirk at the apartment?"

"Hmm." He nodded. "Two things... first, we'd better make sure that they are okay, and secondly, find out if they ever saw Kirk at the apartment or knew of any deliveries he had sent to Scott. Because if they did, they are in danger too. Even if they never intended to tell me. He's killed twice; he won't hesitate to do it again. If Collins turned against him, he knows the girls could do the same thing."

He reached for his phone. Before placing his next calls, he turned off the microphone so Kenzie could no longer hear him in the observation room. His expression was serious.

Kenzie had a lump in her stomach. If it was Kirk, which seemed to be the most likely possibility, they needed to make sure he couldn't get to the other potential victims. He couldn't be allowed to kill again.

45

enzie watched Cameron sit down with Kirk Robertson
in an interview room. She watched via a monitor in a
room down the hall. Kirk was warned by caution signs
on the wall that the interview was being recorded. The camera was
hidden in a bubble in the ceiling, but it was still obvious that was
what it was.

Cameron had confirmed that both Rachel and Anna were alive
and well. He'd had to notify Anna of Collins's death and had given
both women stern warnings that Kirk was dangerous and, if they
knew anything about his visiting his brother or sending him something, they'd better let him know before Kirk managed to get to
them.

Both of them claimed never to have seen or even heard of Kirk.
Rachel knew nothing of any mysterious package Scott had received
from either Kirk or an anonymous source. He hadn't received a box
of chocolate or bottle of daily vitamins.

Kenzie hoped they were both telling the truth.

It was hard to believe that the red-faced, red-haired man sitting
calmly at the interrogation room table might have spent months
poisoning his brother to get his inheritance and then viciously
killed Alex Collins with a hammer.

He looked physically strong enough and didn't have any obvious disabilities that would have prevented him from doing what they suspected him of. He had certainly been bitter about the money his father had left to his brother and had an aggressive manner. He believed that he had been in the right and had been prepared to spend years litigating to get what had been his.

Was he cold-blooded enough to shortcut the process with murder?

"Thanks for coming in," Detective Cameron told him. "I appreciate you taking the time out of your day."

"I don't think you realize how much there is to do when a loved one dies. I have all these arrangements to make, and I guess I'm the only one who can do them. My mom is in Australia," he reminded Cameron.

"Yes, that must make things difficult."

Kenzie and Cameron both knew that Kirk wasn't planning a funeral or memorial service, unless he had recently changed his mind. He hadn't wanted to deal with his brother's remains, and had tried to cajole Kenzie into having the municipality take care of the cremation instead.

So she wasn't sure what arrangements had him so busy, unless maybe it was dealing with his brother's bank accounts and shutting the start-up business down before it ever got off the ground so that he could get his father's money out of the company. Dealing with financial institutions and financiers *could* be mentally taxing; Kenzie knew that. But Kirk's complaint didn't seem to garner much sympathy from Detective Cameron.

"That may be," Cameron agreed. "Unfortunately, I have a job to do, too, and that includes pulling people like you away from their busy lives to deal with murder and other very unsavory topics."

Kirk made a face, demonstrating his dislike of such topics as well. "I suppose we may as well just deal with it," he sighed. "No point in complaining about a necessity."

Cameron nodded. "When I talked to you last, you said you had never been to Scott's apartment."

"That's right."

"But I don't think it is quite true, is it? You have been to his apartment before. More than once, in fact."

Kirk's eyes widened. "No!" He shook his head vigorously. "I had never been there. I wasn't talking to Scott. I didn't have any reason to go to his place. We did not get along. Not since our dad died. Before that, even."

"And you have sent letters and deliveries to his address."

"No way. Why would I? We were not in correspondence. If we were, it would be by email or text. I'm not a letter writer."

"And yet you sent him, what…?" Cameron flipped some pages in his notebook. "Candies? Pills? What was it?"

"Nothing. I never sent Scott anything. Where are you getting this?" Kirk leaned forward, trying to ascertain details from Cameron's notebook. "Who told you that? None of it is true. I don't know why anyone would say that."

"Maybe because it was true. What other reason would they have? No one profits from making this stuff up."

"Was it that roommate of his? I don't know why he would be telling stories like that." Kirk's face got redder. He looked like a boiled tomato. "I'm telling you, I never even met the guy until I went to the apartment to look at Scott's room so I could start making plans to dispose of his possessions. I never even met the guy before that, so I don't know why he would be telling you crap like that. Maybe he's trying to hide something. Maybe he's the one who gave Scott steroids. He was the one in the apartment with him. He was the only one who had access. You should be looking at him."

"How do you know he was the only one with access to Scott's food?"

"Well, I mean, it only makes sense, right? They lived together. They both used the fridge, right? He could just open Scott's food and put whatever he wanted in it, and no one would ever know the difference."

"There were other people in and out of the apartment. Scott's girlfriend. Alex's girlfriend. They were there sometimes, too, so they also had access to it. And who knows what other friends they might have had over, deliverymen, tradespeople. Maybe they gave a neighbor a key in case of emergency or for when they were out of town. It wasn't like there was a log kept of who was there when." Cameron gave Kirk a warm smile. "But we know you were there."

"No. You're wrong. I never went there while Scott was alive. I never had anything to do with him while he lived there."

He did not, Kenzie noted, tell Cameron to ask Alex about it. *Ask Alex; he'll tell you I was never there.*

He knew better than to ask Alex to stand as his witness this time because he knew Alex was no longer around to do so.

He was starting to sweat. Cameron was not, so it probably wasn't a matter of the room being too warm. Kirk was beginning to feel the pressure.

"We know you and Scott did not get along. We know that you wanted the money that had been left to Scott. You felt like it had been taken away from you. He'd already been given money by your father, and you didn't feel like he deserved it."

"He didn't. There was no reason he should get all that money just because he thought he could become the next billionaire with this start-up company. He was never going to achieve that. How long had he been raising the money and 'getting ready' to start the company? He wasn't ever going to get it off the ground. He wasn't ever going to become anything. It was just a dream, and he was never going to accomplish it. Dad should have realized that. He should have known by then that Scott wouldn't get anywhere. He was a failure."

"Really."

"You don't know anything about him," Kirk maintained. "Only what you've been told by Alex and whoever else you've talked to. You think he was the golden child, the brilliant one, but he could not get anything done. All the good ideas in the world will not help you if you can't follow through on them."

"Or if you are dead."

Kirk snorted. "It's not my fault he was dead. That was his own fault, too."

"Oh? How is that his fault?"

"He obviously ticked somebody off. Who was it that was so angry with him that they killed him? You said that he had been feeding poison to Scott for months. Months! Somebody had to really hate him to do that."

"Like you?"

"I didn't hate him. We just didn't get along, and I didn't think that Dad should have been babying him, giving him money, and telling him how wonderful he was. He should have been telling him to get his stuff together and find courage."

"What do you think he should have done with his life? Given up on the start-up company and done what?"

"I don't know. I don't really care. He could sweep streets or collect garbage, for all I care. He would have been more useful to society that way. These guys who spend all of their time *thinking* and on high finance, these big risky ventures and investments... what kind of good are they really doing the world? He should have given it up to take up a good, honest living. Maybe then... he wouldn't have died like that."

"You think it was directly related to his career choice."

"I think it was directly related to him being a dweeb. He had no idea how to get along with other people. To behave like a normal human being. All he wanted to do was all of that financial stuff, and to tell people how he was going to become a billionaire. Because a few people decided he was brilliant when he was a kid, he thought he was something special and could do these things. He should have just gotten along with people. Made friends. Hung out. Had a drink with the guys."

He sighed and looked away from Cameron. Maybe he would have liked to have been friends with his brother. Maybe he wished they could have gotten together for drinks sometime, just hung out as brothers, talking about things Kirk could understand instead of the math and finance stuff Scott was so enamored with. But his brother was gone now, and he couldn't get him back. Those dreams, if he'd ever really had them, were gone.

A phone rang. Kirk reached into his pocket and pulled it out. He frowned, rejected the call, and put the phone down on the table. "Sorry about that. I really do need to get back to work before too long. If you have anything important to ask me… so far, I don't understand why you brought me all the way over here just to ask me if I ever went to Scott's apartment. I already told you I didn't."

"Did you know Scott's girlfriend?"

Kirk shook his head. "No, how would I know her?"

"Do you own a hammer?"

Kirk stared at him. "A hammer? Yeah, I guess. Everybody owns a hammer."

"I'd like to see it."

"Well… I don't have it here with me."

"I'd like to send an officer home with you. You could give him the hammer."

"Why would I do that? Why do you care if I own a hammer?" His face screwed up as he made a show of trying to understand what he would need a hammer for.

"Because that is what Alex Collins was killed with."

"What?" Kirk's face went from florid to deathly pale in a few seconds. "What are you talking about?"

"Your buddy Alex. The guy who was supposed to be giving you an alibi. He's dead."

"With a *hammer?*" Kirk seemed shocked by this news. "How do you kill someone with a hammer?" After asking, he raised his hands in a "stop" gesture. "No. I don't want to know. I don't want to know anything about it. I'm leaving. I don't know why you would think that I would have anything to do with anyone's death. I haven't done anything to hurt anyone." Kirk stood up. His phone started to ring again. He picked it up and again rejected the call.

"Look. Don't call me again," he told Cameron. "I've had all I'm going to take from you. Understood? Just leave me alone."

"We already have someone at your house looking for the hammer," Cameron told him unemotionally.

"I didn't kill Scotty or Alex or anyone else. I certainly never hurt anyone with a hammer. You are crazy. You need to stop looking at me and look for the person who really did this." Kirk tugged at his collar. "Do you really think there is some sicko killer out there who poisoned my brother and beat his roommate to death with a hammer?"

"They're both dead. Who do *you* think did it?"

"I don't know. That's your job. You are going to have to figure it out because I… it's not me, and I don't know who would have done something like that!"

Cameron nodded. "I see. Well, good talking to you, Kirk. I hope that next time, it will be under different circumstances."

He didn't say that he hoped to be arresting Kirk the next time, but Kenzie thought the insinuation was pretty obvious.

Kirk's phone started ringing again, and he looked like he wanted to throw it across the room. He silenced it, jammed it into his pocket, and stalked out of the room. Cameron followed him and escorted him to the elevator.

A few minutes later, Cameron was opening the door to the room where Kenzie had watched the video feed.

"He didn't break," Kenzie observed.

"Not yet. But I think he will."

"You're not going to get him to come in for questioning again."

"It will be interesting to see whether he goes directly home and how he reacts to the police searching his home."

"Have they found anything? The hammer? Blood evidence?" Kenzie already knew the answer. Cameron would not have let Kirk walk out of there if they had.

Cameron shook his head.

"Did you see or hear anything you found enlightening? Anything I might have missed?"

"The overhead camera might catch things at a different angle. It might see things that you can't."

Cameron raised his brows. "Like what?"

"The caller ID on Kirk's phone screen."

"Who was trying to reach him so urgently?"

"Mr. Harris. The landlord."

46

Cameron called Harris on the phone in the middle of the table and switched it to speaker.

"Yes," Mr. Harris confirmed. "I was calling Kirk Robertson. Why does that matter?"

"Why were you trying to reach him?"

"I need someone to take his brother's personal things from the apartment. He's the next of kin."

"Why is that so urgent?"

"It has been more than a week. It's not like I was harassing him the day after Scott died. But I need someone to take those things, and he's the only one I can call. Why do you care about it?"

"We're just trying to get confirmation of everyone's movements," Cameron said. "If you are calling Kirk, I assume you have a history with him. Had you met him before? While his brother was living in the building?"

"No." Harris's tone was confused. "I only met him last week, after Scott died. What makes you think I knew him before that?"

Cameron grimaced and slapped the table softly, not loud enough for Harris to hear and wonder what was going on.

"Well, he must have come to visit before. I just assumed that you might have run into each other on one of those visits. You strike me as the kind of landlord who keeps track of what is happening in his building. One who is concerned about the people and the community within the building, not just whether people's toilets are working."

"Of course," Harris agreed, flattered. "People are what is important. It is much easier to keep things running smoothly if people are willing to talk to each other and support each other. It opens up conversations, and you learn about things before they become a problem. It's much easier to address issues early on."

"Exactly," Cameron agreed. "A building like yours is more than just a structure; it is a living, breathing organism."

Kenzie raised her eyebrows at Cameron, who responded with a sheepish grin and a shrug.

"I'm like a gardener," Harris said, taking up the idea with enthusiasm. "Watering and pruning and training. Creating an ecosystem where everyone works together."

"Right," Cameron agreed. "So you know who spends time hanging around your building, even if they are not your tenants. You recognize people who visit regularly, know who they go see…"

"Some of them," Harris agreed. "Not everyone, of course, not if they've only come once or twice. But regular visitors, you do get to know them."

"And Scott's visitors? The people who came to see him?"

"His girlfriend, of course. And sometimes she had other friends that she brought over with her."

"Uh-huh. And Scott must have had other friends who came over too. And Alex said he sometimes had over investors or other businesspeople he was working with. He was quite smart, you know. He was starting his own company that was expected to really take off."

"I always thought he was a smart boy."

"So, who else did you recognize out of his friends? Who was over regularly?"

"Well," Harris cleared his throat. "He did have some visitors who were dressed up in suits or white shirts. Those corporate types. And the girlfriend's friends."

"But no one else? His own friends?"

"No, I don't know of any. He wasn't a social person, I don't think. He liked his books and computers, you know."

"His brother didn't come over very often?"

"I had never met Kirk until last week," Harris insisted. "If he had been in the building before, I didn't know about it."

"Who would have seen him?"

"Maybe one of the neighbors. Maybe Matt, when he did work in their apartment. Matt is quite friendly with a lot of the tenants. He talks a lot. Or maybe the security camera caught something."

"Security camera?" Cameron repeated. He pulled out his notepad and started to flip through it. "I thought you said there was no security camera in the building."

"I said there wasn't anything useful on the camera footage," Harris clarified.

Cameron frowned, shaking his head and looking for the place he had written down something about this. "No, you didn't. You said you didn't have any security camera footage. If you had said that there was footage, I would have been there looking at it long before this. A lot of these systems only keep three days or a week of video before they start recording over it again!" he said in frustration. "How much do you keep?"

"I don't know... we download it to a hard drive, and then switch out the hard drives when they get full. But they hold quite a bit."

Kenzie could see the hope come back into Cameron's expression.

"So you might still have footage of the days before Scott died?"

"Yeah. It wasn't that long ago. But I looked at it myself. There wasn't anything suspicious on it. That's why I told you there wasn't anything."

"You said you didn't have any footage."

"No, I said I had already looked at it, and there wasn't anything."

Cameron rolled his eyes and shook his head. "That is not what you said."

"Well, officer… what is it you want from me? What exactly do you want me to do?" Harris asked in irritation.

"What I want you to do is send your Mr. Johnson over to the police station right now with whatever footage you have from before Mr. Robertson's death. I want to talk to him about anyone he might have seen in Robertson's apartment, and to go over the security footage now, before anything gets deleted, overwritten, or forgotten."

"Matt has work to do here—"

"And you want to help out with our investigation. You want to know who killed Scott and why. You don't want things like that going on in your building without knowing about it. You don't want a killer living in or visiting your building."

"Well, of course not, but…"

"Send Matt over here ASAP. We need to cue up that video and start reviewing it. It will take time."

"How much do you want?"

"Whatever you have."

"But that's… there are a lot of hard drives. You don't need to go back that far."

"Do you have a month before Robertson's death?"

"I'm sure we do."

"I'll take that. And then, if we need to go farther back, I'll let you know."

"Okay," Harris said doubtfully. "I suppose I'll send Matt over."

Kenzie didn't think Cameron had considered how long it would take to review that much video. Thirty days worth of video would take thirty cops three days to review at regular speed. They didn't have thirty cops to review it. Most of the video was an empty entryway most of the day and the night but, if they watched it at high speed, it was easy to miss someone walking by the camera, they zipped by in a blink.

Zachary was great at reviewing security recordings. Kenzie had seen him do it several times. His hyperfocus and obsessive nature meant he often picked up on details no one else did. She called him to get some tips on how to review that much video efficiently. He recommended apps that analyzed the video for changes so that they could advance from one person walking through the entryway to the next person to come in. It wasn't perfect; sometimes, it stopped because of trees outside the window moving in the wind, a car driving by, or some other movement. But it at least allowed them to skip over large portions of an empty lobby and focus just on the movement.

Matt helped set up the video so that the three of them could view a different drive on their assigned computers, and they chatted with each other as they studied the faces of each person who entered the apartment building.

Of course, they would have to review Matt's video again after he was gone, in case he was trying to hide something but, for the moment, it gave them something to occupy themselves with while they quizzed Matt, trying not to make it feel like an interrogation.

"You don't need to waste your time watching this video," Cameron told Kenzie. "I'm sure you have better things to do. Bodies waiting for you downstairs…"

Kenzie looked at her watch. "It's quiet right now. I am technically not on the clock today. I'm curious to see if we can find anything on the security footage."

"I know this isn't your job, and we do have people we pay to do this kind of thing."

"You mean I'm not getting paid for this?" Kenzie teased.

"'Fraid not, Dr. Kirsch. You are not on my payroll."

"That's okay. I need something to talk to Zachary about during supper, and I don't have any other bodies on the table."

After completing Alex's postmortem, she did not have any autopsies waiting for her. There was still other work to do, but she was curious whether the video would provide a breakthrough.

Whoever had poisoned Scott Robertson in the weeks and months before he died had to have access to his food. And to access his food, they needed to have entered the building at some point.

"So did you see much of Alex or Scott?" Cameron asked Matt. "Did they need a lot of work done?"

"Well, no more than anyone else. Some people are hard on equipment and need things fixed all the time. But Alex and Scott... no, they were pretty normal. Mostly just routine maintenance."

"What about others on their floor?"

"There isn't really anyone else on that floor now because of the renovations. Everyone took the payout and moved out."

"Who gets the payout for Kirk and Scott now that they are both dead?"

Matt frowned. "Why would anyone get it? They aren't there anymore. There is no more lease; there is no payout."

"How much was Mr. Harris going to pay Alex and Scott to move out?"

Matt shrugged. "I don't know. They didn't accept any offer, so... nothing."

"Mr. Harris said Alex had decided to accept it after Scott died."

Matt shook his head slowly. "He never signed an agreement. The other tenants signed an agreement."

"Maybe he didn't have enough time."

"Maybe. Or maybe he changed his mind. He'd gone back and forth a few times."

"That must have made Mr. Harris pretty anxious."

"I guess. He was doing everything he could to get them to agree to it. Or to get Alex to agree to it, since he was the one who held the lease. Offered additional incentives. Wined and dined him." Matt watched the video on his computer start and stop as each person entered the building and walked by the camera to the elevators.

"What about people who don't come in the front door?" Kenzie asked suddenly. "There must be people who come in the service door or loading dock."

She took a break to blink a few times and rub her eyes.

"Not many," Matt said, looking away from his screen to study Kenzie's for a moment, then looked back at his. "The tenants are used to coming in the front, unless they have something special that needs to be brought in through the loading dock. Then, they are supposed to book off the freight elevator rather than use the passenger elevator. People get kind of irritated if you've got a couch in the passenger elevator."

"So there is a logbook?" Cameron questioned. He pulled out his notebook and added a reminder, sighing.

"They're all supposed to use the front," Matt reiterated. "We should be able to see whoever it was on the video." His eyes flicked away from his screen again. "Though… I don't know what I'm supposed to see on the video. How are we going to be able to tell from a video of someone walking into the building what they were there for? How do you draw a line from that to being a murderer?"

"Mostly, you're looking for Kirk. He says he was never there, but he was the one with motive to want Scott dead. The rest are only of interest if they are acting suspiciously. If you see anyone you know was friends with Alex or Scott, I need to know about it."

47

They talked on and off as they watched the footage, getting bored with watching people going in and out of the apartment building. Most faces became familiar. Matt identified the various tenants and their respective apartments. Others were regular visitors, and Matt generally knew who visited which apartments.

Scott had apparently not had a lot of visitors. As Mr. Harris had said, the girlfriends were regular visitors. Alex had a few friends. There were a few business types Matt thought might have been there to see Scott.

"But he didn't have a lot of visitors the last few weeks," Matt said. "I didn't know how sick he was, but I knew he wasn't feeling well. Thought maybe he had picked up one of those viruses going around. They affect some people more than others."

"Different people have different levels of immunity or different levels of health due to lifestyle or genetics," Kenzie agreed.

Matt nodded his agreement, watching the screen in front of him.

"Are we going to get some food?" he suggested. "I'm getting kind of hungry."

Kenzie looked at Cameron. It wasn't like they had planned

ahead of time what they were going to do for food. But it was getting to be dinnertime and, if they were going to impose on Matt to watch the video surveillance with them, they would have to feed him.

And she should let Zachary know that she would be home late. Maybe by the time she got home, they would know something. They would have Kirk's face on the video. Or perhaps someone else acting suspiciously.

"Yeah, we could order in," Cameron agreed, looking at his watch. "I suppose we should do it sooner rather than later. The deliverymen will be booked up."

"I could run out and get something, if you like," Kenzie offered.

"I don't need the medical examiner playing gofer for me. It's bad enough that I'm using you to help review surveillance video. I don't imagine your Dr. Cook would be too impressed if he knew."

"Dr. Cook is pretty chill about letting me do what I want. Especially since I am not actually supposed to be in today."

"We'll have something delivered. What do you like?"

"Pretty much anything." Kenzie shrugged. She and Zachary had probably ordered from or eaten at every restaurant in town at one time or another. She was easy to please.

"Pizza? Mexican?"

"Either is fine."

"Do you like spicy?" Matt asked, a gleam in his eye. "I know this great little Mexican place, but it is quite… fiery."

"I'd be okay with that."

Cameron nodded. "Sure. Why not? I have plenty of time to digest it before bed." His eyes went to Kenzie. "Getting old isn't for the faint of heart. Used to be able to eat whatever I liked without any consequences. Now I have to make sure it will be through my system before I lie down or I get terrible heartburn."

"Well, it's good if you can handle it that way instead of having to take antacids or acid reducers."

"Are you sure?" Matt checked, "I don't want to make anyone

miserable, but they've got some really fantastic food if you can handle the spice."

"I'm game," Cameron confirmed. "I love the stuff, and I've got hours before bedtime."

Kenzie nodded her agreement. She liked a wide variety of cuisines, and it would be nice to have a new place to take Zachary. "Sure. What is this place?"

"Mama Rosa's Authentic Mexican. And my Mexican friends assure me that it is authentic. Not the fast-food franchise stuff that passes for Mexican in this part of the country."

"Sounds great!"

Cameron called in an order, and they watched more footage while waiting for it.

"Alex liked spicy stuff," Matt commented. "He could handle some heat. But Scott was so sensitive. He couldn't handle even Mama's mildest items."

Cameron grunted. "We don't tend to get a lot of spicy stuff around here. It's pretty homogeneous. Burgers and fries. Meat and potatoes. Pasta or pizza with mild tomato sauce."

"I like to be a bit more adventurous," Matt declared.

"And the ethnic stuff tends to be healthier, right Doctor?"

Kenzie agreed. "There's no guarantee, but a lot of the foods from other cultures include a lot more vegetables, less meat, and more herbs and spices. Not as much deep-fried or greasy stuff."

"And serving sizes are smaller," Cameron observed. "I mean a lot of it you get for the table if you're eating out, one dish shared among multiple people. So you can control your serving size. Not like the enormous burgers with a pound of meat in them or super-sized milkshakes with half a gallon of ice cream."

Though Cameron had been worried they might have to wait a long time owing to the dinner rush, less than half an hour had passed when an administrative assistant came in with a couple of bags of food. They cleared a table and spread the food and dishes out. The heady aromas of roasted chilies, fresh cilantro, and lime filled the room.

The flavors were amazing. The food was obviously fresh, and

great care had been taken to select the best ingredients and craft them into the traditional dishes. But Kenzie's nose was streaming, and she occasionally dabbed at her eyes. Matt hadn't been kidding about it being fiery.

"This is great," Kenzie sniffled. "And I'll bet it would clear up any nasal congestion."

Matt laughed. "Great, isn't it? Alex loved it. Ordered it for himself sometimes. He's the one I got the name from, because it's just this little hole-in-the-wall place that doesn't have a sign outside or a website. I don't know if they do any advertising or if it is all word of mouth."

Maybe that was why it had been delivered so quickly. They kept their business to a level they could handle by only using word-of-mouth marketing.

"Did Scott change his mind about the spiciness when his tastes changed? Or did he still find it too hot?" she asked Matt.

Matt shook his head. "Too hot for him. People's tastes don't change that much. You can develop a tolerance for some heat, but to go from the bland stuff that Scott liked to Mama Rosa's? Never."

"But he liked spicy curry."

"No."

"After his tastes changed. He started to eat spicier stuff. Said that everything tasted too bland."

Matt was frowning. He looked at Kenzie. "What are you talking about?"

Kenzie glanced in Cameron's direction for his reaction. "Before he died, he was eating spicier stuff. I think the cat made him congested so that he couldn't smell or taste as well anymore. Something like this…" she indicated the Mexican food, "he would have been able to taste that. And maybe even clear up all of that congestion for a while."

"Huh. No, I didn't know any of that. Knew they'd gotten a cat. There were a couple of complaints about it. But I didn't know he was allergic to it."

"He resented Alex getting a cat without asking him first; there was some friction between them. Who had complained?" Cameron asked, blotting his forehead.

"A couple of neighbors. Heard the cat yowling during the day when it was alone and either thought they shouldn't have one or that it was suffering." He shrugged. "Not much you can do about it if the building allows pets. It wasn't being really bothersome, so the neighbors just had to put up with hearing it now and then."

"And Scott never complained about it?"

"Why would he complain to us about it? He would need to take that up with Alex under whatever agreement they had. That's their business. We wouldn't get involved in it any more than we would a married couple having an argument. Unless one of them was breaking the rules of their lease."

48

Eventually, they had to admit that they were not going to find Kirk's face on the surveillance video. Not the first day, anyway. There was still plenty of video to be reviewed, but Kenzie had to get home and her eyes were tired and gritty from watching the video.

She didn't know how anyone could watch more than a couple of hours at a time. It had been interesting for the first few minutes but had quickly grown tedious and, even with Cameron and Matt there to keep her company and the wonderful Mexican food, she couldn't stick with it any longer. Luckily, it wasn't her job. She had only been helping Cameron out in the hope that they would be able to find something quickly, with all three of them looking at different dates.

"Take some of the leftovers home to Zachary," Cameron suggested. "Does he like Mexican?"

"He likes fast food Mexican. I don't know whether he'll like something this spicy or not. I'll take a bit and find out. Matt can take the rest." She grinned at him. "It was your suggestion, so you should get the benefit of the leftovers."

"I won't argue with that," Matt agreed with a ready smile. "This stuff is like manna. I would eat it every day if I could."

"Good." Kenzie packed up what she wanted to take with her. "We'll talk tomorrow?" she asked Cameron, "Or Monday?"

He nodded. "I'll let you know of any developments."

Zachary accepted the gift of Mexican food left over from their dinner, but was not happy about Kenzie's extended absence. "You usually only put in a couple of hours in the morning on a Saturday. I thought we would have time during the day after you got out."

"We didn't have any special plans that I was aware of," Kenzie said slowly, feeling her way through the argument. Just how upset was he that she had worked all day instead of coming home when she normally did? She had texted him to let him know that she was staying to do other things, and he had not objected via text. But maybe she should have talked to him on the phone to gauge how he felt about it rather than relying on text, which didn't give her any idea of his tone unless he was aggressive about it. "We still have the rest of the evening. And tomorrow. I'm not going in tomorrow at all."

"We've already got your parents tomorrow. That will take half the day."

A couple of hours to drive to the Burlington house, at least two for dinner, and a couple more coming home. That was if everything went well and they got out as quickly as expected.

She suspected Zachary resented going to see her parents instead of visiting Lorne Peterson, his old foster father, and Patrick Parker. Instead of alternating between staying home and visiting the Petersons each Sunday, they now sometimes had visits with Kenzie's parents as well. Zachary said that he didn't mind, that he wanted her to see her family too and have a good relationship with them, but that didn't mean he didn't feel a small amount of resentment over her parents stealing their time together.

"Sorry, yeah, you're right. I forgot about that when I stayed later today. I was thinking we had tomorrow free."

Zachary looked like he was going to read her the riot act about how insensitive she had been, but he closed his mouth and nodded. He couldn't very well complain about her forgetting something. With his ADHD, he held the prize for forgetting commitments, especially ones he didn't want to go to.

"I *am* sorry," Kenzie repeated. "I can call them to cancel."

"No, you don't need to do that. You should still see them."

"I'm tired. I don't know whether this is the best time. We can reschedule."

"Then you're going to be rescheduling to a week when we were supposed to see Mr. Peterson."

"Umm… yeah. I can just skip this time, then. Find out when the next time *after* Lorne's week they are available."

"I don't think that's fair to them. Especially with your mom having so much trouble with Walter right now. She needs someone else to babysit—er—distract him for a while."

Kenzie laughed. "My poor dad. I don't think he knew what a problem it would be when he retired. Other people do it. He had no idea how bored he would be."

But he couldn't unring that bell. The reason he had left his practice was not that he didn't enjoy it or wanted to spend his golden years playing golf or going on cruises. It was because he wanted to get away from the mobsters who were threatening him and his family. If he had a stroke and could no longer work, they couldn't blame him. So, he faked a stroke. But doing so meant he had to stay out of the public eye, so he couldn't see his friends or go out.

Kenzie sighed. "Well, I guess we'll have to go, then. But let's have a nice time tonight. I don't want to be arguing and upset because we will lose out on our couple's time, too." It wasn't fair of her to demand that he overlook her decision to stay and put on a happy face but, aside from apologizing and giving him delicious Mexican food, she didn't see what she could do to make up for it.

Zachary squared his shoulders. "Okay," he agreed. "This looks great," he started to unwrap the Mama Rosa's leftovers. "Why don't you find something on TV while I warm it up? Unless you wanted to go out somewhere…"

"No, not really. I'm wiped out. I probably shouldn't even be watching TV after all of the screen time I've had today, but I don't think I could manage a book, and I'm too brain-dead to think of anything better to do."

"I can think of some things," Zachary teased, waggling his eyebrows suggestively.

Kenzie laughed. "Later, when I've had a chance to rest. Then… we'll see." Maybe there *was* something she could do to help make up for her oversight.

"If your eyes are bothering you, maybe you should put a cold compress on them for a few minutes, and I'll find something to watch when I'm finished getting this ready. Maybe something you've already seen, and you can just listen to it."

She was always bugging him for staring at the screen until his eyes were red and bloodshot. She should be a good example and take care of herself. "Okay. I'll put something on them for a few minutes."

49

Kenzie and Zachary did end up having a nice evening despite her having abandoned Zachary all day. And they had the first part of Sunday to sleep in—which Zachary never did—and spend some lazy time not doing chores and errands and thinking about everything Kenzie had to think about when she was at work.

Then, in the afternoon, it was time to prepare to go to Burlington for dinner. Kenzie had asked for an early dinner so that they could get back home in good time, and Lisa had agreed. She catered rather than cooked the meals, so she just had to arrange for her to have the food earlier in the day. Kenzie also cut the pre-dinner drinks short, trying to get things underway. They would discuss a wide range of topics over dinner, and she didn't see the need to spend a lot of time on small talk and how her personal life was going before the meal started. She was fine. Zachary was fine. Work was fine. She wanted to hear about Lisa and Walter and to be reassured that everything was going fine with Walter and that the worst thing he had to face was boredom and not Russian mobsters.

The dining room looked perfect, as always, with a crisp white tablecloth and the warm glow of the chandelier over the table, sparkling off the dishes. The aroma of curried chicken soup mingled with freshly baked bread filled the room.

"How is work going?" Lisa asked in a measured tone as they started on the soup.

Kenzie shrugged. "The same as usual."

They didn't actually like talking about her work, so she wasn't sure why Lisa felt it necessary to ask.

"It's been pretty dead," Zachary intoned.

Kenzie glared at him. Her parents were not big on ME jokes.

Walter snorted. "Pretty dead," he repeated. "Yes, I suppose it is."

Kenzie nodded.

"She's been working on a poisoning case," Zachary contributed.

Kenzie shook her head. Lisa would not want any talk of dead bodies during mealtime. Or after that, for that matter.

"Poisoning?" Walter asked. "That's not very usual, is it? How many of those do you get?"

"Not very many," Kenzie agreed. "It is far less common than... other methods of homicide. And homicides are the minority of my cases as it is. So you can imagine how seldom I see... that."

"Walter," Lisa reprimanded. "Kenzie, really. Not at the dinner table."

Kenzie noticed that she did not reprimand Zachary for introducing the subject.

"Sorry, Mom. I wonder whether you two know anyone related to the case." She sipped her soup tentatively, and eventually put down her spoon. It was good, but she wasn't really interested in the soup. There would be something more substantial for the main course. She would focus her attention on that. "The man who was killed was Scott Robertson, and his brother was Kirk. I guess I don't know the dad's name, but he died a couple of years ago and his estate has been tied up in court...?"

It was a small community. From what Kirk had said, it sounded like his father was pretty wealthy. And if he was a wealthy Vermonter, especially one from an old family, then chances were her father would know something about him.

"I don't suppose that was Kyle Robertson," Walter said, frowning slightly. "You remember him," he said to his ex-wife. "*His* father was a surgeon, and Kyle disappointed him by going into concrete."

"Concrete?" Lisa repeated.

"Hard to break into," Zachary deadpanned.

Kenzie glared at him, but Walter and Lisa did not appear to catch the joke.

"Yeah. And it *is* hard to break into when you don't have any previous connections to the families who run that sort of thing. But he had his ideas about how things should be run, and some of them caught on. He ended up being a leader in the industry and made a lot of money. I don't know whether his father ever forgave him for going into construction instead of into medicine, but no one could say he hadn't done a good job of it. He made more in concrete than he ever would have as a surgeon."

"And he didn't have to spend his time around sick people," Lisa said with a smile.

"I don't spend time around sick people either," Kenzie pointed out.

"Ah, no," Lisa admitted.

"So Kyle had a lot of money to leave to his sons, then?" Kenzie asked. "If it's the same guy, he has two sons?"

"Yes, it was a very large estate, and I do remember it being quite contentious. His wife was some sort of actress, I think, and moved away to… Switzerland?"

"Australia, if it is the same family."

"Australia… yes, that might be right." Walter set his spoon down, his gaze fixed on Kenzie. "And he was the poisoning victim you were talking about?"

"Yes. Some kind of wunderkind. Scott went into high finance, and was supposed to be starting up his own firm. He needed money from Dad to get things going, and the other brother, Kirk, decided that money should count as an advance on the money from the trust rather than dividing the estate fifty-fifty between them."

"Well, he might be right."

"I guess that's why it is still tied up in court. Or was, until Scott was killed. Now it all goes to Kirk either way, so he is dropping the case so the money can be distributed."

Walter's eyes flashed with interest. "I suppose that makes Kirk a suspect in the murder."

"The prime suspect," Kenzie agreed. "After two years of fighting, he gets all of the money. But the problem is that we can't figure out how he accessed Scott's food."

"Did it have to be ingested?" Zachary asked. "Could he have been exposed another way? Through the air or skin?"

"Well, skin is a possibility. Hormones can definitely be absorbed transdermally. But he would need a patch or something like that. Not just... happening to touch it on a surface occasionally."

She could see the wheels turning in Zachary's brain. He would come up with some wild theories, but maybe one of them would prompt her to look into something. But Lisa was glowering at them. She did not appreciate murder being discussed at the dinner table, even if it did involve one of the socialite families she was familiar with.

"Sorry, Mom," she apologized. "I got carried away."

"Who else *did* have access to the young man's food?" Walter asked.

"Well, number one was his roommate. They shared an apartment."

"Ahh. And did he have a motive? Or a relationship with Kirk? Someone like Kirk wouldn't necessarily decide to do the deed himself. Hiring someone would not be out of the realm of possibility."

"I don't think Alex had a reason to poison him, other than maybe he was jealous of him. They both went through the same program at school, but Scott was the one everyone thought was brilliant. He had all of these plans for his company, which he figured would make him millions, and Alex was more... working stiff. Maybe he could work for a finance company, but he wouldn't be funding his own, and he wouldn't be making millions. Or billions."

"Jealousy is a strong motivator. He had access. And maybe if Scott's brother put a little bit of pressure on him, suggested that his problems could all be solved with a little bit of poison…"

Kenzie sighed, "It's a possibility, I guess. But he wasn't fed just a little bit of poison. He had to keep feeding it to him for months before it killed him. He had to watch Scott getting weaker and sicker and knowing what was happening. That takes a special kind of killer. Most people can't watch that kind of suffering and just keep it up. A lot of potential poisoners give up on killing with poison and choose another method of murder that is faster."

"But that didn't happen with your case?"

"No. They kept administering poison right until the end, according to the hair strand testing."

"Kenzie!" Lisa complained.

"Okay, okay. I'm sorry. I was just answering questions. I won't talk about it anymore."

"Who else had access to the apartment?" Zachary persisted.

Kenzie shook her head at him. It was time to drop the subject. She didn't want the evening with her parents to be ruined. She was supposed to be helping Lisa, not making her more upset.

Zachary chewed his lip. "Friends, family members, neighbors with keys…"

"Yes, but we can discuss it at home later. Now is really not the time."

"Building manager or landlord. You said it was an apartment building, didn't you?"

"Yes. But the landlord wouldn't have any reason to poison him. He—" Kenzie cut herself off suddenly. Because, of course, the landlord didn't have any reason to kill Scott, but he did have reason to dispose of Alex.

And Alex, too, had been removed.

50

One of the drawbacks of being a medical examiner was that Kenzie didn't always get to see the results of a homicide death investigation firsthand. Usually, she only heard about the results through the police gossip mill or on the news. Sometimes, a cop was nice enough to tell her the results directly or to invite her to witness an interrogation, as she had when Cameron questioned Kirk about his involvement in Scott's death.

After watching the surveillance video with Cameron and Matt and discussing the case at dinner with her parents and Zachary, Kenzie needed to talk to Detective Cameron alone. She outlined her thoughts to him and found that he had been on the same wavelength and was preparing the various warrants and requests he would need to move forward.

While she couldn't watch those being executed, Cameron did inform her when he brought Rick Harris—the landlord—in for questioning. Kenzie made herself comfy with a cup of fresh coffee in front of the monitor, which showed the video of their discussion.

On one hand, it was frustrating not to be able to participate in the discussion, but she knew it wasn't her place to interrogate suspects. She could call family members or friends to ask them about medical histories and what they had witnessed, but there was a boundary between those questions and the interrogation Cameron was about to conduct. She was lucky to be able to eavesdrop electronically on the conversation.

And it was nice not to have to face off against a potential killer, not to have to worry about who had seen her face or whether a suspect would get up on the other side of the table and try to assault her. She was perfectly comfortable in her little monitoring room, even if it did stink of sweat and dirty socks.

Harris was already sweating when Cameron had him sit down at the table. So the room they were in probably did not smell any better than the one Kenzie was in. Harris looked around, plucking at his shirt, his face shiny and pale. He was trying to look casual, but this was not a place he was comfortable.

"Have a seat," Cameron motioned to one of the hard plastic and tubular metal chairs. Designed to be uncomfortable within ten minutes of sitting down. Even better if the legs were slightly uneven, making the chair rock and creak whenever the suspect readjusted his position.

Harris sat down. He looked at the metal ring affixed to the table and was probably grateful not to be shackled to it. He rubbed his sweaty hands on his pants.

"I'm not sure what we are here to discuss. I already told you everything you have asked about. I am just the owner and manager of the building. I didn't know the tenants personally and certainly don't know anything about why anyone would kill a nice young man like Scott."

"I'm sure it will only take a few minutes," Cameron told him without addressing the complaint.

Harris swallowed and licked his lips. "Could I get a glass of water? I'm very... it's very dry in here."

"Yes. I'll have someone bring you a drink. But if we could get started right away... The sooner we start, the sooner you will be out of here."

"Yeah, sure."

Cameron didn't ask anything. Harris shifted in his seat, waiting for a question that never came.

"So… did you find anything on the surveillance recordings? I told you that Kirk had never been there that I was aware of. We had never met before, whether he had been there or not. That was the truth."

"As opposed to the rest of the lies you told me?"

"No, I didn't lie to you about anything. I'm just saying, that's what I can prove is the truth. So now you know I tell the truth."

"I know that you *sometimes* tell the truth, but that isn't the same thing. I also know that you lie."

"I don't! I've answered all of your questions and I told you the truth. Why do you think I'm lying?"

"Do you know that at the same time as I asked you to come in for a conversation, we had cops going to your apartment and the outbuildings with a search warrant?"

"A search warrant?"

Kenzie would not have thought Harris could get whiter, but he did.

"I suppose you know what we were looking for."

"No. No, I have no idea. Obviously, you are not going to find anything in my apartment. I didn't have anything to do with Scott's death. I don't know where you got this mistaken idea."

"Sometimes detectives make mistakes."

"Yes." Harris breathed a sigh of relief at this statement. "Yes, of course, anyone can make a mistake. I know you're doing your best to sort this out."

"I didn't say I made a mistake. Just that it can happen."

"I don't… you just said…"

"I told you we got a search warrant for your apartment and the outbuildings. Are you concerned about what we might find there?"

"No, not at all. I didn't get a chance to clean, but…" He shrugged. "If you're going to descend on other people's houses without warning, you have to accept what you get."

Cameron laughed. "We don't care what people's houses look like. What we care about is what evidence we find."

"Well, I guess you found that there wasn't any evidence in my apartment."

"That's not quite accurate. In fact, we did find a couple of bottles of steroids."

"Steroids?"

"Oxymetholone. The anabolic steroid that killed Scott."

"Scott died from steroids? How awful. I knew they were bad for you. Unless you're taking them for a medical condition, of course."

"What medical condition are you taking them for?"

Harris didn't answer.

"Mr. Harris, you want to tell me why you had anabolic steroids?"

"You must be mistaken," Harris bluffed. That was pretty bold. If they found steroids, they found steroids. He couldn't really get around that one.

Cameron turned to the next page in his notepad.

"There were tools in one of the outbuildings."

"Of course. That's what they're for. To store tools."

"This one in particular had a hammer in it."

"So? Everybody has a hammer."

"You probably should have replaced it with a new one instead of just trying to wash the blood off…"

"Blood? What blood? If somebody… used it for something bad, that's not anything to do with me. Anyone could have broken into that shed."

"It didn't seem to have been broken into. We had to cut the lock to get into it."

"That was a new lock. If the police can come along with a set of bolt cutters and cut off a lock, so can anyone else. They could get in there and…"

"And plant a bloody hammer?"

"No. Yes. I don't know why anyone would do that. It isn't mine."

"It has your fingerprints on it."

"Well, it's my hammer. So it would."

"But your fingerprints are in the blood. That means that you handled it while the blood was wet."

Harris shook his head wordlessly.

It was hard for Kenzie to believe that Harris could have been framed. But it was still possible. Someone could plant steroids in his apartment. Plant the bloody hammer in his shed. The fingerprints were damning. Was there any way someone could have fooled him into handling the hammer? And then taken it back and planted it? She didn't see how.

"We also used something called an ALS or Alternative Light Source to look for blood and bodily fluids in your apartment. Just in case it was where Alex was killed."

"My apartment was clean."

"Didn't you just say how messy it was because you weren't expecting company? That's the funny thing. It was untidy. But it had been thoroughly cleaned. Apparently, you did some internet searches on the best way to clean up blood so that it could not be detected by an ALS or reagent like Luminol or BlueStar."

Harris swallowed. He looked around. "Where is that water? My mouth is so dry."

"Someone will be in with it in a moment. So you cleaned the apartment the best you could, and you did a good job of it. But even someone trying to clean blood up thoroughly can miss microscopic spatter. An expert knows where to look for blood, when an amateur doesn't. Just like our medical examiner knew to test for what kind of steroids Scott had been given and to find out that it was not the same type of steroid that Alex had taken when he was bodybuilding. Not the same thing as he had in his apartment, but disposed of before we could find it there."

Harris shook his head, confused by the change in direction. "What?"

"The steroids you used were not the same ones as Alex used."

"Alex poisoned Scott?"

"No. You poisoned Scott. And we know that because you used the wrong product. Not the same thing as Alex used."

"Maybe... he changed. Or wanted to confuse you."

"Maybe you didn't know what steroid he used and didn't think we would know the difference. But you were wrong. Did you know that when you hit someone with a hammer, you get what the experts call high-velocity spatter?"

"I might have heard of it on TV."

"Like those true crime shows, do you? And do you know how far that high-velocity spatter can spread? You might think you cleaned every surface the blood could have gotten onto. But how closely did you examine your ceiling for high-velocity spatter and cast-off? Even though you might not be able to see it with your naked eye, microscopic droplets can remain behind. And a good crime scene tech can find those. Even though you couldn't see it."

"I don't know what you're talking about."

"It took us a while to figure it all out. You see, we were distracted by the fact that you didn't have any motive to kill Scott. So when Alex was killed, it was only natural to assume that he was killed by the same person, or else that Alex had killed Scott and was killed in revenge. But that wasn't the case at all, was it?"

Harris shook his head wordlessly. Whether he meant that he didn't know or that it wasn't the case was not immediately apparent. Maybe he now admitted that he had killed both men, but not for the reasons that the police had assumed.

"You killed Scott by accident," Cameron suggested.

Harris put his face in his hands and moaned.

"You had plenty of time to figure out your mistake, but you didn't. You kept looking at Alex and not seeing any changes in his health, but you did not realize how sick Scott was getting until it was too late, since Alex was your contact. Did you figure it out in those last few days? That for months, you had been poisoning the wrong person?"

"I didn't do it," Harris groaned.

"You had the steroids in your apartment. There was no other reason for you to have them. You had access to all of the apartments. So it was not difficult for you to go into Alex's and Scott's apartment every few days when they were out and dose his food."

"No. Why would I do that?"

"You thought you were poisoning Alex. You had wined and dined him, to use Matt's words, and you knew that he was the one who preferred spicy foods, and that Scott couldn't tolerate them. Scott liked meat and potatoes. Bland food."

Harris raised his head slightly, nodding at this.

"But Scott was allergic to the cat. It plugged up his nose, and he couldn't taste anything. So… he started eating foods that were more highly flavored. Foods that would more easily hide the taste of the steroids. Spicy curries and other dishes. And those were the ones that you dosed with the steroids. Because you knew those were *Alex's* dinners." Cameron paused dramatically. "Except that they weren't. You discovered too late that you'd poisoned the wrong man."

51

Harris ran his fingers through his hair, making it stand on end like a fright wig.

"What? What are you talking about? I didn't kill anyone. I didn't have any reason to hurt either of those boys. What happened to them is tragic, but you can't railroad me for it. I had nothing to do with it."

"The poison in your home that exactly matches the profile of what was given to Scott, Alex's blood on your ceiling and the bloody hammer found in the shed with your fingerprints on it. You think any juror in their right mind would be able to ignore that kind of evidence? You are going to prison for a long time. All because you were greedy and wanted to renovate that apartment."

"They knew I needed it for the renovations. I couldn't do the upgrades that I needed to without it. Without upgrading that building, there is no way I can bring in the money I need to survive. Do you have any idea what a money pit a place like that is? Everybody wants work done. The plumbing is falling apart. The electrical needs to be stripped out and replaced. I can't afford to do that. Not without apartments that cost a lot more than the ones I've got in there right now. And people are not going to pay a higher price for the same apartments. Not unless they are upgraded.

With luxury suites, I can charge two or three times as much, and make that building profitable."

"And Alex was standing in your way. He was the only one who wouldn't take your payout. Why was that?"

"He was an idiot. He said he didn't want to move, but he was just holding out for more. I couldn't pay him more! Why did he think I was trying to do the renovation? I needed the money. I only had a short-term loan from the bank to do the renovation and then start paying them back."

Harris's voice was a snarl like an animal's, no longer whining and acting like he was the victim. Here was the predator. The color-less, nondescript man who had whispered his greeting the first time they met him was gone. "They were in the finance game! How could they act like they didn't understand? Alex would say he would take the deal, but then he would never sign the agreement. The next day, he would change his mind again, saying that he didn't really want to go. You think I don't know that the only reason he did that was to squeeze more money out of me? Money that I didn't have!"

"And you just blew," Cameron suggested sympathetically.

"After Scott died… I thought it would be easier to get Alex out of there. He would want to leave the apartment where it all happened behind. Bad memories. He would need a new roommate anyway. With the cash that I could give him to terminate the lease early, he could put down a nice deposit on a new place and he and his new roommate—or maybe even that nice girl—could get a new place without all of the memories. And it worked. He agreed. He said he didn't want to be trapped there anymore and wanted out of the lease."

"Until he'd slept on it, and then the next day, he'd flip-flopped again."

"How could he survive in the real world when he couldn't even make a decision? Every time he said he would take the money and go, he changed his mind again. It was maddening."

"And you blew."

"I didn't want to hurt anyone. You need to understand that. I never planned to hurt anyone. It was just… I just saw red. He pushed me too far. It was like I went crazy for a few seconds, and then it was too late to do anything about it."

"You couldn't control yourself."

"Yes. I don't know what happened. I don't even remember doing it. I was just talking to him, and then there he was, lying on the floor. I don't know how it happened."

Kenzie rolled her eyes. She knew what a bludgeoning scene looked like, and the amount of force that had been used to kill Alex. She had seen the number of times he had been hit. It had not been an impulsive shove down the stairs, easy to do and quickly regretted. It had been a vicious attack that had taken a great deal of effort and had not been over in a second or two.

"If it was an accident, something that just happened out of the blue, why didn't you call the police?" Cameron asked. "You had my card. If you didn't want to call 9-1-1, you could have dealt with me personally and explained yourself. Told me how it had just happened. We could have gotten you some help." Cameron leaned forward. "But instead, you decided to hide what you had done. That shows a consciousness of your guilt. And understanding of what you had done. A decision to keep anyone from finding out and throw the police off your trail. The cleanup must have taken hours. And it was well done, if it weren't for those microscopic traces on the ceiling. You even thought you could make us believe that Alex was still alive, using his phone as a beacon, taking it out of town to make it look like he had run."

Harris shook his head, but didn't voice his protest or try to give another explanation for what he had done.

"It didn't occur to you that we could look at your geo records as well as Alex's? That we could see that the two phones had traveled together almost all of that day. Maybe you should have shut your own off before you left town. But you couldn't, could you? Because you had to deal with your bank to tell them that you were proceeding immediately with the renovation, and you had to talk to your subcontractors to tell them that the apartment would be empty by the end of the week."

Harris shook his head. "I needed to do that. I had to get the renovations going. We had already started at the other end of the floor and every extra day it took to get Alex out of there would cost me money. If he hadn't changed his mind so many times, it would never have happened."

"It was his own fault."

"Yes, it was," Harris said sullenly.

"And Scott? What did he do wrong?"

Harris shook his head. "I should have made it a pet-free building. I thought that by allowing small pets, I would get more business. Could charge a little more for apartments because people with pets needed somewhere to live. I had no idea…"

Who would ever have thought that Alex getting a cat would one day result in Scott's death?

52

After congratulating Cameron on getting a confession from Harris and wrapping the investigation up like a Christmas bow, Kenzie returned to the medical examiner's office to report to Dr. Cook and add the necessary details to the Robertson and Collins files.

"Two homicides put to bed," she said with satisfaction, as she marked each file as complete. "One more killer off the street."

She wondered what would happen to the apartment building with Harris going to prison. He would have to sell it or let it go into foreclosure, probably. He wouldn't have the money to pay someone else to manage it while he was behind bars. And to finish the renovations and pay his legal fees. It would be someone else's headache now.

She tried calling Zachary, but her call went to voicemail immediately. Kenzie hesitated, then checked his location.

No location found

Kenzie checked his calendar, but didn't find any appointments on it. She double-checked that he hadn't sent her a message telling her where he would be. There was nothing from him. She checked her email just in case, but Zachary rarely emailed her, so she didn't expect to see anything from him in her inbox.

There was no reason to panic. There were lots of reasons his location might not be showing up again. It didn't necessarily mean anything sinister. He could have traveled to a cellular dead zone. He might be in a fancy restaurant that required cell phones to be turned off. He might have run out of juice and forgotten to bring a charger with him wherever he had gone.

She checked for the last known geographic coordinates of his phone. That would give her a better idea of where he might be and why he wasn't broadcasting his location.

The hospital.

Dread clutched at Kenzie's heart.

While there was nothing inherently bad about Zachary being at the hospital, she knew enough about his history to be concerned. She had visited him there for months during his last stay in the psychiatric ward while he had worked through his last depressive cycle and med change.

It was the best place for him to be if he were having psychiatric issues. Things had been difficult for him since he had taken on the Kymchuk case. Kenzie didn't think it had gotten *that* bad, but she couldn't always tell what was happening in Zachary's head. He had admitted himself to the hospital a number of times in the past, when he knew that he needed additional help. That should reassure her rather than causing that tight knot of dread in her stomach.

Zachary was the best judge of what he needed and, if he had decided he needed to be admitted to the hospital, then it didn't matter that she hadn't seen it coming. After the months of couple's counseling, she thought he would tell her when he was struggling. Maybe he had tried, but she had been too wrapped up in her work or too impatient about other things.

Or maybe it had been sudden, a trigger that neither of them had foreseen, like the woman hitting her child in the parking lot of the grocery store. If he'd had a public meltdown, he might have been transported to the hospital for evaluation. A cop or doctor could have decided to put him on a Title 18 72-hour involuntary hold.

He hadn't been admitted on an involuntary hold in all the time she had known him. One of the psych nurses Kenzie knew had said that he had never been put on an involuntary hold while she had known him. He had been admitted on an involuntary basis while he had been in foster care but, as a minor, he had no say; that had been up to his guardians and did not have to be invoked by the police or a doctor.

She went to find Dr. Cook, who was working through a stack of paperwork.

"Kenzie?" He looked up at her. "What's wrong?"

She must have looked worried. She tried to smooth out her expression, forcing a smile. "Oh, probably nothing to worry about. It's just… Zachary's gone off the grid again, so I just want to make sure everything is okay."

He made a shooing motion. "Go, go. I've got everything covered."

"Okay, thanks." She felt she needed to explain more or say that she wouldn't let her work suffer, but Dr. Cook didn't expect anything more from her. He had said before that he trusted her to run her own schedule, and he knew that Zachary had some health issues. It was nice not to have to justify herself, but it was also a little disconcerting. "I'll see you later."

"Drop me a text later if you need anything. Any time."

"Okay." Kenzie nodded and left.

She tried not to rush down the hall or to her car, reminding herself that there was no reason to think anything was wrong, and there was certainly no need to panic if Zachary had admitted himself to the hospital. If he were having problems, it was exactly the right thing to do. He should have let her know, of course, but that was secondary to making sure he was safe. If he'd been admitted involuntarily, he might not have been able to use a phone or tell anyone how to get ahold of her.

She took a few deep breaths before starting the engine, then drove to the hospital, carefully observing all rules of the road.

She went to the emergency room first and looked around. She hadn't expected to find Zachary there, but it was always possible that he'd hurt himself or gotten sick, or that he needed to go through the ER to be admitted, which was sometimes the case. She shook her head at the nurse, who looked at her questioningly, and withdrew. She would try psych, which was bound to be where Zachary was, rather than going through admitting, where they were getting more and more picky about privacy issues and who they would talk to about a patient being admitted.

She walked across the hospital to the psych ward and approached the nurse at the front desk there.

"Hi. I'm Dr. Kenzie Kirsch, and I believe Zachary Goldman may be here?"

The nurse looked confused. "Zachary Goldman? Maybe…"

"I'm his partner. His emergency contact. You can talk to me about him."

"It's just that I don't know. Can you wait here for a minute? I need to talk to someone."

"Yes, of course," Kenzie agreed.

There was no point in badgering her about not knowing the protocol to follow, especially since Kenzie was basically breaking the protocol herself, which was exactly why she had introduced herself as a doctor. She wanted them to make an exception for her, not to make her jump through the usual hoops.

The nurse motioned Kenzie to sit in one of the plastic chairs lining one wall. Kenzie sat down and pulled out her phone to occupy herself while she was waiting. Still no notifications from Zachary.

She sat there for a long time, shooting a glance toward the nursing station every now and then, but generally ignored by the nurses coming and going. Then she looked up from her phone screen and saw a familiar face.

"Nurse Val!"

Val smiled at her. "Kenzie, right? It's nice to see you. Did you want me to take you to Zachary?"

"That would be great!" Kenzie got to her feet. "It's nice to see a familiar face. I'm sure Zachary was glad to see you."

"We always have a soft spot for Zachary and our other regular patients." She leaned closer to Kenzie. "The ones who are nice to the staff, at least," she said in a lower, confidential tone, and chuckled.

Kenzie laughed too. "I'm glad he's one of the good ones. What happened—do you know? I didn't know he was having problems. Was there a trigger? You might not even know..."

Val looked at her, frowning, as if trying to work out what Kenzie was talking about. Of course, she expected Kenzie to know exactly why Zachary was there. They lived together, and Kenzie should have had some idea as to what had sent him back there again. Val stopped, and put her hand on Kenzie's arm to stop her.

"You think Zachary was *admitted*."

"Well... yes." Kenzie tried to wrap her head around the reason for Val's surprise. Was Zachary just there for some tests or to pick up a revised prescription? Or something else that Kenzie hadn't thought of?

Val shook her head. "No. He's just here to talk to someone."

Normally, Zachary just went to Dr. Boyle. Was there something he couldn't talk to her about for some reason? Maybe it was something to do with Kenzie, and Zachary didn't want to bring it up with Dr. Boyle since she was their couple's therapist as well, and he was afraid she would bring it up with Kenzie or it would affect how she treated them.

"A patient," Val clarified. "He's here to talk to another patient."

"Oh." For a minute, Kenzie was silent, stunned by the revelation. She had been worrying so much about Zachary's condition, the possibility that he was there to see someone else had never occurred to her. She thought about Rhys, who they had been there to see before. He had seemed like he was in a pretty good place recently. Had something happened to him? Kenzie laughed. "I honestly had no idea! Who is he here to see? I feel so stupid. His phone location put him in the hospital, at this end of the building, and I just assumed that he couldn't talk to me because he had been admitted."

Val shook her head. "No, no. Just visiting."

They continued their walk down the corridor. Kenzie nearly

tripped, her knees suddenly weak with relief. She shook her head at the confusion caused by her assumption.

Val led her into the common room where visits usually took place, and Kenzie saw Zachary seated across the room, facing her. She couldn't tell who he was sitting with, but it was not Rhys, a skinny black teen. The man sitting across from him was white, chunkier, in his thirties or forties if Kenzie could accurately gauge that from the back of his head. The full head of hair and style of haircut suggested a man who was mature, but not old.

Zachary rose to his feet, looking surprised to see Kenzie there. Kenzie's face heated in embarrassment. It had been perfectly logical to assume that Zachary was there for his own mental health, but now she was going to have to explain herself.

"Kenzie. Hi. I wasn't expecting to see you here."

"I was in the area," Kenzie told him, keeping it casual. She would tell him the details later, when it was just the two of them. "Val said you were here visiting and I just came over to say hi."

She turned to look at the patient who had previously had his back to her. The face was familiar, but it took her a minute to sort out who he was.

Jason. Lydia Kymchuk's husband. The man who had held her hostage and nearly blown up his city block with the conflagration he'd planned. He seemed smaller and weaker now. Not a threat to anyone, sitting there in the visitor's room with no weapon or hostage.

"Uh... Jason. Hi, I'm Kenzie. Zachary's... partner."

He held out his hand, looking down at his feet. "You know who I am?"

"I was... I was around that day. How are you doing?" Kenzie forced herself to breathe some enthusiasm and sincere concern into her question. This was a man who'd had an unfortunate mental breakdown. He was not a danger to her. He was embarrassed and concerned about how she would see him, or that she might even call him out in front of his fellow patients.

He was somebody she had seen on his worst day, and he was there to get help. That was why Zachary was there. He knew something about what it was like to be in a bad relationship and to do something impulsively that he would live to regret. Zachary had never hurt anyone or threatened to, but he knew what it was like to lose control and to lose the person he loved.

Jason looked uncertain. He gripped her hand and then let go. "I'm... I'm okay, I guess. Just need to... figure out my life from here. I screwed things up pretty badly."

"Well, I'm glad you're here to get back on track. I hope you can get things straightened out."

"Thanks. I'm trying, and I'm clean. I guess... I'm never going to be with Lydia again, but... I hope I haven't ruined her life." He choked up and cleared his throat. "We'll get divorced and go our separate ways and, hopefully, she can have a good life."

He seemed sincere. Kenzie hoped that he would be able to stay clean from whatever substances he had been on and be able to control himself better in the future. Next time, the right people might not be there to talk him down. Hopefully, he would get a lot of intensive therapy and long-term medication and supports.

Kenzie looked at Zachary. "I'll see you at home?"

He nodded. "I'll be there."

53

D r. Kirsch?"

Kenzie looked up from the postmortem she was working on to see Dr. Cook in the observation ante-room. He didn't normally interrupt her in the middle of an autopsy, so she was surprised by his appearance.

She turned off her recording. "Yes, doctor?"

"There is a woman here to see you. I realize she does not have an appointment, but it seemed urgent."

"You think it's important enough to interrupt the procedure?"

Dr. Cook gave a nod and didn't explain further. Kenzie sighed. If he thought it was important enough to interrupt the post-mortem, then she would. She could probably use a break anyway. She pulled off her gloves and headed to the door to take off the rest of her protective gear and make herself presentable. In a few minutes, she was greeting an older woman in the boardroom. She stood when Kenzie entered, emphasizing her height. She was a tall, severe-looking woman. Very tanned. Not someone Kenzie could recall meeting before or seeing a picture of.

"Hello, I'm Dr. Kenzie Kirsch."

She offered her hand, and the woman shook. Then she stepped back slightly.

"My name is Lynnette Robertson."

"What can I do for you?" The name rang a bell, but it took a few seconds while Mrs. Robertson composed herself before Kenzie figured out where she knew it from. She had called and left this woman several messages.

"You're... the mother. Scott Robertson's mother. And Kirk's."

"Yes."

"Have a seat." Kenzie motioned for her to sit down at the table, and pulled a chair out for herself. "I'm very sorry for your loss."

"Thank you."

"I hope... you have found everything to be in order. Kirk claimed the remains..."

"It has been a difficult time," Mrs. Robertson said, not really answering the question. "I'm afraid you must think me a terrible mother."

Kenzie blinked. "No. I don't think that at all. You were on the other side of the world; you couldn't exactly drop everything and rush back here."

Of course, she could have, and many women would have. As far as Kenzie knew, Mrs. Robertson wasn't in the armed services or in some other position where she was not allowed to leave of her own free choice. But there were all kinds of people in the world and Kenzie hadn't been shocked that she hadn't shown up at the medical examiner's office a day or two after being informed of her son's death.

"I left both of my sons here to sort things out themselves and fled to another country so as not to have to deal with their problems. Maybe I should have stepped in and told them what to do, told them what their father would have wanted and how to interpret the will. But you know, they would have just resented that."

"Sometimes it is best not to choose sides."

Mrs. Robertson nodded. "I couldn't choose one without alienating the other. So maybe I alienated both instead."

"There wasn't a winning answer."

"No."

They both sat in silence. Kenzie wasn't sure what to say to her.

What had she come home for? What had she traveled all this way to find out or do?

"I wanted to thank you for what you did," Mrs. Robertson told her. "For finding out what happened to my Scotty and who was responsible."

"I was just doing my job. And the police were responsible for the criminal investigation and finding out who was responsible. I am sorry that he was killed... for the terrible mistake that was made."

"It doesn't really matter whether he was the target or not... I'm glad that the person responsible will be punished. But that doesn't change anything."

"No. I don't suppose it makes it any easier."

"I am glad... that Kirk had nothing to do with it. It has hit him hard, realizing that because of how they fought over the estate, they separated on bad terms and never had a chance to make up. If he had accepted his father's wishes... they could have been friends until the end. And that is a hard thing to accept."

Kenzie could see how it would be. "You and Kirk still have each other. I hope you can have a good relationship."

Mrs. Robertson considered this seriously. "I don't blame him for Scott's death. So I think we can. We are the only two left now. And the money is his, aside from my portion."

Kenzie nodded. "Does Kirk have a girlfriend? Any future plans?"

"Grandchildren, you mean?" Mrs. Robertson gave a little laugh. "I hope so, someday. And maybe if he does, I won't be on the other side of the world when they are born." Mrs. Robertson sighed. "Life is too short, Ms. Kirsch. I hope you know that."

If there was anyone who knew how fleeting mortality was, and how permanently death ended all disputes eventually, it was the medical examiner.

Kenzie put her hand over the older woman's. "I do know. I hope that you will be able to find some peace, after you have worked through your grief. And future happiness."

Mrs. Robertson gave a small smile and stood up. "Thank you for taking the time, Dr. Kirsch. I appreciate it greatly."

"You're welcome… I hope it can give you some closure."

They shook hands, holding them clasped for a moment, before Mrs. Robertson released her grip.

"We are… Rachel has planned a little memorial. I don't know if you would be interested in attending. We're having…" She gave a little laugh, her cheeks growing pink, "It's sort of an open mike at an Indian restaurant. Curry. You might think that's morbid, but…"

"But it's something Scott had come to love."

Mrs. Robertson nodded. "Come if you like." She gave Kenzie the details and patted her on the arm. "Again, thank you."

Kenzie watched her go with a mixture of melancholy and wistfulness. Her role as assistant medical examiner was many-faceted. She hoped that it could bring some healing to bereaved family members like Kirk and Lynnette Robertson.

She walked through the corridor back to autopsy, to take up the tools of her trade to begin another journey.

Did you enjoy this book? Reviews and recommendations are vital to making a book successful.

Please leave a review at your favorite book store or review site and share it with your friends.

Don't miss the following bonus material:
Sign up for mailing list to get a free ebook
Read a sneak preview chapter
Other books by P.D. Workman
Learn more about the author

DON'T MISS A THING! GET THE LATEST NEWS AND A FREE EBOOK

Your First Taste

PDWORKMAN.COM/SIGNUP

PREVIEW HEALED TO DEATH

CHAPTER 1

Kenzie's phone started ringing loudly on the side table, jarring her awake. She grabbed it and tried to silence the noise, her fingers clumsy with sleep. She wanted the noise to end as quickly as possible, but finding the button to mute it took precious seconds. She considered getting out of bed and stepping out into the hallway to take the call so that her voice would not disturb Zachary's sleep, but by the time she had formed the thought, she knew there was no use. Zachary woke more quickly than she did, and if he was awakened at night, it was pretty much guaranteed that he would stay that way. Even if Kenzie could go back to sleep after the sound of that klaxon, there was no way Zachary would.

So she saved herself from the risk of stubbing her toes or other accidents that might occur stumbling around in the dark or blinding herself by turning on a light and stayed in bed. She blinked a couple of times to clear her vision, then swiped the screen to accept the call.

"Dr. Kirsch," she acknowledged. "Sorry, took me a minute there."

"Good morning, Dr. Kirsch," the operator at the other end of the line greeted pleasantly. "I'm afraid I have a call-out for you."

"Sure," Kenzie agreed. "Where are the remains? Any details about the situation?"

The operator gave her an address and directed her to a back lane, which was not particularly surprising. Kenzie thumbed the address into a note on her phone and read it back. The operator confirmed.

"Police have secured the scene."

"Great, thanks."

"Have a great day, doctor," the operator told her pleasantly and disconnected.

Kenzie looked at the window. Though the blinds were pulled, she could still see through the crack between them. It was dark—streetlights shining. Though the dispatcher had wished her a good morning and told her to have a good day, it was still in the middle of the night. Kenzie looked at the time on her phone screen.

Two o'clock in the morning.

At least she had a few hours of sleep under her belt. She wouldn't be getting any more. While in theory, she could go back to sleep, and the police would hold the scene until it was *actually* morning, she would never do that. With her heart hammering after being startled out of sound sleep, she wouldn't be able to get back to sleep if she wanted to, and she wouldn't make the law enforcement officers who had secured the scene stand around for hours waiting for her. That would just be rude and would guarantee she would not get the friendly cooperation she was used to from the police force in the future.

She took a few deep breaths to settle her heart and try to get the oxygen to her brain to help her wake up and focus on the business at hand.

"Got a call out?" Zachary asked in a quiet, calm voice intended not to startle her.

Kenzie stretched and turned partway around to look at him. She couldn't see much in the darkness of the room, just his shape beside her. Her brain filled in what her eyes could not see—his very short, dark hair, a scruff of several days' growth of whiskers, the mixture of concern and reassurance on his face.

"Yup," she agreed, "body in a back alley. Those are always nice."

He chuckled. "Who knows, it could just be a heart attack. A businessman who went out for a breath of fresh air."

"It's never just a heart attack," Kenzie countered. If it was earlier or later, it could be. A businessman having a nightcap before bed, or an early morning heart attack on his commute to work. But two in the morning was rarely anything so benign.

Of course, he might have died hours or even days before. There was nothing that said he had died within the last hour or two.

In her experience, it would not be pretty.

Zachary stirred beside her. He untangled himself from the blankets and got out of bed, stopping momentarily to feel around for some clothing. "Do you want me to make coffee?" he asked. He was already moving, heading toward the door. There was no point in telling him no. He'd already made up his mind. He'd be making coffee for himself. She might as well take advantage of it.

"Sure," she agreed, "that would be nice. But just regular strength. None of that high-test stuff."

"You sure you don't need an extra boost?"

"If I need more caffeine, I'll drink another cup."

"Aye-aye," he agreed.

Kenzie rubbed her eyes and got moving. She didn't want to keep the police waiting longer than necessary.

By the time she had splashed water on her face, combed her curly hair, and finished making herself presentable, the smell of coffee was wafting through the house. On her arrival in the kitchen, Zachary handed her a large travel mug filled with the fresh brew. He leaned in for a kiss, bristly, still smelling of sweat and musk.

"Have a good day," he told her. "Shoot me a text or call me over lunch and let me know how it is going."

"Will do," Kenzie agreed. She slipped on her jacket and shoes, grabbed her purse, and entered the garage where her "baby"—a sporty red convertible—awaited her. Her small scene-of-crime kit was stowed in the trunk as usual. If she found she needed additional equipment when she got to the scene, she would have Carlos bring it to her when he drove the medical examiner's van to the scene for transportation.

CHAPTER 2

Despite the fact that it was not yet a decent hour of the morning, it was not lonely and creepy to go into the back alley where the remains had been found. A police perimeter had been set up, and large lights banished all thoughts of night. Kenzie was happy to see that the police mostly stayed outside the perimeter until she and the forensic unit gathered the evidence they needed and turned the scene over. They did not need a scene that had been trampled all over. She pulled on the prescribed protective gear and approached the scene.

"Morning, everyone," Kenzie greeted. "What've we got?"

A detective had arrived ahead of her and was patiently waiting with his own cup of coffee, an extra large from the nearest coffee shop. He took a sip of the coffee, considering her. He had wavy, sandy-colored hair and was young for a detective. He looked as if he, like Kenzie, had been woken up by the call. His name bar gave his name as Samuels.

Kenzie knew she wasn't what most people pictured when the title "assistant medical examiner" was mentioned. Most people expected a gray-haired man, not Kenzie, with her wild dark curls and bright red lipstick. Her red sports car didn't advertise that she was from the medical examiner's office either, although if Samuels got close enough, he would be able to see her medical examiner parking pass hanging from the mirror. Kenzie smiled and nodded, indicating the identification on the lanyard around her neck in case he doubted who she was. He cleared his throat and nodded.

"Just an old homeless guy," Samuels told her. "No sign of violence or anything out of place."

Kenzie nodded. "Great. This should be quick, then."

He escorted her to the officer who was logging the visitors to the scene and Kenzie signed in. The detective pointed to the body in case she couldn't see it, which she could, and suggested that she walk around the edges to preserve any evidence. Kenzie didn't push back about being told how to preserve the crime scene. She was happy to have them cordoning it off and controlling foot traffic in and out of the scene as they were supposed to. It didn't always turn out that way and she was never happy to arrive at a crime scene where people were just wandering around or, even worse, had touched or moved the body for one reason or another.

Kenzie walked as close to the brick wall of the building on her right as she could, shining a flashlight ahead of her at an angle to detect any footprints, fluids, pocket debris, or other piece of evidence before she stepped on it. When she reached the body, she checked the ground carefully before setting down her kit and leaning in to examine the body.

The first matter of business was to confirm that he was, in fact, deceased. That was apparent just by looking at him. Yellow, waxy skin, and lifeless eyes. But she checked for a carotid pulse anyway and shifted his jaw slightly. Either he didn't yet smell, or the other smells of the alley were overwhelming the beginnings of decomposition. It had not been long since he had passed.

"Who found him?" Kenzie asked, projecting her voice toward Detective Samuels, standing outside the tape.

"Another homeless guy."

"You got him? To get a full statement?"

"Didn't seem like he knew anything. We got his details in case we need to reach him again."

The homeless did have the unfortunate habit of disappearing when the police were looking for them. They had the ability to disappear without a trace for long periods of time, swallowed up by the streets, with no address and often no phone number to reach them at. Kenzie wished she'd had a chance to talk to the homeless man before he had been allowed to leave.

"What did he have to say?"

"Just that he knew his friend was sleeping close by and was looking for him. Found him here, deceased, and called it in."

"He is very recently deceased. No rigor. Are you sure he was already dead when the friend arrived?"

Samuels frowned, a crease appearing between his eyes. "Why would he call it in as a death if he was still alive? He would call 9-1-1."

Kenzie nodded slowly. Usually, people went with 9-1-1 even when calling in a dead body. Sometimes, they thought the person could be saved, even if they knew their hopes were most likely unfounded. They wanted to do *something*, and preserved the hope of revival long after it was reasonable.

"I would like to talk to him, if you would please be sure to include his contact information in your report."

"Of course," he agreed.

"If you have his friend, then I assume you also have his identity? A name for our victim?"

"John Lane. Jack. A longtime resident of these mean streets."

Kenzie nodded, not surprised. The man's clothing and rough-looking appearance suggested that he was not new to homeless life. She looked around for his possessions but did not see a shopping cart or stash anywhere close by. He might live some distance from there, maybe in a tent or other shelter, and that was where his belongings were.

She looked at his hands and fingers for any sign of what he had been doing recently. They were stained yellow, obviously a smoker of many years. She could smell alcohol and vomit on him. She pushed up one of his sleeves. No tattoos. No track marks. But there was something.

"There is an IV puncture mark here," she observed. "Would you call the hospital and find out what he was being treated for?"

"Sure," Detective Samuels agreed. He pulled out his phone and tapped the screen a few times. Like most other first responders in town, he had one or more of the hospital's numbers in his contact list. He called admitting and talked to them while Kenzie made her next few observations.

There were bloody stains on the collar of his shirt. Kenzie leaned in closer. There were no cuts on his throat or face. That fact, combined with the smell of vomit, told her that he had likely been throwing up blood.

Certainly not unheard of for an alcoholic. Long-term alcohol use did terrible things to the digestive tract. And alcoholics just kept drinking despite the pain. His skin and eyes were yellow. Jaundice. The elevated bilirubin told her there was liver damage.

The detective was probably right. He had probably died of natural causes, the destructive effects of long-term alcoholism, and not any street violence.

She examined the rest of the victim's limbs as far as his clothing would allow and checked his torso, front and back. There was some bruising, which was concerning, but she didn't think he had been beaten up. More than likely, it was just another sign of impending organ failure. He had been pretty hard on his body for some years.

"Okay," Kenzie called over to Samuels. "I'm going to call for transport and see how long we are waiting on the forensic team."

"Hospital says he was not admitted."

"Not admitted? But he was treated."

He shook his head. "They don't have any records of him being there. Not recently, and I assume you meant the IV mark was new."

"Yes. It's fresh. The IV was just pulled out in the last few hours. He *must* have been at the hospital."

"Maybe some kind of private clinic?" Samuels suggested.

A clinic. Kenzie nodded slowly. What kind of clinic was nearby that might have treated Mr. Lane? Someone might have noticed that he was dehydrated after throwing up. A doctor's office, rehab center, or some mobile clinic or outreach center that treated the homeless.

"We'll have to find out where he was being treated. Or maybe he was admitted to the hospital as a John Doe if he wouldn't give his name or was unconscious when he was taken there."

"Already asked that. No John Does treated in the last week. Few patients that meet his demographic.'"

"Hmm. We'll have to check around. Where was he living? Was he in a shelter?"

"More than likely. Ninety-five percent of the homeless population in Vermont is sheltered. We'll make a few calls around. I'm sure it won't take long to find out where he was being treated and for what."

"I can tell you the what. Alcoholism and ulcers in the upper GI. Vomiting, dehydrated, throwing up blood. It wouldn't have been pretty."

He sniffed and nodded in agreement.

"Wherever it was, he shouldn't have been released in this condition," Kenzie pointed out.

"He probably snuck out or signed an AMA."

"Against medical advice," Kenzie agreed, sighing. And there wasn't really anything anyone could do about it. They could try to have him declared incompetent and to put him under some kind of conservatorship, but other than a locked ward in a nursing home, there weren't many places that would physically prevent him from walking away if he wanted to leave.

Most doctors and social workers would shrug and let him leave if he insisted. Choosing to live a high-risk lifestyle was not cause to have someone declared incompetent. If he knew the likely consequences of his behavior and was coherent, it was pretty hard to convince a court to take away his freedom.

Healed to Death, Book #12 of the *Kenzie Kirsch Medical Thriller* series by P.D. Workman
Order your copy now!

ABOUT THE AUTHOR

P.D. Workman is a USA Today Bestselling author and multi-award winner, renowned for her prolific output of over 100 published works that span various genres. With a knack for crafting page-turners, Workman captivates readers with everything from cozy mysteries like the Auntie Clem's Bakery series to gripping young adult and suspense novels.

A prolific reader and writer since childhood, P.D. Workman crafts emotionally powerful stories that don't shy away from hard topics. Her books tackle mental illness, addiction, abuse, and trauma with raw honesty and compassion, giving voice to the often unheard. If you crave authentic, character-driven page-turners that hit deep and stay with you long after the final page, you're in the right place.

With each new release, fans eagerly anticipate another thrilling blend of thought-provoking storytelling and relatable characters that define P.D. Workman's brand as an author of unforgettable page-turners—gripping tales that leave a lasting impact long after the last page is turned.

> P. D. Workman, does not shy from probing the deep psychological scars of childhood trauma, mental illness, and addiction. Also characteristic of this author, these extremely sensitive issues are explored with extensive empathy, described with incredible clarity, and portrayed with profound insight.
>
> — —KIM, GOODREADS REVIEWER

Some of Workman's titles have been translated into Spanish, French, Portuguese, German, and Italian.

Workman began writing at an early age and is a prolific reader as well as writer. She is also passionate about teaching and learning, expresses her creativity through art and cooking, and loves exploring the Calgary parks and green spaces where the Parks Pat Mysteries are set. She was a legal assistant for many years and has done extensive charitable work.

Workman was born and raised in Alberta, Canada, and is married with one adult son.

———

Please visit P.D. Workman at pdworkman.com to see what else she is working on, to join her mailing list, and to link to her social networks.

———

If you enjoyed this book, please take the time to recommend it to other purchasers with a review or star rating and share it with your friends!

tiktok.com/@pdworkmanauthor

facebook.com/pdworkmanauthor

x.com/pdworkmanauthor

instagram.com/pdworkmanauthor

amazon.com/author/pdworkman

bookbub.com/authors/p-d-workman

goodreads.com/pdworkman

linkedin.com/in/pdworkman

pinterest.com/pdworkmanauthor

youtube.com/pdworkman

Find P.D. Workman's books at

PDWORKMAN.COM

Scan the QR code below

www.ingramcontent.com/pod-product-compliance
Lightning Source LLC
Chambersburg PA
CBHW030936260626
47169CB00002B/496